THE
FORGOTTEN
BOY

THE
FORGOTTEN
BOY

LAURA ANDERSEN

OPEN ROAD
INTEGRATED MEDIA
NEW YORK

ISBN: 978-1-5040-9045-2

Published in 2024 by Open Road Integrated Media, Inc.
180 Maiden Lane
New York, NY 10038
www.openroadmedia.com

THE
FORGOTTEN
BOY

CHAPTER ONE

JULIET
NOVEMBER 2018

The house is a miniature St. Pancras . . .

Juliet thought *miniature* was hardly the word to describe Havencross. *Mammoth,* maybe. *Gargantuan. Titanic.* The rambling house might not take up as much literal space as London's iconic railway station/hotel, but then St. Pancras was surrounded by buildings and people and the thrum of city life that kept the eye moving every moment to look at something new. Here in Northumberland there was nothing to see except Havencross, a flamboyant Gothic Revival structure thrusting its redbrick turrets, spires, and exuberant outlines against the gray sky.

And windows. Windows with sharp points and decorative tracery. Leaded glass and gable windows. Clover-shaped windows tucked beneath turrets. A hundred people could be watching her from as many windows. For the next five months, the only person looking out the windows would be her, in a house refurbished nearly two hundred years ago for a family of fifteen, not to count the servants and staff. When Juliet had undertaken this position, she'd never imagined such a daunting wealth of style and space.

Then her thoughts flitted to how it would look after dark. Hastily, she pulled back from that. She was an expert at ignoring the unpleasant until it grew impossible.

"Cowardice," some said. *Not borrowing trouble* had been her grandmother's term, one Juliet preferred.

Nell Somersby-Sims, the solicitor who had engaged Juliet, hovered outside the grand double doors. When Juliet pulled up and lowered the car window, Nell said, "Drive on round the far left. You'll find a spot to leave the car."

"Do you want to get in?" Juliet asked.

"I'll go through the house and meet you at the scullery door."

Just as well, since Juliet was not yet entirely comfortable with driving on the left side of the road. Not that she was likely to encounter another car between here and the back of the house, but still. It was important to her these days to appear competent. At anything.

Around the back of Havencross, the Gothic flourishes gave way to the bones of the original fifteenth-century house that had been nearly swallowed up by renovations. Fewer windows, Juliet noted, but centuries more history. If she believed in ghosts, this would be the place for them.

Nell Somersby-Sims (distant cousin or not, it was impossible not to think of her by that full upper-class name) hovered at the solid oak door leading into the scullery while Juliet grabbed her bags. Nell wore four-inch spiked-heel boots that were meant for cities, not overgrown farmyards.

Juliet dumped her suitcase and messenger bag on the tiled floor of the scullery and looked around at the copper tubs and

4

the creaky drying racks meant to be cranked up to the ceiling with heavy armfuls of wet linen.

Hastily, Nell said, "You won't be responsible for the heavy things, of course, or anything attached to the walls or floor. We'll have a removal company come in and take away all of that once you leave. You'll be sorting through old chests, wardrobes, shelves, that sort of thing."

"Yes, you were very clear on the nature of the job."

It wasn't a job, exactly. For one thing, Juliet wasn't being paid. It was a convenient trade-off. After three years as an adjunct Victorian history professor in Maine, she'd needed to escape—both Maine and her imploded marriage. Thirty years old, living once more with her parents, her savings account just a distant memory. Not a pretty picture.

Desperate for something to do but without the energy to actually do it, Juliet had ended up in England hardly knowing how she got here. It started when her mother had been contacted three weeks ago by a British lawyer—solicitor?—about the sale of an old and abandoned family property.

Havencross.

Juliet had been hired partly because of her impressive Skype interview and partly because of her mother's offer for Juliet's salary to come out of her own profits from the sale. But mostly she'd been hired because she was willing to live all alone in a fourteen-thousand-square-foot house in the middle of Northumberland National Park, next to a fast-flowing river and ten miles from the nearest village. For five months. Five winter months.

Havencross was on its way to being transformed into an exclusive country hotel, the kind that offered shooting parties in autumn, snowshoes and roaring fires in winter, fishing and walking in spring and summer, with a foreign chef and four-star luxury bedding. But before any of the costly renovations could begin, the house had to be cleared of generations of debris.

Nell took her on a brief overview of the ground floor, but Juliet waved off the offer to take her around the rest of it. She could see that the younger woman was eager to get away. And she was eager to be rid of Nell, no matter their relationship. Which, considering she'd never heard the name until three weeks ago, might as well not exist.

Not that Juliet had anything against her personally. No doubt Nell Somersby-Sims—with her glossy, shoulder-length bob and gel-manicured nails and size 2 pencil skirt—was a perfectly nice woman. But Juliet could practically hear Nell's doubts: *Surely it will be all right; we haven't hired this woman to do anything crucial. She's little more than an early alarm system. And it's not as though anyone will miss an unhappy academic for a few months.*

Juliet had always felt defensive around beautiful, professionally accomplished women. Three years of careening hormones, indifferent husband, and grief had convinced her that she was basically invisible.

"It's in your head," Duncan had said impatiently. "If you don't like how you look or how you feel, if you don't like feeling invisible, then do something about it!"

Right now, invisibility was what she craved. *So yes, Miss Somersby-Sims, I'll be quite all right. There's a house plan—very helpful—and all the necessary keys. And how kind of you to have laid in a week's worth of groceries. I can hardly wait to get to work.*

Her lawyer-cousin lingered at the scullery door on her way out. "Rachel Bennett will come in every Thursday to clean the living areas. Theirs is the nearest house, almost three miles by road but closer on foot if you cross the fields this side of the river. Her family's been here forever—she's your best bet for local knowledge and history."

"Lovely, thank you."

At last Nell lowered her expensive sunglasses. "You can reach me on my mobile at any time if you have questions or find anything unexpected. Best of luck."

Juliet closed the door before Nell had cleared the yard in her sleek Audi and leaned against it, eyes closed and head pounding.

Alone. Exactly what she wanted.

Wasn't it?

CHAPTER TWO

JULIET
2018

The first thing Juliet wanted to do was the first thing she always did when she traveled: unpack and organize so that she wouldn't be living in a state of chaos. Nell Somersby-Sims had directed her to a ground-floor arrangement of sitting room, bedroom, and a 1940s en suite that had been Clarissa Somersby's last home. Clarissa had been born at Havencross in 1894 and died in this downstairs space at age ninety-eight. Juliet wasn't superstitious about death—she'd spent a large part of the last six months thinking of little else—but she found the indicated suite claustrophobic and defiantly dragged her bags upstairs before making her own tour of the second floor. *First floor*, she corrected herself, though it hardly seemed to matter when she was alone and didn't have to worry about pressing the wrong elevator button.

Juliet had always loved the eccentricities of English architecture, but a house like this pushed that love to the limit. It had been built as a family home at a time when large families and even larger belowstairs staffs were the rule, then adapted for the needs of a boys' boarding school before being commandeered as a military training center in the Second World War. With that history, it took her a few minutes to identify what each particular room had been originally used for.

There were two very large rooms on either side of the open staircase landings that must have been reception areas of some sort, though not as large as the cavernous and more formal spaces on the ground floor. She guessed that one had been a music room, based on the carvings of various instruments and musical notations that adorned the fireplace surround and the frieze work. The other might have been a morning room, that space reserved for upper-class women to attend to their private correspondence; here they could appear in less formal dress than the public spaces.

Both rooms had a smattering of furniture, as varied as a Chippendale sideboard, a reproduction medieval settle that would have fit ten school boys side by side, and army-issued metal desks. Clearly Clarissa had chosen not to use these rooms upon her return to the house in the late seventies.

Beyond these rooms, on both the east and west sides of the house, stretched long corridors. The west wing contained bedrooms of various sizes and one massive bathroom fitted out in full art deco glamour, including mint-green tiles on both floor and walls.

The largest bedroom at the far western end had four narrow windows across the side of the house and two overlooking the river, stretching nearly floor to ceiling with heavy green damask curtains, a mahogany four-poster bed that must have been constructed inside the room for even in pieces no one could have carried it up here, built-in bookcases flanking the marble fireplace, and a beautiful dressing table. An inner door led to a Victorian dressing room and another door leading to a smaller bedroom that would have been for the husband whose wife did not always welcome his presence in bed.

There were plenty of things here to be cleared through, for someone had repopulated these rooms with personal books and files of papers and even trunks of vintage clothing. This must have been Clarissa's room before age had forced her downstairs. Though Juliet looked forward to going through it all—and the side windows gave a lovely view of the original walled garden— she had no desire to sleep here.

She finally chose a room in the oldest section of the house. Not overlarge but charming with its multiple angles of wall and ceiling, a window seat, and hand-painted wallpaper whose jewel-bright colors had faded to a pleasing background. The woodwork had been painted a Dresden-blue at some point; it reminded Juliet of the décor in the House of the Seven Gables in Salem, Massachusetts. (She and Duncan used to love Salem.) There was a similar room across the corridor that she could use as a study or small sitting room.

By the time she'd unpacked and decided it was safe to use the nearest toilet—though she would have to trek to the downstairs suite if she wanted to shower—the sun had gone down. Nell and her bosses had already updated the wiring in the most critical sections of the house. But even with new bulbs in the corridor and hall, Havencross seemed to swallow the light.

Juliet used to be afraid of the dark. A neighbor once noted that she always knew when Duncan was gone, because there were lights burning all night long in the house. But since May, Juliet had no room left in her for imaginary fears. So after heating up soup in the kitchen, she went back up to the first floor and then kept climbing to the top of the Victorian section of the house.

She meant to just get an idea of where the most work and clearing would be required. And yes, she surveyed any number of small servants' rooms filled with boxes and discarded household objects. But the most surprising space was high-ceilinged and airy, and seemed to be used much more recently than World War II if the cordless telephone was anything to go by.

It could only have been Clarissa—as far as she knew, no one else had lived here in sixty years. Juliet inspected her surroundings with curiosity. It was not the room or office of a sad and eccentric recluse; even empty for all these years, it retained a vibrancy and individuality of mind that made Juliet think she would have liked Clarissa. And why not? Clarissa had been her mother's great-aunt. That made Juliet her . . . well, they were related somehow.

The lighting up here was dim, so Juliet could only take a cursory look. There were drawers filled with both typed and handwritten pages, and a quick scan of the shelves left an impression of a great interest in English history.

She was about to switch off the light when something glinted in the corner of her eye from one of the lower bookshelves: a silver frame, much tarnished, with a vintage photo of a small boy. Dark hair, round cheeks, starched white shirt, and knee-length breeches of an era before World War I; even in the frozen photography of the past, he possessed an irrepressible charm, as though at any moment he would burst into a wide grin and jump into your arms for a hug.

Juliet stared at the boy for much longer than the photo itself warranted, until grief threatened to choke her and she fled for the safety of her bedroom and sleeping pills.

CHAPTER THREE

JULIET
2018

Juliet had always used to notice how poorly she slept her first night in a different place. But these days sleeping badly was her usual, so she was no more tired than normal when her alarm went off. She checked her texts and replied to the one her mother had sent at midnight Pennsylvania time when she'd been asleep: *How's the haunted house?*

She typed back, *No ghosts yet, just a lot of dust and boxes.*

When the job had been offered, Juliet's mother had spent an afternoon hour reminiscing about her great-aunt Clarissa. Juliet's English grandmother had moved to Philadelphia when she was ten, and family visits back had been mostly confined to London. But one August week when Juliet's mother was fourteen, she had spent a week with Clarissa at Havencross while her parents toured Switzerland.

"Brilliant," Juliet's mother had stated. "I mean really brilliant, like genius level. She had a master of arts from Cambridge

12

and studied mathematics in Germany. She was in Paris when the French surrendered in 1940 and spent the rest of the war doing . . . something. She wouldn't talk about it. It was 1974 when I visited, and she'd only returned to Havencross the year before."

"And the house?" Juliet had asked, since that would be her job.

Her usually talkative mother had taken her time answering. "It didn't feel like a house that had been empty for years. Even with just Clarissa and me there, Havencross felt lived in. It had its own life, that house, or a memory of life. You felt that the house itself carried on no matter who might be there at any given time."

And though her mother had laughed off any ghostly sightings, she'd left Juliet with a lingering sense of . . . possibilities. If Juliet's life hadn't fallen off a cliff six months ago, she might have been interested in possibilities. Now she just wanted to work.

The best part of working all alone in an empty house was that she needn't think twice about wearing leggings and an old high school sweatshirt. She ate toast and yogurt standing up in the small kitchen and decided to begin where she was, in the rooms Clarissa Somersby last occupied.

The kitchen was as anonymous as a rental apartment, save for the blue-and-white willowware that would fetch a good price in an antique shop. Or maybe one of the far-flung family members would want some pieces. Making a note to ask Nell about it, Juliet took a quick look through all the cabinets and drawers, found nothing further of interest, and moved into the back bedroom.

More than twenty-five years after Clarissa's death, the room retained the scent of extreme old age, a mix of powder-fine skin and stale heat. The mattress was wrapped in a mix of linen and canvas to keep out small wildlife, but the bed frame was beautifully crafted of cherrywood with garlands of vines and flowers. There was a small fireplace with glazed Victorian tiles, and a mantel with two empty cut-glass vases on it.

Juliet opened a wardrobe—that had obviously been made by the same craftsman who made the bed—and made her first fascinating discovery: a wealth of vintage clothing.

Gorgeous wool in gray and ivory and houndstooth. Fine cashmere and velvet and floral cottons in the bias-cut, high-waisted, butterfly-sleeved fashion of the 1930s. In a hatbox that was itself worthy of collection, there were several confections that wouldn't look out of place at a contemporary royal wedding. Juliet decided Clarissa's bedroom was as good a place as any to begin collecting those pieces that should be evaluated separately for sale.

She spent the next hour putting things in boxes, wrapping the sturdier pieces in acid-free paper, and made a note on her phone to call Nell and ask for appropriate garment storage bags. When she had an array of boxes neatly lined against the wall, Juliet considered the dressing table.

It was not as expensive-looking or ornate as the bed and wardrobe, but charming with its delicately curved legs and scrolled edges. It reminded Juliet of the desk her parents had bought for her twelfth birthday. Something meant for a girl between childhood and adolescence. Had Clarissa clung onto this piece from her childhood until the very end?

The drawers contained only thick writing paper, embossed at the top with Clarissa's initials, and various beautiful fountain pens that Juliet set aside for sales consideration. And on the dressing table's surface sat three photographs in silver frames matching the one she'd found upstairs last night. The one in the middle, a family grouping of the same period as the boy's photograph, could have been entitled *Successful Victorian Gentleman Surrounded by His Picture-perfect Family*. Next to the mutton-chopped, middle-aged man sat a younger-looking woman with the upright carriage of one wearing a whalebone corset. There were four children: one fat baby in its mother's lap, a small girl of three or so with an enormous bow encircling her head, a much older girl, and a boy—the same bright-eyed, impish-faced boy of the upstairs photograph. Juliet felt a sharpness in her chest, barbed wire tightening around her beating heart, and turned the family photo face down on the dressing table.

The largest photograph was of Havencross itself, as seen from the long, sweeping driveway. She had a sudden image of Clarissa touching her fingers to the photo's glass, as perhaps she grew too old to walk comfortably outside and see that view for herself.

The third one was the most candid. As close to a snapshot as one could get in that time—Juliet considered the clothes and guessed World War I—of two women sitting on what she recognized as the front steps. They both wore light-colored blouses and dark skirts that just reached their ankles. One of the women had a bountiful, generous smile and looked as though she'd been caught midlaugh—indeed, she looked as though she were often caught midlaugh. In the black-and-white photo, her hair could only be said to be a lighter color than her companion's. Little drifts and tendrils of it floated around her cheeks and neck from however she'd secured the bulk of it.

The other woman's hair was more neatly pinned up, but even a hundred-year-old photo managed to hint at its glossy darkness. Something about the starkness of her cheekbones and chin reminded Juliet of her own reflection in the mirror—not a physical likeness, more an imprint of suffering. Her smile was smaller and shyer than her companion's, and an open book rested on her lap.

After a good deal of pointless staring—the photographs were hardly going to introduce themselves to her—Juliet moved on to the last room of the ground-floor suite. It was a smaller version of the study she'd found upstairs last night. She imagined Clarissa, forced by age and unsteady balance to move to the ground floor, choosing her most important books and papers to bring down with her. As such, she figured it would give her a good overview of Clarissa's mind at the end of her life.

The books confirmed her interest in English history, though in this low-ceilinged room the reference books and histories had narrowed to the fifteenth century. Juliet scanned the titles on the low bookshelf next to a burgundy leather recliner. Mostly nonfiction, fifteenth-century English history. The Wars of the Roses, then. Clarissa even had a well-read copy of Josephine Tey's *The Daughter of Time*, the popular novel dedicated to rehabilitating Richard III's character from its Tudor-era blackening.

There was also a shelf of local histories, including that of Havencross itself, some little more than photocopied pages bound together.

Juliet sat cross-legged on the floor before the bookshelves, wondering about the source of Clarissa's interest. The house, of course, she might reasonably be interested in the history of her family's home. But why the focus on the York–Lancaster conflict? Had Havencross been caught up in that long-ago war? Juliet's own academic specialty was Victorian and Edwardian social history; her knowledge of earlier centuries was sketchy.

Impulsively, she chose a random selection of histories to read at meals and in bed. If she was going to spend five months here alone, she needed something to think about besides cleaning and throwing stuff out. In that same mood, she picked up the photograph of the two women. Nell Somersby-Sims had said that the cleaner was part of a family that had lived here for generations. Maybe she could tell Juliet the story behind the unexpectedly moving portrait.

CHAPTER FOUR

DIANA
SEPTEMBER 1918

Diana Neville arrived at Havencross afflicted with serious forebodings even before the house came into sight. *Who lived in the middle of nowhere?* she thought crossly, but knew her crossness to be anxiety. And to be fair, Havencross had not been a private home for some time now, although the Somersby family had retained their own quarters upon turning it into a school. But still . . .

There was a slight, narrow bridge from the west bank of the river. If she'd been in any vehicle heavier and wider than her motorcycle, she might have been worried. As Diana carefully navigated her Douglas across, she eyed the steel-gray water below with misgiving. Even if she knew how to swim she wouldn't trust the icy waters of the North.

HAVENCROSS SCHOOL FOR BOYS proclaimed the austere sign on the other side of the bridge, and in less than a minute the house began to reveal itself. Spires and turrets first, like a medieval fairytale against the washed-out blue of the sky above the small hollow that held the house. Quickly enough the vast building revealed itself and, despite her best intentions to remain unimpressed, Diana's mouth dropped open. *Ninety schoolboys? This place could fit three times that. It must cost the earth to heat.*

She had sent her trunks ahead with a warning that she would arrive on motorbike so no one would be alarmed when the new school nurse appeared in canvas trousers, knee-high boots, and leather gloves. She had a ready collection of phrases to both introduce and defend herself, but the woman standing at the front door greeted Diana with a warm smile.

"Miss Neville? I'm Mrs. Willis, the school secretary. Welcome to Havencross."

The entrance hall stretched up three floors, with a grand staircase that split onto open landings on each level. The hall was tiled in a cream and dark green William Morris design, with mahogany paneling to head height and buttercup yellow paint above.

"I'll give you a quick tour of the general layout before I show you to your quarters," said Mrs. Willis, neat and trim as an English sparrow. "Including the infirmary, of course. If you're not too tired."

It was a speech that could easily have sounded condescending if delivered by the right sort of woman. But Mrs. Willis was young—early to midthirties at a guess—with soft brown eyes, a quick smile, and a black ribbon pinned to her blouse. A widow? There were widows to spare in England these days. Diana wondered if the woman had children.

She did, it turned out: two boys at the school. "Though my youngest will just be starting his studies this year," she confided.

The building was as efficiently laid out as possible in such an idiosyncratic space. Everything to the right of the central hall belonged to the school: a dining room with five long tables on the ground floor, classrooms on the first that stretched along a connecting corridor to the long east wing, and dormitories on the second floor.

The top floor of the central block was given over to staff bedrooms. "But you'll be housed in a more private area," Mrs. Willis ('Please call me Beth') said. Separated from the male staff, she meant. Other than Beth, who said that she lived in a suite in the west wing, and Diana, there were only two other women in residence: the cook, who lived near her kitchen domains, and Clarissa Somersby. Not only was Miss Somersby the school's headmistress, but the last family member in residence. *She'd* hardly be living in an attic floor bedroom.

The infirmary was at the end of the east wing on the second floor, an airy, high-ceilinged space with freshly whitewashed walls and a long line of windows that gave it the feel of a mini-cathedral. There were four beds set up, with room for twice that if needed, and Diana gave a delighted half laugh when shown the connecting examination room that doubled as an office. Situated in one of the turrets, it had a view right over the roof-tops to the river. If she stood on tiptoe, she could just see part of the bridge over which she'd come.

"I hope you like it," Beth said. "Our last nurse was a bit old-fashioned. She'd been here since the school opened in 1898, and the space reflected that. Miss Somersby gave me leave to update things. I hope it's acceptable."

"Acceptable? I spent the last three years in field hospitals and military tents. This is beyond beautiful." Diana turned away from the window and surveyed the pale oak desk, the cream-and-blue rug over freshly stained floorboards, the examination table covered in a white drape so clean that it looked as though it would actively repel anything except minor colds

20

and sprained ankles. More softly, she added, "It almost makes me feel guilty."

"Don't." The word came out with a sharpness that was surprising from the mild-faced secretary. "Don't feel guilty. My husband died in a field hospital near Verdun. He lived for three days before infection took him. I know what the nurses did for him there—I know they sat with him and helped him write a last letter to me and the boys. I know he was not alone when he died. So don't ever feel guilty about life being better now. You deserve it."

Diana blinked, then squeezed Beth's hand. "We all deserve it."

From the infirmary, Beth led her to a door that opened onto a corridor with lower ceilings and uneven floors.

"Fifteenth-century manor house," Beth said. "Built strongly enough to be worth preserving all this time."

Even if Beth hadn't confirmed it, Diana realized they'd crossed into a much older section of the house. The walls were stone and very thick, judging by how deep-set the windows were. Diana's bedroom was the lone unoccupied one in a short corridor with four rooms. One of them had been converted into a large bathroom that, even in September, made Diana shiver with cold and hope the water ran hot in the bath. The bedroom's low-beamed ceiling, charming angles, and linenfold paneling were generations removed from the décor of the main house, but the large fireplace and bright linens made it cozy.

Thankfully, her trunks had arrived. After bidding Beth a temporary goodbye and promising to join her and her boys for dinner that night, Diana set about unpacking. As comfortable as her motoring clothes were, she couldn't stay in them forever.

She only made it partway into her "I am a respectable nurse to be trusted with the health of ninety boys and not to be disturbed by fifteen male teachers" transformation. Her blue-striped shirtwaist and gray flannel skirt were demure enough. But she had just taken her hair out of its tight braids (the better to fit her helmet on) and it was still in a riot of loose, tangled curls when she heard a quick rapping on the door. "Come in," she called, figuring it was Beth with something she'd forgotten.

But the woman who entered was clearly not a secretary. Though Diana had not met her in person, she was certain this was Clarissa Somersby, headmistress of Havencross. She looked younger than Diana had expected, and prettier. Weren't all headmistresses gray-haired and iron-browed? Miss Somersby had dark hair pulled back in satin-smooth loops to frame a delicately-boned face and cheekbones Diana would have killed for. Even when she'd lost weight as an overworked battlefront nurse, her face had remained stubbornly round. Diana had always described herself as average height, average weight, average hair color somewhere between brown and mousy blond. Mostly it didn't bother her, except when facing a woman like this.

In a plummy upper-class voice, the woman said, "I am Miss Somersby. I know we're meant to meet later, but I wanted to ensure everything is in order. You are content with what you've seen thus far?"

Calling upon hard-won lessons about dignity and strength no matter if one had been working twenty-four hours straight and had blood up to their elbows, Diana straightened her back and said, "More than content. Havencross seems a lovely school, and the infirmary is wonderfully modern. Especially considering where I've been."

"Good." Miss Somersby took in Diana's tousled hair and the driving coat tossed across the bed. "I have no objection to your motorcycle, but of course the boys are not to be allowed near it."

As if Diana would risk her precious Douglas. "Of course not."

"Then I will see you in my office in one hour, Miss Neville." She paused and, in a much cooler tone, added, "It is a northern name, *Neville*. Are you part of that particular historical line?"

"As in the Wars of the Roses and Warwick the Kingmaker? If so, it's very distant. My family has been in London for generations. The only war we know is the current one."

Apparently Miss Somersby was not one for small talk. As abruptly as she'd entered, she was gone, leaving the door open. Diana blew out her breath and went to the dressing table to tame her hair into proper order.

Behind her, the door slammed shut with a suddenness that made her drop the hairbrush. An unexpected gust of air from the window she'd opened? Or Clarissa Somersby, deciding to . . . what? Warn her new employee to always be on her guard?

But on guard against what?

CHAPTER FIVE

DIANA
SEPTEMBER 1918

The boys began to arrive three days later. The staff was kept busy in every corner of the house: checking students in, overseeing luggage, tactfully separating parents as quickly as possible from the younger boys while keeping the older boys from running wild. Diana spent nearly six straight hours in her new office.

It was her job to accept any updated medical records for returning students and go through a thorough health history with the parents of new ones. It was a luxury she'd rarely had— to make note of such minor issues as measles and chicken pox, a broken ankle from falling out of a tree or stitches from a bicycle accident. She reassured the anxious mother of an asthmatic nine-year-old that his physical activity would be closely monitored and politely deflected a father who wanted assurances his son wouldn't be coddled despite a bout of rheumatic fever last winter.

Some of the parents had lost older sons in the war; some

of the boys had lost their fathers. Diana listened patiently to a mother whose only child was beginning here this fall.

"I didn't want to send him away," she admitted. "My husband has been in France since 1915 and has only just been invalided out with lung damage. But Luke has been asking me for a year to go away to school. I've told him he can change his mind at any time, that I'll come get him at once if he wants to come away. I just wish I knew what was best to do."

"I'm sure he'll be fine," Diana said reassuringly. "He'll be well watched over."

"Truthfully," the mother said, in a much softer voice, "I think he's glad to get away from home. His father is not . . . not exactly as he was before. Too much noise, too much bother. The littlest things make him angry."

Diana thought of her older brother, once so lighthearted, whom she hadn't seen smile in months. "I'm very sorry. The war exerted a terrible price, even on those who survived."

In a whisper that did not disguise despair, the mother asked, "Will it ever get better?"

"Time heals many things." And that, Diana thought despondently, is about the most useless thing she'd ever said. Time could heal. But not always, and not everyone. When the mother had left, Diana made an extra note to keep a personal eye on her son.

The flow of parents and a few grandparents slowed to a trickle as the afternoon wore on. Diana ensured the infirmary was in perfect order and that the store closet was stocked with medications and dressings for small injuries. Then she began putting her notes into a concise report for her meeting she had scheduled with Clarissa Somersby before the whole school gathered for dinner.

Diana had spent the afternoon listening to approaching

footsteps—the ones she heard now were different: male, firm, but with a slight hesitation in gait that her medical mind instantly categorized as *soldier, wounded.*

"Nurse Neville? Diana Neville?"

She turned in her seat, prepared with her professional smile to greet whatever father awaited her.

He had brown hair, a slender build but with the erect carriage of, yes, a former soldier, but too young to be anyone's father—at least of any boy old enough to attend this school. One of the school masters, then; there were still several she hadn't met.

But as these logical thoughts and impressions flashed through her mind, her body buzzed with something more instinctive that brought her to her feet. She took several steps closer, and he broke into a smile.

"It is you," he said. "Well, Nurse Neville, it's a long way from Thiepval."

Diana had met a lot of soldiers in three years of war nursing, but she didn't even have to search for this man's name. "Lieutenant Murray. What are you doing here?"

"Me? I'm from Northumberland. I grew up not five miles from here. The question is, what is a London-born nurse doing this far north? And it's not *lieutenant* anymore. It's Josh."

"What's your name?" she had asked the soldier with the bone sticking out of his lower left leg. It was a way of trying to keep him conscious, to keep shock from stealing him away, to make him focus on the here and now.

"Josh," he'd said through gritted teeth. "Joshua Murray."

"Stay with me, Josh. We'll get you straight into surgery. We'll take care of you."

"Promise?"

It wasn't the first, or even the five hundredth, time Diana had been asked that. But when she looked into his eyes, hazel ringed with green, and said, "I promise," the words tugged at something deep within her chest. Her heart? It didn't matter. A war zone was no place for hearts. And so she'd assisted in his surgery and got him through the first forty-eight hours and shipped him back to England for rehabilitation, as she'd done with every other soldier that had survived.

But now he was standing in front of her—standing, not lying on a bloody stretcher—at least five inches taller than she was, his face clean-shaven and no longer hollow-cheeked, wearing a three-piece suit instead of a uniform or hospital gown. It was all so odd. Was it really happening?

His expression changed, a mark of concern between his eyes. "Are you all right? Do you need to sit back down?"

Diana began to laugh. "Do *I* need to sit down? I can't believe you're on your feet. Not after the last time I saw you."

"You promised you'd take care of me. Are you telling me that was just a line you feed every soldier? That you fully expected me to die?"

There weren't a lot of smiles in field hospitals, at least not the kind of smile Joshua Murray gave her now. All at once, Diana thought it might be a good idea to sit down. But she wouldn't let him have the last word.

"What I never expected was to have you walk into the infirmary of a boys' school as though you owned the place. Really, what are you doing here?"

He gestured to her chair and she sat gratefully while he pulled out a wooden straight-backed chair and straddled it, elbows braced on the back. Diana shot a quick look at his leg, but there was nothing to see beneath the carefully-tailored trousers. She

27

was pretty sure he wasn't wearing a brace, which, truth be told, *was* more than she'd expected.

"Considering I was in and out of consciousness most of the time you knew me, I will forgive you for not knowing that before I was Lieutenant Murray, I was Joshua Murray, with an MA in classics and history. I meant to stay at Oxford when I finished my degree, but my father had a stroke and I was needed at home. Fortunately, our farmhouse is the nearest neighbor to Havencross and the Somersbys were kind enough to take me on. I'd only been here a year before war broke out." He eyed her intently. "Now your turn. How did a nurse born and bred in London find herself all the way up here in the wild?"

"There aren't a lot of jobs available for nurses, at least not those who want to leave the war behind. I didn't want to work with soldiers anymore. I know that's selfish, but—"

"Not selfish."

"Maybe. My mother doesn't understand. Certainly not the Northumberland part. As far as she's concerned, civilization ends somewhere around Coventry."

There was more to it, but Joshua didn't need to know that. No one needed to know how London had just too many damned people. After years of living on top of one another in tents and field hospitals, after the constant pressure of wounded men in crowded wards, after the relentless, eternal thrum of heavy guns pounding day and night never more than three miles away . . . Diana had craved silence. Solitude. Ninety schoolboys might not sound like the perfect escape, but it had to be better than what haunted her dreams.

Those hazel-green eyes of Joshua Murray looked far too knowing. But bless the man for discretion—and probably a measure of understanding—for he simply said, "You're going to be very popular, Miss Neville. Ninety boys and fifteen schoolmasters—half of them will be in love with you by Michaelmas."

"And the rest?"

He grinned—there was no other word for it: "The rest are fools." He stood up and swung his chair back against the wall it had come from. "I'll see you at dinner."

She listened to his footsteps receding. Yes, he had a definite hesitation in that left leg. It must still be considerably weaker than the right one, but he covered it well. Those who'd been to war knew how to cover lots of things.

There was no use trying to get any more work done. Diana tidied up her files and desk and checked her watch: ten minutes to her meeting with Miss Somersby. As she picked up the notebook that went with her everywhere, another set of footsteps sounded in the corridor.

For one moment her heart leaped at the thought of Joshua returning, but these were too light. One of the boys, perhaps? But no, there was a distinct clicking sound—the sound made by the heels of a woman's shoes.

She crossed the room, expecting to find Beth Willis. Although she was even busier than Diana, they had spent a little time together each day since her arrival.

The footsteps were just outside the door when Diana opened it with a greeting on her lips.

A greeting that died instantly. It wasn't Beth. It wasn't anyone. The corridor was entirely empty.

CHAPTER SIX

JULIET
2018

The great advantage of any physical work after months of lying in bed watching Netflix was how easily it exhausted Juliet. She was in pajamas by seven o'clock her first full day, which didn't seem so early considering it had been dark outside three hours earlier. She intended to read, but when she jerked awake hours later, the book had fallen on her chest still open to the first page. She rubbed her breastbone where it had hit her and thought that at least there wasn't anyone to see a bruise.

Rolling over, Juliet checked her phone: 4 a.m. With a groan, she realized she had to get up and pee.

Why did beautiful old English houses have to be so freaking cold? Even in her thermal tee and wool socks, Juliet was shaking by the time she reached the toilet at the other end of the corridor. She pulled the cistern chain and dashed back to her room to the sound of creaking pipes.

And not just the pipes. As the banging subsided along with

the flow of water, Juliet heard something soft and whispery snaking through the air. Like the intake of breath just before someone speaks, or the echo after a footstep.

She whipped around in her bedroom doorway, but of course it was empty—the entire fourteen-thousand-square-foot house was empty. It was freezing outside, and anything she thought she heard was only mice moving through the walls in search of warmth and shelter. *Oh please, let it only be mice*, she thought as she took refuge back in bed. No rats. Or raccoons.

She didn't hear anything else before finally drifting back to sleep around dawn.

When she woke again, Juliet was astonished to realize that she'd slept until ten—and that she was starving. Two things that had not happened in so long. She scrambled into jeans and a wool sweater and was halfway down the main stairs when she heard the definite sounds of someone in the house. Someone real, unless ghosts had learned to vacuum.

She was prepared with a smile when she reached the ground floor and found a woman vacuuming in the room to the right of the central hall. This must be Rachel Bennett, whom Nell had said would come once a week to clean. Juliet moved carefully into her line of sight so as not to alarm her.

Rachel switched off the vacuum the moment she saw her. She was younger than Juliet had expected—midthirties, at most, with a cheerful face and round cheeks with matching dimples.

"Ms. Stratford, I hope I didn't disturb you."

"Juliet, please. Of course not. I just wanted to say hi and then I'll get out of your way."

"Do you want breakfast? I'd be happy to make something."

"Oh no," Juliet said, horrified. "You're not—I mean, I can cook."

Rachel clicked the vacuum into a standing position. "You'd be doing me a favor. I'd rather cook than hoover any day. Besides, I'm dreadfully nosy and this will give me a chance to find out your darkest secrets."

You're far too happy-looking to want my darkest secrets, Juliet thought. But she couldn't think of a graceful way to continue saying no without sounding like Rachel *did* work for her.

"Thank you, Ms. Bennett. When I say I can cook, I use the term loosely."

"It's Rachel. I brought fresh bread with me. Come tell me what else you want."

When Rachel Bennett said *fresh bread*, she meant "kneaded by hand and taken out of the oven an hour ago." Also raspberry jam ("simple to freeze jam in the autumn"), a dozen eggs that had never seen a supermarket, and local bacon. While Rachel fried the bacon and eggs, she chatted away about herself.

"I went south for university and stayed in Leeds when I got married. My wife, Antonia, is in IT and I temped in between having three boys, but all I've really ever wanted was to come back to the farm. Then my mum died last spring, and my dad needed help round the house and caring for my great-aunt, so the boys and I moved up here in June. Antonia was able to negotiate working remotely two days a week, so Tuesdays to Thursdays she's in Leeds, and the rest of the time she's here. Drives me mental complaining: 'the sky is too big' or 'the farm is too smelly.' But she's just taking the piss—she knows we love it."

It wasn't easy getting a word in, which was rather restful. Not like with Duncan, who had simply loved the sound of his own voice. Juliet even managed a couple questions: "Your boys didn't mind moving? How old are they?"

"Eight, seven, and five. The oldest complained about

switching schools, but his heart wasn't in it. They love running wild outdoors and the farm animals. What boy wouldn't?"

Would you have loved it, Liam? Would you have run wild through the Maine woods and along the beach?

"So you're here taking inventory and throwing out the junk," Rachel continued, neatly slipping two over-easy eggs onto a plate and handing it to Juliet. She poured herself a cup of tea and leaned against the worktop. "Word around here is you're a professor too." This argued some very good sources of local gossip.

"Not quite that grand. I haven't even finished my doctorate yet." She took a bite of egg and nearly moaned in delight.

"What's your subject?" Rachel asked.

"Overall, I focused on Victorian and Edwardian women's history. For my doctorate, I started out researching the history of women in the workplace before and during World War One. But these days I mostly teach introductory history courses."

Duncan hadn't liked that. Teaching freshman students how to properly use the university library for research wasn't impressive enough for his wife. He'd been pushing her to finish her dissertation for years. Which was probably why she'd dragged her feet for so long. Her own passive rebellion.

With Rachel looking at her as though she were truly interested, Juliet expanded on the idea that had seized her the moment she'd learned about Havencross. "I've always been fascinated by the 1918 flu pandemic. I know Havencross was a school then. I'm considering writing about Clarissa Somersby. She was very young to be a school headmistress, and I'm curious how she coped when the flu swept through the area." Juliet took a sip of tea. "Of course, I'll need to dig deeper to see if there's really enough here to support a book-length dissertation."

"I should think so," Rachel said, with an unexpected hint of amusement. "The flu hit the school just as the war ended. They only had one medical officer, a nurse who'd served in France. For two weeks, everyone at Havencross who didn't fall ill worked themselves that way taking care of the others."

Juliet laid down her fork—she'd eaten almost embarrassingly fast—and eyed Rachel thoughtfully. She sounded as though she were speaking about something that had happened just a few years ago. "How do you know all this? Because if this is the kind of local oral history available, then I'm very interested."

"We've got more than just oral history," Rachel said, with a grin that hinted at smugness. "The Havencross school nurse was actually my great-grandmother. Some stories have been passed down in the telling, but my great-aunt Winnie has written sources if you'd like them. I'm pretty sure they're packed away in trunks in the farmhouse attic."

"Would your family mind if I went rummaging through them?"

"Mind?" Rachel laughed. "Aunt Winnie will be delighted. She's tried to get us interested in that stuff, but only the major points have managed to stick. Come over some afternoon, stay for dinner. No need to phone ahead. Just be prepared for more stories than you'll know what to do with. She'll probably even throw in the Havencross ghost too, so I hope you're not easily frightened."

"I imagined there must be a ghost. No house stands this long without collecting tragedies." Juliet knew all about tragedy and ghosts. She'd left home because she was being haunted. No stranger's past and death could be worse.

Rachel returned to the vacuum and Juliet decided to take a look at the pile of local histories she'd gathered from Clarissa's rooms. She took out her notebook and began skimming for references to Havencross School, 1918, and influenza. But she got sidetracked in the very first one she picked up. It was so old it was mimeographed, with the overwritten prose of a certain kind of local historian.

Havencross, though known today primarily as the showplace of Gideon Somersby, his large family, and his even larger railroad fortune, has a much deeper past. The name comes from Havencross Priory, a monastery active from the twelfth to the late fourteenth century. Though little remains standing, parts of the cloister were built into the foundation of Havencross Hall in 1430. The land was the gift from the boy king, Henry VI, to a useful local lord who helped patrol the Scottish border. It remained in the Deacon family only until 1471, when the last family members vanish from the records.

Legend, which must always be treated with care, claims violence in the family's end, and there have been many reports in the intervening centuries of the sighting of a small boy. Though one does not wish to encourage a belief in the supernatural, one also admits that the Wars of the Roses were a time of upheaval and death, not least in 1471 during Warwick's Rebellion. Some few claim the boy must be one of King Richard III's murdered nephews, but one need only note that the eldest was barely born in that year and so could hardly have to do with any mystery of that decade.

Juliet thought, *Well, that explained Clarissa's interest in the Wars of the Roses.* It was an intriguing story, though she wondered why it had caught the attention of an old woman in her last years. She made herself a note to ask Rachel's great-aunt what she knew of Clarissa Somersby. Maybe the woman could tell her more than the few stories Juliet had gathered thus far.

CHAPTER SEVEN

ISMAY
MAY 1453

In these times sprang up between King Henry VI and Richard, the Duke of York, those quarrels which ended only with the deaths of nearly all the nobles of the land. For those who were rivals of York brought accusations against him of treason, insisting that he was endeavoring to gain the kingdom for himself and his sons. A solemn oath was demanded of York that he would never aspire to the rule of the kingdom, and he was most strictly ordered not to go beyond his own estates or to pass the boundaries of his castles. Many of York's friends took it very much to heart that injuries so great should be inflicted upon an innocent man, and they determined to remove York's enemies from the side of the king.

Ismay Deacon stood as tall and straight as any fine lady as she waited in Ludlow Castle's hall to meet her new guardian. Ten years old was practically grown-up, and so what if the Duke of York was the richest man in England behind the king?

Ismay was a descendant of Scottish kings, and she must do her mother proud.

But thoughts of her mother threatened tears, so she blinked hard and made herself think of other things. Ludlow was a fine castle, bustling and busy with the duke's household. Seven children survived, and Ismay had memorized their names: Anne, Edward, Edmund, Elizabeth, Margaret, George, Richard. It was a little bit frightening for an only child. Now an orphaned only child.

A burst of noise made her flinch, and before she could locate the source, someone barreled into Ismay hard enough to knock her over.

"Sorry! I didn't see you there. Are you all right?"

Ismay swallowed hard and looked up at a very tall boy, who bent over and offered his hand to help her up. Maybe not so much a boy. He had blond hair and a breathtaking smile that didn't waver even when a commanding female voice said, "Edward! What have I told you about playing games indoors?"

"Sorry, Mama. At least I didn't break anything this time. Or I don't think I have." He looked at Ismay quizzically. "I haven't broken you, have I?"

She shook her head, for her voice had deserted her. So this was Edward of York. He seemed much older than eleven.

Duchess Cecily came down the steps and turned her gaze from her son to her new ward. "Forgive my son, Lady Ismay. His carelessness is exceeded only by his impudence." But there was more affection than criticism in her voice.

"I am all right," Ismay said. "I wasn't paying attention."

"You've had a long journey. My husband is away for several days. Until his return I have put you in a private room. I know you are unused to other children."

"Thank you, my lady."

"I'll show her, Mama," said Edward.

The offer terrified Ismay. She would never be able to think of anything to say to him that wasn't childish or stupid.

But the duchess shook her head. "You were expected with the clerk fifteen minutes ago. You have business to attend to."

Edward grinned and kissed his mother's hand before taking the stairs two at a time.

The duchess studied her as though she were a perplexing household problem. She was as terrifying as her oldest son but in an entirely different way. Ismay's mother had been all laughter and music. Cecily of York looked as if laughter would be beneath her.

In the flow of people that had continued in and out of the hall, one caught Lady York's eye and she motioned. "Will you show Lady Ismay to her room? It's in the same corridor as mine."

It was another boy, younger than Edward, a slightly paler copy, but clearly related. "She's not to be with the girls?" he asked.

"Not just yet. Your father will decide." The duchess turned her cool regard on Ismay once more. "I will have a maid bring up water to bathe. You may dine in your room tonight. In the morning I will send for you."

It might have sounded as though Ismay was being accorded great favor as an honored guest, but for all that Duchess Cecily called her Lady Ismay, she knew that she was being kept apart from the York children until such time as the duke decided whether she was good enough to remain in their household. Just because they wanted the wealth of her wardship didn't mean they needed to keep her. She could just as easily be sent to a convent.

She thought a convent might be very nice. Quiet, at least. And no superior duchesses or beautiful boys who could talk rings around their mothers.

She felt a tentative touch on her shoulder. "Are you all right?"

It was the other boy asking, in a much kinder way than his brother had. As though he truly cared.

Ismay nodded, then found that her voice had returned. "It's a long way from Havencross."

"And you came by yourself?" He managed to ask without sounding judgmental or pitying.

She lifted her chin, feigning bravery. "I had no one to come with me."

I have no one, she repeated in her head. *I am alone in the world.*

"Well, you have us now. If you want us." His smile was not as breathtaking as Edward's. "I'm Edmund," he said. "Welcome to the family."

CHAPTER EIGHT

DIANA
SEPTEMBER 1918

The second Saturday after term began, Diana took advantage of her first free afternoon to put off her nurse's uniform and put on her leather boots and goggles. She pushed her beloved motorbike out of the old stables, where it was stored with several automobiles belonging to the school. And, to the admiring looks of the boys playing cricket on the front lawn, she rode out of the courtyard with a little more flair than was strictly necessary.

Her father had bought her the Douglas after sixteen-year-old Diana had tried to ride her older brother's Enfield. There was no better training ground for riding through traffic, making quick turns and stops, than London, and within weeks of war being declared she was a messenger for the War Office. In December 1914, an army medical officer had spotted Diana, by now twenty-one, as she'd made a hairpin turn on her motorbike, tracked her down, and asked if she wanted to be an ambulance driver in France.

Almost four years ago, but it seemed much longer when she thought of herself back then, cheerful and innocent and eager to dash toward adventure and embrace danger. That girl had died in France, somewhere between ambulance driving, nurse training, and the forward medical post she'd helped set up in 1916 just a hundred yards from the front.

Only on her Douglas did Diana feel that maybe not all light and joy had died in the war. And to ride out here—beneath enormous skies, across rivers, up and down hills—was what she imagined flying must be like. There was only air and light surrounding her, until she reached Steel Rigg and caught her first sight of Hadrian's Wall.

She parked the bike and took off her goggles and gloves, tucking them into one of her panniers. She didn't know exactly where she was, but it didn't appear to be private land—it certainly wasn't farmed or foraged—and this was England; nobody here would shoot her for walking in the wrong field, and the Romans hadn't left landmines behind.

The old stone wall marking Rome's farthest border tracked along the natural geography. In some places it had tumbled down to little more than a suggestion, and everywhere it had grass growing along the top as though Britain had told her invaders, "Build your wall, but we'll make it our own and endure long after you are gone."

One section, going sharply uphill, had a path beside it. Diana went partway up until she found a convenient rock outcropping to sit on. She had never been anywhere so silent. It was tangible, but not in an oppressive way. Rather, the silence stole inside her limbs and her mind until she had never been so at peace in her life. She had been right to come to Havencross. This silence and space was what she needed.

Diana sat there long enough to grow stiff, and in all that

time saw only one person, walking a dog in the far distance. She reluctantly started down the path when she saw a rider on horseback approaching from the west. The rider must have seen her as well, for the horse angled its direction and met up with her as she reached the bottom of the track.

Joshua Murray wore an open-necked shirt on this unusually warm day with the sleeves rolled, showing off his forearms. He smiled at her wryly. "You're a hard person to catch up. That motorbike is fast."

"And it requires less feeding and care than a horse." She kept a wary eye on the animal. Horses had played little part in her life, save for speeding around horse-drawn carts in parts of London.

With easy grace, Joshua swung off the horse and dismounted with brief hesitation when his injured leg touched the ground. "I'll walk you back to the bike if that's all right."

"You don't have to."

"I want to."

Seeing him so at ease on horseback had reminded Diana that she knew what regiment he'd served in. "You were a cavalry officer."

"Northumberland Fusiliers, yes. Family tradition. My grandfather was in the Crimea. I could ride almost before I could walk."

"It was a horse that broke your leg," she said, details returning as those distinctly intense eyes of his pulled out memories from the field hospital.

"It was a bullet that broke my leg," he corrected her. "The horse falling on me just compounded matters. No pun intended."

"Compound fractures are notoriously difficult healers." An ambivalent sentence at best.

The corner of his mouth quirked up. "Are you trying to be discreet? It's all right, I don't mind talking about it. Not to you. It took me eight months to walk without crutches and a year without a cane. Even now I still have one, for when I get tired. My hill-walking days may never return, but I can still ride. For a Murray, that's as important as breathing."

"I feel that way about the motorbike. As long as I can get away somewhere by myself, independent . . ."

"And alone? I shouldn't have bothered you. I apologize."

"I don't mind you." The words slipped out before she knew it, and heat bloomed in her cheeks. "I mean, I don't mind out here. Where it's so empty and quiet."

"A big difference from France," he agreed.

"Is that why you came back here?"

When he answered, it wasn't at all flippant. "Yes."

Diana cast around for a topic not so laden with war memories. "Tell me about the Somersby family," she asked. "When I interviewed with Sir Wilfred Somersby in London, he told me that his daughter was brilliant, but not easy. I wondered if he was warning me away, though he seemed eager enough to offer me the job."

"Clarissa Somersby," Josh said with a meditative air. "I didn't know her well, she's five years younger than I am, but our families spent some time together before the school was founded. Before Thomas died."

Diana raised her head sharply. "Thomas? Who's Thomas?"

"You really haven't been anywhere near the village, have you? Thomas Somersby was Clarissa's younger brother. He vanished during a storm in '07. They never found his body. He was six years old."

Beneath her war-deadened sensibilities, Diana felt a fierce pluck of sadness. She had thought the soldiers she'd nursed too young to die. But a six-year-old, one who wasn't even sick . . . "He and Clarissa were close?"

He nodded. "She and Thomas were the only children of

Sir Wilfred's first wife. He married again when Thomas was a baby, had a few more children, but my mother always said that Clarissa blamed herself for losing Thomas. The family usually only spent a few months each year at Havencross, but after her brother disappeared Clarissa refused to leave. She searched every day, and then she was ill for a very long time. And ever since, she has not left Havencross for a single night."

"Not once? But surely—"

"Her father objected? Of course he did. But Clarissa has never lacked for willpower. She was only thirteen at the time, but she was the driving force behind the founding of the school. Her father made sure she was educated to the best standards by those who came here to teach, and by the time she was twenty she was already his second-in-command. When her father chose to return south in '16, it was Clarissa who ensured the school kept functioning. She is a remarkable woman, yes. *Brilliant* is certainly accurate."

"Brilliant but broken," Diana whispered.

Josh shrugged. "Aren't we all, these days?"

They'd reached her motorbike. He didn't linger but mounted his horse with the same ease and gazed down at her. "I didn't just tell you this for gossip's sake, or to make you feel sorry for her. Like all boys everywhere, the students get to know these things. There have always been stories running among them about the ghost of a boy who died there. The older ones use it sometimes to frighten the youngest. Death is not a stranger to most of them now, and it will be easy for them to transmute their grief into a safe haunting. You might want to be on alert for that."

With a flick of his hand to his head, almost a salute, he rode off. Diana watched until he was long out of sight, thinking of Thomas and the many lost and forgotten boys she'd known in the last four years.

CHAPTER NINE

JULIET
2018

After Rachel's visit, Juliet decided to create a schedule for herself. That was the problem with spending months without a job. As an adjunct history professor for the last three years, her schedule had changed with every new semester, but the basics had remained the same. Getting up early, doing some yoga, teaching class, attending office hours in a squashed corner of whatever space the tenured professors allowed, grading papers, prepping for the next day's classes, eating dinner with Duncan on the nights he came home, and going to bed. When doctor's visits began creeping into her life with depressing regularity—even in the aftermath of three miscarriages in two years—Juliet had clung to the structure of her days.

For months now, she'd hardly been able to tell the days apart, broken only by her parents' insistence that she see a therapist weekly. And though Juliet had gone simply because resisting would have taken too much energy, slowly she had begun to pick up the various threads of daily life.

"Start small," her therapist had said. "Take a shower every day. That's all you have to do for now."

Showering had been followed by getting dressed, then leaving her bedroom during daylight hours. Instead of watching *Parks and Rec*, pick up a book. Instead of lying on the couch, do stretches for ten minutes.

Clearly, it had worked well enough to get her here. Now that she was here, Juliet didn't want to lose her momentum. She didn't want to just drift anymore. She wanted to accomplish things. And the therapist's stepping-stone process had shown her the value of a schedule.

So . . . split each day between cleaning and organizing the many rooms of Havencross, and doing the research needed for her dissertation. She would aim for a seventy/thirty split at first, but if things went smoothly in the house she could spend more time writing as she went along. And she needn't feel guilty, because a large part of her job was simply to be at Havencross through the winter to ensure there were no structural disasters or opportunistic thievery. It's not as though they had her keeping a timesheet.

They meaning the law firm who represented the hotel investors, which meant in practice Nell Somersby-Sims. While she was being so productive, Juliet sent off an email to Nell with a list and photographs attached of the various valuable items she thought would be worth selling, and a couple questions about heating and water supply.

She added one last question after dithering back and forth: *Do you have any paperwork on the previous ownership and/or history of Havencross?* It was worth a shot. Probably lawyers didn't care about ownership past a certain time—it wasn't as though the inhabitants of the medieval priory were going to suddenly make a claim on the estate.

For two days, Juliet kept strictly to her schedule of early bedtime and early rising and moved through the old army offices in a flurry, tossing out old papers, cleaning decades of grime off desks and chairs and stacking them neatly against walls. With each hour, it became easier to see the house as it had been when a family had lived and loved there, or when dozens of boys had scrambled through corridors between classes and meals.

On Friday afternoon—having called first, despite Rachel's open invitation—Juliet drove her rental car across the narrow bridge then three miles to White Rose Farm. Another reference to the fifteenth century and the North's support of the Yorkist cause, she noted. They seemed to be popping up everywhere.

Winifred Murray opened the door to the low stone farmhouse herself and greeted Juliet with a formal courtesy that made her nervous. Rachel's great-aunt must be in her eighties, and she dressed like Juliet imagined a World War II country-house matron would: tweed skirt, cardigan, and discreet pearls. But the woman's dignity was paired with genuine warmth, and Juliet found it surprisingly easy to talk to her.

Juliet accepted tea, and they sat in a shabby but welcoming room with books jammed onto shelves and piled haphazardly on almost every flat surface. A fire—of course there was a fire, there was probably a nanny upstairs somewhere too—burned cozily, and she thought it one of the most relaxing rooms she'd ever been in.

"Rachel told me you grew up in this house," Juliet said.

"Yes, there have been Murrays at White Rose Farm for hundreds of years. No matter how far we roam, most of us remain anchored here."

"I hope you don't think me unbearably inquisitive, but I'm curious about the family tree. Rachel's surname is Bennett—"

"Why isn't she a Murray?" Winifred anticipated the question. "Goodness, child, never apologize to an old woman for asking questions. There's little I like better than talking about myself and the past. My parents had four children. Two girls and a boy in quick succession, then me nearly a decade later. Sadly, my brother Andrew died on a Normandy beach on D-Day. In the sixties, the farm passed to my sister Ellice and her husband Charles Bennett, then onto their son Josiah, who is Rachel's father. But make no mistake—just because her name is Bennett doesn't mean Rachel hasn't inherited every last bit of Murray love for this farm."

"I could tell," Juliet agreed. "It must be lovely to be surrounded by your own history. My mother's mother is English, but I couldn't even tell you where the rest of my ancestors were three hundred years ago. I think that's one reason I was always drawn to history."

Winifred eyed her intently over her teacup. "Rachel says you're interested in Havencross and the influenza pandemic of 1918."

"I am, yes. Havencross was still a school when you were young, correct?"

"Until 1939. The school had survived one war; no one had the heart to keep it going for a second. And of course, Clarissa Somersby had moved on long before then."

"Did you know her?" Juliet asked.

"She was my godmother. I knew her mostly through letters when I was young, but after the war—World War Two—I often spent summers with her in London or Paris or Rome. She helped me prep for university and encouraged me to think beyond teaching or nursing. Not that those aren't honorable occupations, but I was never suited for caretaking. I worked in the Foreign Office for thirty years instead."

Winifred levered herself up carefully from the chair—only her cautious movements revealed her advanced age—and searched for something on the overfilled bookshelves as Juliet stood. Instead of a book, she selected a silver frame with a black-and-white photograph. She handed it to Juliet, who had stood up when Winifred did.

It was a familiar photograph—two women in ankle-length skirts sitting on the brick garden wall at Havencross. One woman with laughing eyes, and one with defined cheekbones and glossy, dark hair.

"I've seen this," Juliet said. "I found it at Havencross, among Clarissa's belongings."

Winifred pointed to the dark-haired woman. "That is Clarissa, and that"—she pointed to Clarissa's laughing companion—"is my mother. They were the best of friends until the last days of their lives."

"The school nurse," Juliet noted, remembering what Rachel had told her about her great-grandmother. "And that's why you have records about the school and the influenza."

"Indeed. I've already had Noah bring down the most pertinent items from the attic. They're in the dining room."

For a historian, the trove of primary source materials spread out on a twelve-foot-long refectory table was as enticing as alcohol and arguing was to Juliet's ex-husband. She had to restrain herself from attacking it all at once and forced herself to listen to Winifred's overview.

"Here is the school register for 1918, the curricula vitae of the teachers and staff, maps of the dormitory wings with boys' names penciled in, copies of the rules and regulations, standard curricula by year, etc. Also, my mother's diary and casebook, covering November 1918."

Juliet was itching to open that casebook, but she forced

herself to pay attention as Winifred indicated a number of newspapers encased in clear plastic. "Local reporting during that last autumn of the war, lots of good background details about domestic and farm life here at the time. And then, of course, all the news about the pandemic, including casualty lists by area and week."

"This is perfect," Juliet said. "You won't mind me coming over to research for a week or so?"

Winifred laughed. "Trying to work here would be a waste, what with three active boys running around. You came by car? I'll have Noah help you load the boxes. Keep them as long as you'd like."

She stepped out for a minute to ask Noah—Juliet assumed he was one of Rachel's sons—and Juliet ran her fingers lightly over the items spread across the table.

When Winifred returned, Juliet asked, "What's this?" while touching the cover of a vintage photo album. When Winifred nodded for her to go ahead, she opened it to find not photographs, but newspaper cuttings.

LOCAL BOY MISSING IN STORM

DOZENS COMB THE WILDERNESS IN SEARCH OF MISSING CHILD

SIR WILFRED SOMERSBY OFFERS REWARD FOR NEWS OF SON

SHOE LOCATED ON RIVER BANK; THOMAS SOMERSBY PRESUMED DROWNED

Juliet looked at the dates—all 1907. If she remembered correctly, Sir Wilfred had been Clarissa Somersby's father, which meant the lost boy had been her brother. This had not been one of the—admittedly few—stories her mother had passed on.

"Is this where the Havencross ghost story comes from?" asked Juliet.

"Oh no, the ghost sightings go back much further than Thomas. I think somewhere there's a monograph that attempted to collate all the sightings, but I couldn't locate it offhand. I'll keep an eye out. But no, the Forgotten Boy"—Winifred capitalized the phrase with her voice—"goes back centuries. Perhaps all the way to the Wars of the Roses."

"That's what Rachel mentioned. But surely not really Richard the Third and his nephews?"

Winifred shrugged. "Who knows? There have never been any credible accounts of their disappearance. The North was always Richard's power base. Who's to say the boys didn't end up here—maybe to be quietly killed, maybe on their way to being smuggled out of the country?"

Juliet didn't believe it—or at least, she didn't believe anyone would ever prove it. It was just another in a long line of centuries' old rumors and legends. Besides, the Havencross ghost references were to a single boy, not brothers.

Next to her, Winifred straightened and said, "If you want to know more about the ghost, you should ask Noah. He's got a story. And here he is now. We'll just pack up these papers and he'll get them in your car for you."

Juliet turned, prepared to greet Rachel's son with a friendly smile. But Noah could not possibly be her son. Her brother, she guessed. He was in that indeterminate age between midtwenties and midthirties, his hair a common shade of light brown. He had a quick step that brought him to Juliet with outstretched hand before she'd recovered from her surprise.

"Noah Bennett. It's awfully nice of you to entertain Aunt Winnie for us." But the teasing was good-humored and made Winifred roll her eyes as she might at a teenager.

"All the pleasure is on my side," Juliet said, wincing inwardly at how artificial she sounded. "I am truly interested, I mean. In Havencross. And I need something to do during the long winter nights."

She was babbling like an idiot. Duncan had always told her she should think about how she presented herself in professional settings. Not that this was professional. Nor was it personal. What exactly was this?

Up close, Noah Bennett's eyes were hazel-green, with the kind of long lashes that women always envied on men. At least he was polite enough not to draw attention to her awkwardness. He merely shook her hand, then helped his great-aunt with the papers and boxes.

When all had been secured and she'd bid Winifred Murray goodbye, Juliet directed Noah to her car.

He deposited three boxes on the back seat. "You sure you don't want me to follow you and help unload?"

"If I can't manage three boxes, then I should hardly be left in charge of Havencross on my own," she said.

"You know you can ring the farm anytime if you need, well, anything. You've met Rachel. She's got enough energy to run a small power plant. And you've got my number, I think."

"I don't—"

"Should be on the information the solicitors left for you. My surveying company did some work around Havencross when the investors were looking to buy. Mine is the contact number in case of fire or flood, that sort of thing."

"Oh, right."

He hesitated, one arm resting against the car's back window. "In fact, they thought it a good idea if I dropped in every week or so and checked things over. Heating, plumbing, you know. Preventing problems beforehand. I'm based in Newcastle, but since I'm visiting home this weekend anyway, I could come by tomorrow?"

Juliet didn't recall anything about weekly checks from surveyors. Could it be Noah simply wanted to see her? "Yes, of course. Anytime."

With a pat to her car roof, as though seeing off a busload of kids, Noah said, "One o'clock, then. See you."

Ghosts, she thought as she drove away from White Rose Farm. *I was expecting ghosts. And the flu. And Clarissa Somersby. I was not expecting a man with beautiful eyes and a sexy accent who makes me want to forget that I thought my life was over.*

CHAPTER TEN

DIANA
OCTOBER 1918

The tricks began in mid-October—or at least that was when Diana began to take note. At first she thought herself simply absent-minded when she couldn't find her favorite fountain pen, only to locate it that night balanced precariously on the edge of the bathroom sink. And it wasn't so odd to misplace a file for *McArdle, James* in the *A*s instead of the *M*s. When she found her tea tray on her desk with the cup smashed on the floor, Diana assumed one of the boys had been looking for her and, having broken it accidentally, fled the scene.

Ink flooded across her notebook, messages that never made it to her so that she missed meetings, even a long rip in her favorite skirt—all of it, though annoying, could be explained.

But when the knocking on her door started in the middle of the night, Diana knew she had to get things under control. It wasn't that she was surprised; she'd grown up with two brothers and knew that putting ninety boys under one vast roof would entail a certain amount of high spirits and pranks. She also knew how quickly things could get out of hand in that same environment.

She brought it up in the weekly staff meeting, held every Sunday while the boys attended an evening service, presided over by a local priest in the dining hall. Present were all those who both worked and lived in Havencross: fifteen masters, Mrs. McCann the cook, Beth Willis taking notes, Diana herself, and Clarissa Somersby. Though she presided, Clarissa was not a dictatorial headmistress. She was also highly efficient: there was always a printed agenda never longer than one page handed out by Beth, and so far no meeting had lasted over an hour. Today's agenda covered the upcoming half-term holiday and the activities planned for those boys not going home, behavioral reports from the six teachers who were resident supervisors of each dormitory wing, and academic issues, which were handled by Joshua Murray as Clarissa's newly named second-in-command. Last was always Diana's report of weekly infirmary visits.

Because Diana was last, she segued straight from her medical report into the knocking on her bedroom door at night. It had happened three of the previous four nights. After asking if anyone else had been a victim, she looked expectantly around the room.

There was silence.

Diana waited for Clarissa to take control, but she looked unusually remote, even for her. So Diana mentally shrugged and queried the dormitory supervisors herself. "Have any of you noticed a boy or several boys out of bed after hours?"

It had to be asked, though she was pretty sure if they had, they'd have mentioned it earlier. Sure enough, all six denied knowledge.

Luther Weston, who taught Latin and Greek, shot a question

back at Diana: "Are you quite sure you didn't . . ." he hesitated meaningfully. "That you weren't dreaming?"

He spoke with an arrogance that could not be learned, only inherited. Diana knew everyone there heard his real question: "*Are you quite sure you didn't imagine it?*"

"Once might have been dreaming. Not three times."

"It would be very difficult for any of us to have missed seeing or hearing an out-of-bound's pupil." He would have been less offensive without the forced politeness or the condescending smile. "We do know our jobs."

Little girl, he might as well have added.

Prick, she thought back. Army nursing had a way of expanding one's vocabulary.

Joshua intervened. "We all know our jobs well enough to know how very ingenious the young can be when in pursuit of mischief. This is an old house. Surely you don't pop out of bed to investigate every creak, Weston, or you'd never get any sleep. It's not hard to believe that some of the older boys have learned the quickest and quietest methods of going where they want without being noticed."

And vanishing afterward, Diana almost added. It was the part of all this she most disliked—that no matter how quickly she moved, by the time she heard the knocking and crossed the room, whoever it was had vanished out of sight in the corridor. Could they really hear her padding across the floor in her bare feet?

The alternative—that they could somehow see inside her room—she liked even less.

Beth Willis put down her pen and cleared her throat. "If you like . . ." she began, a little tentative since she rarely spoke in these meetings, "I can speak to my boys about any rumors going around."

"We could do that," said Weston insultingly.

Diana decided she liked him less every time he opened his mouth.

Just as she liked Beth Wills more when she retorted, "No offense, Mr. Weston, but I rather think my boys are more afraid of me than they are of you. If there are any tales being spread about mischief at night, I think I can find them out quicker than you can."

After her sphinxlike silence, at last Clarissa spoke in command. "Good, thank you, Mrs. Willis. And I think it best to set up night patrols for the next week—every hour on the hour. I'm sure you won't mind taking tonight, Mr. Weston."

"It's a waste of time," he muttered, just softly enough that Clarissa could plausibly ask, "What was that?"

There weren't enough jobs going spare in England that Weston could afford to get himself thrown out of this one. So he plastered on a neutral expression and said, "I don't mind at all."

As everyone pushed back chairs and gathered up notebooks and calendars, Joshua lingered near enough to say softly to Diana, "Can we talk privately?"

Clarissa chose this moment to say more loudly, "Stay, please, Miss Neville. I'd like a word with you."

Diana pulled a quick face at Joshua where Clarissa couldn't see, and he smiled. "Later," he mouthed, and followed the others out.

When Clarissa did not invite her to retake her seat, Diana wondered if she was about to be fired. Or at least reprimanded for causing trouble among the staff. Maybe the headmistress, too, thought Diana was imagining things.

"I assume, Miss Neville, that you do not drink in the school?"

Worse: Clarissa thought she might be *drunkenly* imagining things.

"I do not."

Clarissa's whole expression lightened. It was almost a smile. "You needn't look so wary, Diana. May I call you that?"

"Of course."

"How old are you?"

Didn't you even read my application? she thought. That was quite a degree of trust in her father's judgment. "I am twenty-five."

It wasn't often that Diana was reduced to such brief sentences, but standing here felt a lot like standing before the nursing matron while being examined for the slightest infraction. Diana was almost tempted to check her uniform and stand to order.

"I'm twenty-four. I've never really known those my own age," Clarissa continued, almost musing. "Being privately schooled, my only companions were my much younger siblings. I have wondered what it might be like to have someone to speak to. Someone I don't pay."

"You *do* pay me."

Clarissa sighed. "Yes, but a nurse is not the same as a secretary. You have your own . . . dominion. Your own status. And no doubt plenty of other offers of employment. You are not beholden to me in the way others might be. Would you be willing to call me Clarissa?"

Her very awkwardness proclaimed how little social interaction Clarissa Somersby had enjoyed. But there was an appealing innocence in her awkwardness. "If you'd like."

"I would."

When silence fell again—Clarissa was very good at silence—Diana furrowed her brow, trying to divine the atmosphere. "Is that all?"

Eyes downcast, fingers playing with a pen, Clarissa asked,

"Have you seen anything, Diana? Anything that seems . . . that doesn't belong? Lights or movement?"

Diana blinked. "Are you asking me if I've seen a ghost?"

"Have you?"

It was asked with such eagerness, that Diana was almost sorry to say, "No."

"And your expression proclaims you do not expect to. You do not believe in ghosts."

Diana chose her words carefully. "If I were ever going to see the spirits of the damned, I would have seen them in France, Clarissa."

With a curious look of disappointment, Clarissa said, "Just because one is lost does not mean one is damned,"

Oh no, Diana thought guiltily. *She's thinking about her little brother, lost and never found.* "I didn't mean—"

Clarissa waved a hand and instantly retreated behind her headmistress-in-charge shield. "No matter. Our primary concern is always the boys themselves. Whether they are teasing you, or whether there is something more going on, we must find out and put a stop to it. The war is grinding to an end. Our students have already, most of them, lost a great deal. We must ensure that they are healthy both in body and mind."

Which was so very much the expected thing for a headmistress to say that Diana wondered if Clarissa had read it in a book. She exited the room thoughtfully, and with a sense that there was more going on with this school and its occupants than could be seen by the unwary.

That didn't mean there were ghosts running around.

She'd forgotten that Joshua had wanted to speak to her until she nearly walked into him leaning backward against the balustrade.

"Aren't you afraid of losing your balance?" she asked, for it was a long drop to the stone-flagged hall below.

"After France? Normal fears don't really apply, do they?"

Not normal fears, no. But France had hardly made her fearless. It had just sharpened and focused her fears into one, all-encompassing terror. *The high whine of the shell, the roar of the explosion, the crushing weight of wood and dirt and rocks, she couldn't see, she couldn't move, she couldn't breathe . . .*

Fortunately, that was easily dealt with: just stay out of confined spaces.

Joshua chose that moment to announce, "I've got an idea about the nighttime knockings on your door. Tunnels. And secret passages. Havencross has both."

Of course it does, she thought wearily. *Of course it does.*

As they could hardly throw themselves into exploring in full sight of curious schoolboys, Joshua had to be content for the present with providing descriptions and drawings. That suited Diana just fine.

To the logical question of "How do you know this?" Joshua had given an equally logical answer: "The Murrays have been entwined with this house since its beginning. My great-grandfather helped build it, and my grandmother was housekeeper here for forty years."

Diana left unasked the second and third logical questions: *Wouldn't Clarissa know this? And if so, why didn't she mention it as a possible solution to the knocking?*

They had retired to the infirmary, being both a private space and yet official enough that no one would think them suspiciously intimate. Something else she'd learned in France—how to function as a rare woman in a sea full of military men without drawing undue disapproval. Joshua attempted to sketch each floor of the house on its own piece of paper, but there were so many wings and asymmetries and towers that there was no way to lay it out in perfect order. He did his best, standing at the examination table with the papers scattered across it.

"See?" He grabbed the first one he'd sketched, showing the entrance hall with the school dining room on one side and a similar space on the other that he pointed to now. "The drawing room. I know there's a passageway going from there to the music room on the floor above. Gideon Somersby, who built the house, apparently liked to come and go from the ground floor without using the central staircase. He would pop out at guests without warning. Legend says it's how he discovered his first wife was cheating on him with a violinist."

"But my room isn't anywhere near there. And that's the private part of the house, anyway. I understand Clarissa keeps the outer doors locked against curious boys. Probably to keep them from playing tricks."

"It's not the only secret passage. Gideon was either truly paranoid or had a whimsical sense of fun. I know of two others, here"—he pointed at one spot and then a second on another piecemeal map—"and here."

Diana leaned in and attempted to decipher them. "That's the kitchen," she said of the first.

"That one is less exciting—simply a roofed-over passage from the scullery to the outer storerooms. This one is more pertinent."

"The staff quarters?"

He nodded. "Right at the end of the corridor. The entrance is at the back of one of the linen cupboards. It's the only one I've ever been in. It was actually Clarissa who showed me, when I was here one day with my grandmother. I was—thirteen, maybe?—so she was still a little girl. This one takes you inside the walls of the house before climbing up a story and coming out in the old servants' quarters."

Well, that answered the question of whether Clarissa knew about the passageways. And gave greater urgency to the question of why she hadn't said anything about it in the staff meeting.

"The problem is," Josh continued, "I'm pretty sure that last one is boarded up. Or at least it was, during my first year teaching. And it takes a particularly bold set of boys to traverse an entire corridor filled with schoolmasters, even in the dead of night."

"The real problem is that every one of these tunnels appears to begin and end in the main house," Diana pointed out. "Which makes sense, if Gideon Somersby was the one who wanted them. It would have taken a lot more work to incorporate hidden passages into the oldest part of Havencross, where my bedroom is—and why bother, when he had so much space to construct whatever he wanted?"

"All right, so we haven't quite sorted out how the boys are getting to you, but we will."

What if it's not the boys? Diana didn't dare ask it aloud. She didn't know Joshua well enough for such imponderable questions. But despite her honest answers to Clarissa about ghosts, there was one detail she had omitted from her statement in the staff meeting. A tiny detail, almost inconsequential: the sound of footsteps receding down the corridor as she approached her door. And not the soft whisper of bare feet or the slap of a boy's slippers.

The distinct tapping of a woman in heels.

She'd left that part out because saying it aloud was tantamount to an accusation—against the inoffensive Mrs. McCann, or Beth Willis, or Clarissa Somersby herself. Clarissa, who had sat so silently as Diana explained the mysterious knocking. But who had also decided on nightly patrols of the boys' dorms. Which could merely be her way of deflecting attention.

But why on earth would Clarissa Somersby be sneaking around her own home in the middle of the night simply to tease Diana? And why the other tricks—the missing or moved items, the smashed teacup? There didn't seem to be any purpose to any of it, except to annoy Diana.

Or frighten her. Frighten her enough to leave? But Clarissa ran the school. If she wanted to get rid of Diana, she had only to fire her.

She realized that Joshua had stopped talking—probably some time ago, judging by his quizzical expression—and she shook her head as though waking herself up. "Sorry. Look, I don't think you're necessarily wrong that these passageways could be tempting to schoolboys if discovered. And dangerous. We should keep an eye on that."

He had tidied his various map sketches into a neat, squared-off pile that he set on her desk. "Don't worry. Weston won't be the only one patrolling tonight. I'll be on the lookout for any mischief-makers." He hesitated, then asked, "Your door does lock, doesn't it?"

"It does, but look . . . I didn't mean to set the cat among the pigeons like this. It's disconcerting, but hardly terrifying. As you say, the standard for horror is extremely high after France."

"You could move out of the old wing. A little closer to Mrs. Willis, perhaps."

Just the thought of leaving her private aerie with its wide-open views and silent solitude made Diana's skin crawl. Not that she wouldn't be private enough in the main house—Havencross was hardly lacking for space—but logic had little to do with it. She felt safest where she could see the farthest.

"And let whoever it is know that they've succeeded in frightening me?" she said with a laugh. "That would hardly do my authority any good. Don't worry about me. As long as the knocking is on the other side of the door, I'll be just fine."

She should really have known better than to say such things.

CHAPTER ELEVEN

DIANA
OCTOBER 1918

One might have expected that all the odd happenings would have affected Diana's ability to sleep. But she hadn't been in France for a week before she'd mastered the ability to sleep whenever and wherever she had the chance. And Havencross had lived up to the first part of its name—since her arrival, she had slept more deeply than she had since childhood, secure in this northern haven. Which made being dragged awake in the middle of the night even more disconcerting.

This evening, though, it wasn't a sound that woke her but the cold. Swimming up from a dream of Joshua making her ride a horse, Diana realized that her grandmother's wedding-ring quilt had slid to the floor. She leaned over, hoping to snag it with her hand without having to leave the bed, and with sudden swiftness the remaining blankets and sheet were pulled off her.

She shot off the bed without thinking, then jumped back on

the mattress in case someone grabbed her like they had done with the blankets. *But who?*

"Who's there?" she asked, even as she switched on the bedside lamp. To reveal an empty room.

Of course it was empty. She had locked her door, after all.

She stood on her bed, breathing harder than she liked, and said aloud, "This is ridiculous!"

It gave her the courage to climb down, grab her wooly dressing gown and slippers, unlock her door, and march to the dormitory wing as though fully confident of receiving answers.

"Miss Neville."

Damn it. Of course the first person she'd run into would be Luther Weston, managing to make even his torchlight insolent as he moved it up and down her body.

"If it's Murray you're looking for—" he drawled.

"Has anyone been out of bed?"

"Besides you?"

Before she could well and truly lose her temper, someone switched on the corridor lights. Diana turned to address the newcomer and saw Joshua, with his hand resting on a young boy's shoulder. A very young boy. Austin Willis, Beth's nine-year-old son, had the scrunched-up face of a child trying not to show fear. Beneath the weight of Joshua's hand he was trembling.

"Hello, Austin," she said, modulating her voice into the trademark nurse's mix of kindness and brisk practicality. "Are you feeling ill?"

"No, miss. That is—"

"What are you doing out of bed?" barked Weston.

"More to the point," Joshua barked back, "how did *you* miss the boy being out of bed?"

"The dormitories aren't your responsibility, Murray. You shouldn't be here."

"It's a good thing I was, or who knows where young Willis might have wandered off to."

Diana had zero patience for aggression between territorial males. She extended her hand to Austin Willis. "Come with me to the infirmary. I'll just make sure everything's fit."

He took her hand gratefully, and they left the bristling school-masters behind to fight or retreat as they chose. She didn't press the child with questions until they were in her cozily lit study off the infirmary. Diana chose to seat the boy in her squashy armchair rather than on the examination table. She didn't really think he was ill, and didn't want to frighten him any more than he already was.

"Do you want to tell me why you were out of bed?" she asked gently, when she'd wrapped his thin shoulders with a blanket.

He had the high, uncertain voice of a boy just edging out of childhood. "I wanted my mother."

She'd thought it might be that; Diana knew that Beth had debated having her youngest sleep in their suite at night instead of the dormitory.

"Did you have a bad dream?"

His eyes were dark pools in his thin face. "It wasn't a dream. He wanted me to follow him."

"Who?" Diana braced herself. An older boy intent on mischief—or worse? She certainly hoped not. And surely he didn't mean Joshua.

But she hadn't braced herself sufficiently for Austin's answer. "The ghost boy."

By the time the sun rose, Diana was dressed and on her way to report last night's occurrence to Clarissa Somersby. After getting what broken pieces of information she could from Austin, she'd kept him in the infirmary for the remaining hours of the night, shamefully glad of a reason not to return to her own room in the dark. Joshua had checked on them shortly after their retreat. (He didn't appear to have been engaged in a fistfight.) She'd asked him to return at dawn to escort Austin back to the dormitory, leaving her free to speak to Clarissa before informing Beth Willis of her son's broken night. Diana was prepared to knock long and loudly to rouse the headmistress.

It wasn't necessary. Clarissa's study door was partly open, and a light shone from inside. Diana stopped short at the raised voice—a male voice. Had Weston preempted her?

But almost at once, Clarissa broke in. "Father . . ."

That was even more surprising. What was Sir Wilfred Somersby doing here at the break of day? He'd told Diana when he hired her that he preferred to keep out of his daughter's way now that he'd left the day-to-day running of the school in her hands. What had brought him to Northumberland without warning?

"The war is ending, Clarissa. The German navy has mutinied. Turkey has asked for terms. The Allies control all of France and most of Belgium."

"What does that have to do with me?"

"For four years, the world has been in stalemate. But now time is turning again, and your life must turn with it."

"I am—"

Sir Wilfred's voice rode right over his daughter's. "Thomas would not want you to throw your life away in mourning him."

There was a long, terrible silence. Diana knew that she should not be hearing this, that she should walk away. But she didn't.

"I have indulged you for years, Clarissa. I thought allowing you to remain here would help you heal. Then I thought that creating the school would be the impetus you needed to go into the world, attend classes, learn new things to bring back here . . . but all you've done is populate your self-appointed prison with dozens of Thomas replacements."

"No one could ever replace Thomas."

"Do you think I don't know that, my dear? You were not the only person who loved him. We have all mourned."

"Not Sylvia."

Even without knowing who Sylvia was, Diana knew that Clarissa had just crossed a line. Out in the hall, the temperature seemed to drop ten degrees.

"What are you implying?" he asked.

"Sylvia never cared for me or Thomas. She accepted us as the price of marrying you and gaining a title. But once she had her own children—once she had her own *son*—she was all too glad not to have Thomas around to split your attention. Or your money."

The sound of the slap was so loud Diana flinched, then grimaced in sympathy. That would leave a mark.

When Sir Wilfred spoke again, he sounded sorrowful rather than angry. "Clarissa, I'm only trying to do what is best for you. And I'm afraid that doesn't always mean doing things you like. I lost Thomas here. I will not lose you to the same place. You are twenty-four years old. The war is winding down. I want your word that when this school year is ended, you will come to London for the summer. You will mingle with those your own age. You will be social. If it were a hundred years ago, I would insist on marriage—any marriage. But at the very least, you will leave Havencross for the summer."

"Or?" Clarissa asked, the steel in her voice more brittle than she'd no doubt intended.

"Or this year will be the school's last. Come to London, or

the school closes. I will sell the land, and raze Havencross to the ground."

Sir Wilfred left his daughter's office so abruptly that Diana had no chance to dart into hiding. He stutter-stepped when he saw her, but strong emotion kept him charging past with nothing more than a glimpse of an anguished face. She would never have imagined the upright gentleman she'd met in London could have looked like that.

Diana cast a glance at the open office door, but wisdom—or self-preservation—kicked in belatedly and she retreated before Clarissa could discover her eavesdropping on such a sensitive matter. Now was not the moment to pass on tales of a ghostly boy to a still-grieving sister. The last thing she wanted was to precipitate a crisis that might hasten Sir Wilfred's threat.

She may have only been at Havencross a few weeks, but already she could feel the place working its way into her heart. She loved it here. She adored the Northumberland sky and the moors and the hills and the complete absence of shellfire and blood. There weren't a lot of jobs on offer in the middle of nowhere for a war nurse.

There aren't any jobs on offer that also have Joshua Murray working there, her mind whispered traitorously.

Whatever was happening at Havencross—middle-of-the-night knocking, irritating pranks, invisible footsteps, schoolboys seeing ghosts—Diana would just have to figure it out on her own. As for Clarissa, Diana had only one goal: help the damaged headmistress heal from her brother's loss. At least enough to get her to London next summer and keep the school open.

She'd dealt with dying men by the hundreds. Surely she could cope with a single ghost and one traumatized woman her own age.

CHAPTER TWELVE

ISMAY
MAY 1455

Then was there a mortal debate between Richard Duke of York and Edmund Duke of Somerset, who ever steered the king against York. But the people loved the Duke of York because he preserved the common good of the land. Then York, seeing that he might not prevail against the malice of Somerset, gathered privately a great many men about the town of St. Albans. And when the king was there, York beseeched the king to send out the Duke of Somerset, who was an enemy to all the land. The king, by advice of his council, answered and said he would not.

Ismay's twelfth birthday passed entirely unnoticed at Ludlow Castle. It wasn't because of her status as ward rather than family member—for the York family had been as welcoming as they were capable of being, and indeed Ismay had made great friends with Elizabeth and Margaret, who were only a little younger than she was. Once the Duke of York had decided it worthwhile to keep her in his household, Ismay had joined the girls in their rooms and in their tutoring and, like them, watched the eldest daughter enviously. Anne, now sixteen, was already a duchess in her own right; she had officially married the Duke of Exeter when she was only eight. Now of an age to be a wife, she still spent a great deal of time with her mother, and the younger girls thought her impossibly grown-up and glamorous.

But as Ismay's twelfth birthday dawned at the end of May, the entire York household had been on edge for days. The Duke of York and his wife's nephew, the Earl of Warwick, had marched their personal troops south more than a week ago after being summoned by the king. It wasn't King Henry they feared—it was Lord Somerset, who had been thrown in prison by York during the king's last illness. Ismay didn't understand all of the story, but she knew that anyone as wealthy, as powerful, and as royal-blooded as the Duke of York must always be worried about enemies.

The household was kept well informed during their lord's absence, with a constant relay of messengers riding from the south, so they all knew that the king had marched out of London with an army in response and camped at St. Albans. (Of course, by king, they meant Queen Margaret. Henry might have been present, but it was his queen who had the backbone.)

The children had been haunting the battlements as often as they could sneak away from their various tutors and servants, not least because both Edward and Edmund were with their father and the siblings were eager for news of their brothers' adventures. Today Ismay had been sent after six-year-old George by the exasperated nursemaid who'd lost him for the third time since breakfast. He was forever wishing to catch up to his older brothers, always complaining that he couldn't go off with his father and ride into battle. Not that Edmund had been in battle—he was only twelve—but Edward at thirteen was as tall as many soldiers and skilled beyond his years.

Ismay caught George in one of the turret stairs before he could reach the open air. But they were near enough to the top that she heard the shout from the guards: "Rider coming! Banner's ours!"

The impulse was to dart up and look out. Instead, Ismay grabbed George by the hand and hurried him down the stairs. When he protested, she said, "We'll meet him in the courtyard. Maybe we'll beat the others."

But Duchess Cecily was there before them. For a woman who appeared constantly unworried and unhurried, she always had the strings of her family members in her hands and each twitch brought her directly to the critical point.

George tore himself from Ismay's grasp and ran to his mother. Next to her, Elizabeth held three-year-old Richard in her arms. Margaret grabbed Ismay by the hand, and they hovered just behind.

The messenger was a familiar face, and he wasted no time in formalities. "A victory, my lady. A great victory at St. Albans! Somerset's army is defeated, and King Henry is safe in our lord-ship's hands."

"Casualties?"

"None of note in our ranks, but Somerset was killed in battle." Then, with a smile that could only be described as jubilant, he added, "And so was Henry Percy."

Everything happened very quickly after that. Duchess Cecily was often noted for her efficiency, and at no time was it put to better use than immediately following the news of the Yorkist victory. Without any outward sign of hurry or fuss, the entire household—children and all—was transferred to London in just over a week. That was no minor feat, considering the duchess was also heavily pregnant.

Though she had maintained her perfect composure in victory as well as defeat, her daughters and Ismay were as jubilant as any common Yorkist soldier. Somerset was a bitter enemy of the duke, and the Percys . . . well, the bad blood between the Percys and Duchess Cecily's brothers had long ago hardened into the deepest hatred. With this victory, not only had the Duke of York been named Protector of the Realm, but his wife's brother and nephews could glory in having the North firmly under their control.

Ismay had never been to London; she was overwhelmed by the crowds and the noise, yet dazzled by the luxury of Baynard's Castle along the Thames. She would have been content simply to watch from the fringes as important visitors came and went, as the duchess dressed with care for court, as they attended mass at St. Paul's Cathedral.

The older boys were in and out of Baynard's Castle. Edward, now Earl of March, came with his smile and his charm, trailing the glamour of the battlefield behind him. And Edmund, the Earl of Rutland, came as well. Always a shade paler, a shade less noticeable, many shades less outrageous than his older brother, Edmund came with less glamour, but with lots of stories—not of himself and his own exploits but stories of the court, lively sketches of men and women that made his sisters and Ismay laugh.

But even in his most devastating impressions, Edmund was never vulgar or cruel. Queen Margaret's loathing of the Yorks might be returned a hundredfold, but Ismay felt that Edmund would be able to find something good in Satan himself.

And though nothing was ever said, Ismay was certain that Edmund was behind the great honor bestowed on her and

Elizabeth: to attend a court reception at Westminster Palace. They were only twelve and ten, respectively, but an important family is an important family. Especially an important family just a few heartbeats removed from the English throne.

Ismay was no fool. She did not have Elizabeth's bloodline, but she was an heiress of no small fortune. An heiress with no family to negotiate for her, meaning her marriage was in the hands of the Duke of York. With him in the ascendant, there might not be a better moment to create an alliance.

She just didn't expect a proposal to happen at the reception itself.

They were escorted by the Countess of Warwick—for Duchess Cecily had given birth to a stillborn daughter ten days ago and was still in bed—and introduced to a handful of men and women. Edward was extravagantly welcoming, and Edmund was touchingly anxious that they enjoy themselves. Ismay would have been glad to spend the whole evening ignored by everyone else. But no possible York connection could be ignored by the crowd, not even two young girls.

Though most were eager to speak to Elizabeth, Ismay found herself captured by John Neville. The younger brother of the Earl of Warwick, and thus another nephew to Duchess Cecily, John was best known for one thing: his overriding hatred for all things Percy. Since the age of eighteen, he'd been involved in raids against his family's powerful northern adversaries and been called to account by the king himself. But for a Neville, a king's demands ranked somewhere below their own family honor. With the death of Henry Percy at St. Albans, John was in a very good mood. Between telling Ismay all about the battle—indeed, more than she cared to know—he asked her about Havencross and seemed both surprised and pleased by her grasp of estate matters.

"Not many girls immerse themselves in questions of land and

tenants," he told her. "You have a good steward, after all, and an excellent guardian."

"No matter my steward or guardian, Havencross is mine. My father made sure I understood that as early as I was able."

"You were fortunate in the estate your father left you."

"I would rather have my father than the estate."

Edmund, who stood close enough to hear without making himself part of the conversation, flashed her a look of sympathy and approval. John flushed, and almost Ismay apologized for making him uncomfortable. But she was saved the dilemma when a servant wearing the white rose of York appeared in front of their small group and announced that the Lord Protector requested Ismay's presence. Alone.

Since she'd had exactly one private interview with the Duke of York since arriving in his household, Ismay bit her lip and queried Edmund with her eyes. Across the ten feet that separated them, he gave a small shrug of ignorance, but also a smile calculated to raise her spirits.

The Duke of York was in a small, square room down one of Westminster's innumerable corridors. The black walnut paneling swallowed up light so that the elaborate candelabras appeared like islands in the midst of a dark sea. York looked the same as he always had: thin-faced, dark-haired, with severe lines, and hooded, searching eyes. He sat behind a desk, reading from a stack of papers and making notes. Standing next to him, younger and taller and far more dashing, was his wife's nephew Richard Neville, Earl of Warwick.

"My lords." Ismay executed a painstakingly practiced curtsey.

While the Lord Protector continued reading, the Earl of Warwick ran his eyes up and down Ismay as though assessing a horse he wished to buy. Or not buy, if his expression was any indication.

"How old are you?" Warwick demanded.

"Twelve."

He snorted. "I've seen ten-year-olds better developed."

Ismay flushed, and was suddenly grateful for the shadowy room. Then the Duke of York addressed Warwick: "My wife tells me the girl has been bleeding for six months now. She's thin but no longer a child."

Ismay nearly burst into flames. Keeping her eyes fixed on the toes of her shoes, just peeping out from beneath the heavy blue silk skirt, she tried to pretend she was elsewhere.

"Look at me, girl," commanded Warwick.

She lifted her head and set her face into the chilly, neutral lines she'd learned from Duchess Cecily. That seemed to amuse him. "A little spirit. That's good. Johnny would soon tire of a bloodless bride."

Ismay froze, her eyes locked on Warwick's. *Bride? Johnny?*

Johnny. All at once, she understood why John Neville had gone out of his way to speak to her tonight. Not about herself or the things she liked, but about Havencross— her manor house and estate that ran across a good part of Northumberland. Of course Ismay had understood that there would be men who wanted Havencross. But understanding was a completely different thing than thinking of that rest- less, impatient, twenty-three-year-old she'd just left wanting to marry her. Ismay didn't want to marry Johnny. She didn't want to marry anyone yet. She knew what the onset of her monthly bleeding meant, she understood—as did all who lived around animals—the nature of what happened in the marriage bed. But the thought of being left alone with a grown-up man who expected her to do . . . that?

Ismay must have looked as appalled as she felt, for Warwick growled, "It's not as though I intend to drag you to the altar tonight. But it's just as well that plans are made. And it would be a fine match."

For Johnny, she thought spitefully. A younger son in a family of twelve without any land of his own.

The Duke of York had a knack for reading the undercurrents of any situation and speaking to the point when necessary. "You may think Johnny too old, but I assure you, Ismay, there are men a great deal older who have approached me. Do you really wish to marry a man with children older than you are? There need be no announcement at once, but I wish you to seriously consider the matter."

The words *I wish* coming from the senior duke in England, the Lord Protector of the Realm, and her legal guardian meant "I command." Ismay could only be grateful he had confined his "wishes" to her considering the matter rather than requiring her immediate assent. Maybe she could make herself so disagreeable to John Neville that even Havencross wouldn't tempt him.

Maybe she would ask Edmund to help.

CHAPTER THIRTEEN

JULIET
2018

After depositing the three boxes from White Rose Farm on the long table of the enormous dining room, Juliet went straight for the neatly bound pages of *Information and Instructions* that she'd so far ignored. She conceded that Nell Somersby-Sims was every bit as efficient as her image: the pages covered everything from how to restart the boiler to where to find candles and flashlights in case of a power outage. That gave Juliet pause—it was one thing to blithely anticipate that a winter storm might knock out the lights from the safety of home, but another thing entirely when inside the belly of the beast, as it were. Nevertheless, she went ahead and gathered two flashlights, ten candles, and three boxes of matches to take upstairs to her bedroom.

But what Juliet really wanted she found on the last page, under the *Pertinent Telephone Numbers* heading. *Noah Bennett, Newcastle Surveyors, Ltd. Call in case of structural issues.*

So he was on her list. Not that she'd thought he was making it up. But the pages didn't say anything about weekly checks. She thought of the way he'd leaned against her car, looking at her . . . No, not looking—*seeing* her. Duncan had appeared to look at her all the time. But he'd never really seen her.

Juliet shook her head as though trying to escape a circling fly. There was no point in her thoughts wandering down that path. Or any path that involved a man. Her divorce was barely final, and it's not like she had any intention of crossing paths with Duncan ever again. Any love between them had died a long time ago. It was Juliet's own fault that she hadn't seen it until forced by humiliation at the very moment she'd been drowning in grief. She was finished with Duncan Whittier. That didn't mean she had any intention of starting anything with someone else. Maybe ever.

In light of that virtuous resolution, she made a sandwich (then, considering, made a second) and piled them on a paper plate with some of the brownies Rachel had pressed on her before leaving the farm. She opened the box that contained the nurse's notebook and shoved it—along with the flashlights, candles, matches, and a cold can of Diet Coke—into her tote bag and made her way upstairs to eat and read in bed.

The notebook wasn't especially riveting if one were reading for personal interest, but it held a wealth of details about the infirmary at Havencross School, including what supplies and drugs were on hand. It was tempting to leaf through and skip to the interesting bits, but Juliet had enough academic discipline remaining in her to refrain. Best to take things in context, always. She made notes on her laptop with questions to be researched and lines of inquiry to be followed, as well as a few of the seemingly trivial kinds of details that made for the best narrative history. For example, that one of the schoolboys had already been in the infirmary at the time of the influenza outbreak, suffering from exposure and a broken leg. If she could learn the story behind that injury, it would make a good counterpoint.

She yawned at last and set the nurse's notebook on the bedside table with her laptop. Then she slid into a comfortable position against the pillows and used her cell phone to check social media.

It's all part of returning to the world, she told herself. *I used to scroll Twitter at least twice a day.*

Her curiosity tonight was repaid rather in the manner of the proverbial dead cat. She opened Twitter and saw someone had sent her a direct message with a photo. The account wasn't one she knew, but she didn't have to. She knew exactly what she was looking at. The photo showed a tiny infant swaddled and capped with a rose-bud mouth and a perfect button nose.

Welcome to the world, Marcus Dane Whittier. @duncanw and I are head over heels for you.

Duncan's son. Fathered not with his wife of eight years but with a twenty-two-year-old graduate student. The girl he'd been in bed with while Juliet labored alone to deliver a baby boy whose heart had inexplicably stopped beating when she was eight months' pregnant, a baby boy with perfect features and a secret smile on the mouth that never drew a breath. The baby boy she had named Liam months before.

Juliet fell asleep with wet cheeks and a sore throat and a heart that felt as though it would never be whole again. It was like the first weeks after Liam's death, so it was no surprise when she woke up in the dark, knowing she hadn't slept more than an hour or two. She lay there with that dull feeling that she hadn't realized she'd started to leave behind. Now it had returned full force. The kind of dullness that meant she didn't have the energy to do anything more than lie there and breathe.

The kind of dullness that meant she didn't realize for some time that a faint light was glowing through her open bedroom door.

She had shut that door when she came up. And locked it.

Nothing like adrenaline to jolt one fully awake. Juliet sat up so fast that her head swam, giving her a moment to consider what to do. Grab her phone? If someone was in the corridor, they would hear her talking. Her best bet was to get the door shut and locked before anything else. Maybe drag the desk in front of it for good measure.

She threw back the covers and stepped cautiously onto the floor. The door was no more than eight steps away.

She'd only made it three steps when the light flared up and died back almost instantly. Juliet froze while she blinked away the spots in her vision. Only it wasn't just spots—the light had coalesced into an outline. A small, fuzzy, but distinctly human outline.

As Juliet stared, unable to move, the outline took on details: a young boy, no more than nine or ten, a cloak over his pale shirt, and a sweep of fair hair over wide eyes.

And then the boy extended his right hand and, without opening his mouth, said straight into Juliet's head, *Come hide with me.*

The spell broke.

Juliet crossed the space in a violent movement and slammed the door shut. Even before she'd finished locking it and dragging the desk to block it, she knew that it—whatever it was—had gone.

That didn't keep her from staying awake the remainder of the night.

CHAPTER FOURTEEN

DIANA
OCTOBER 1918

As the sun rose, Diana woke Beth Willis and succinctly filled her in about Austin's nighttime excursion to find his mother, as well the "ghost" sighting that had prompted it.

Beth blessedly maintained the calm demeanor of the school secretary, with only her furiously tapping fingers betraying the worried mother. "Austin didn't say any more about what he saw?"

"I didn't want to press him. I kept him in the infirmary the rest of the night. I've asked Mr. Murray to escort Austin here once you and I'd had a chance to talk." She checked her watch. "They'll be here in a few minutes. I can give you the room to speak with him."

"No, stay. And perhaps Mr. Murray could go back for Jasper. Where one is involved, the other will know something."

In the event, Beth asked Joshua to remain as well. Diana was afraid that three adults facing them would overawe the brothers, but they clearly gained courage from each other. And though he was only thirteen, Jasper had the cocky surliness of an adolescent.

"Have you been telling Austin stories?" Beth asked her older son.

"No."

"Jasper—"

"It wasn't me, mum. Honest. Everybody talks about the ghost."

Diana asked, "What do they say?"

He attempted a casual shrug, but there was definitely a flicker of nervousness there. "A boy died here. Murdered, probably. That's why he's a ghost."

"Have you seen him?"

Jasper shook his head. "It's only ever the first-years who see him."

Well, that was definitely the kind of thing that would prime sensitive, grieving nine-year-old boys—with the right kind of imagination—to see ghosts. In a school full of students who had all suffered losses from the war, it was a wonder all fifteen of the first-year boys weren't wandering at night.

"Austin," Beth asked gently, "was this the first time you've seen the boy?"

He shook his head.

"When did it start?"

He spoke under his breath, looking down. "The second week."

"Why didn't you say anything?"

His eyes fluttered to his mother, then back to his lap, where his hands were twisted together. He shrugged.

"Was last night the first time you left your room?"

He nodded. "He wanted me to follow him. He kept saying, 'Come hide with me.' So I finally did."

"Why?"

In a heartbreaking whisper, Austin said, "I thought he could help me find Papa."

Diana met Joshua's eyes in a shared glance of empathetic agony as Beth gathered her youngest boy into her lap. Austin sobbed like a toddler, and even Jasper's adolescent shield melted away and he moved to his mother's side.

Without a word, Diana and Joshua left the little family to mourn alone.

Diana leaned against the wall at the far end of the corridor and put her hands over her eyes. Her head ached from exhaustion and sorrow. She felt a brief, gentle touch to her shoulder and straightened up, eyes opening.

"You all right?" Joshua asked.

She ignored the question. "So the youngest boys are being fed stories of a ghost their own age—a ghost who beckons them to follow—and then . . . what? Are there any stories about what the ghost boy wants?"

A sarcastic snort came from her left, and she snapped her head around. How did Luther Weston manage to be everywhere she didn't want him? He appeared at the top of the staircase having clearly heard them, and answered before Joshua could: "Don't all ghosts want revenge? Or justice? Maybe Miss Somersby should get a medium up here to find out."

Joshua spoke without noticeable heat; his threat all the more chilling. "If you say one word about mediums and séances within earshot of a boy, I will throw you out of this school myself."

"Doesn't it get exhausting being so righteous all the time? You're not the only one who watched men die in France, Murray."

"No, I'm not. And I'd wager Miss Neville has witnessed more men die than either of us could count."

"For heaven's sake, shut up. Both of you," she said, with a warning glance at Joshua. "What do you want, Weston?"

"Miss Somersby asked for an update on the Willis boy. I take it he will not be sleeping in the dormitory tonight?"

"I'll speak to Miss Somersby directly."

His sour smile lingered unpleasantly as he clattered down the stairs with a quick ease that Diana thought might be aimed at Joshua. Weston may not have been a frontline soldier, but he'd also returned without frontline injuries.

She turned to the matter at hand. "Whatever is going on in this school, there's no way Austin Willis is my midnight prankster. He hasn't the nerve. Perhaps we'll get somewhere if Beth can discover which boys have been spreading stories."

"If you can get any of the boys to focus long enough."

"What do you mean?"

"You're not in the classroom every day, so maybe you haven't caught the undercurrents running through here. Everyone knows the war is drawing to an end. Getting the boys to focus on history or chemistry is getting more difficult. The tension is becoming unbearable."

"We'll all feel much better once it's over."

"Do you think so?"

Diana was taken aback by the bitterness in his voice as much as by the question. "Of course we will. We must. It's been four years of hell. The relief of no more war . . ." She shrugged.

"Just because the fighting stops doesn't mean we're free of hell. People think it will all just go back to normal. Tell me true, Diana—did you leave hell behind? Or has it followed you every day since leaving France?"

She wanted to deny it. She wanted to look him in the eye and tell him yes, of course, life was normal again and it soon would be for everyone. But one can't lie to someone who has walked the same battlefields you have.

"No, life is not what it was and it never will be. We cannot go back. But equally we cannot stand still. The world will make a new normal. We must," she repeated, as though saying it could make it so.

It was Joshua's turn to close his eyes and lean against the wall. "That is the most exhausting thing I can imagine. I just want to sleep until all the treaties are signed and all the soldiers have come home. Then maybe I can believe in the future."

CHAPTER FIFTEEN

DIANA
OCTOBER 1918

Like a weight, Diana carried Josh's despairing outburst with her throughout the rest of the day. It fit in next to other new weights—like pity for the fatherless Willis family and worry about wandering boys at night—and older ones that she preferred not to look at head on. "One apocalypse at a time" one of her nursing supervisors used to say. Though sometimes that just resulted in lining up your disasters in a seemingly never-ending line. All in all, enough for a pulsating pain at the base of her skull by the time she made it to breakfast.

In any but the most strictly disciplined schools, mealtimes with dozens of boys were always a dull roar of voices and silverware and dropped plates and the scraping of chair legs.

Diana nearly backed out of the dining room, but when she caught sight of Clarissa Somersby, sitting straight and ghastly-pale alone at the head table, she grabbed a bowl of oatmeal and sat next to the headmistress without worrying about whether she was wanted. If Clarissa didn't want company, she should have stayed in her room.

Anyone would have asked it: "Are you feeling quite well, Miss Somersby?" Even if Diana hadn't overheard this morning's ultimatum from Sir Wilfred, she would have guessed that something was wrong with Clarissa. Strands of her glossy hair slipped from crooked pins, and up close her skin had the green tinge of nausea.

Clarissa turned her head, her eyes the only glittering, alive part of her face. She put down her fork and seized Diana's wrist. "Tell me about the ghost," she commanded.

"I don't . . . what ghost?" Diana would have liked to look around for reinforcements, but she was afraid to break eye contact. Quite why she was afraid, she couldn't say.

"I heard about the Willis boy, Austin. He was out of bed in the night because the ghost boy was calling to him. You stayed with him, right? Can you tell me exactly what he said? Beth does not want me questioning him. Not yet."

Not ever, Diana thought, *if this wildly intense version of Clarissa were going to stick around.* Forget ghosts calling children out of bed—if Clarissa Somersby were to get at Austin Willis right now she'd frighten him much more than any story.

With the decisiveness of a field nurse, Diana pushed her chair back and used Clarissa's hold of her wrist to get them both standing. "Let's speak in your office," she said in a low voice. "Best not to let any whisper of ghosts be heard by the boys. The only thing that flies faster than rumors is fear."

The walk, or perhaps the reminder of her position, did Clarissa good—she had herself under better control when they reached her office. But instead of taking a seat behind the desk, she gestured Diana to a settee and joined her. So, a conversation between equals, or as near as the two of them could come.

Before Clarissa could ask again, Diana gave her a detailed—and purposefully dry—account of Austin's nighttime wanderings. The last thing they needed just now was more atmosphere. She ended by saying firmly, "Mrs. Willis is right to keep him calm and resting today. The last thing he should be doing is answering further questions. At least, none that aren't asked by his mother. I'm sure Mrs. Willis will be forthcoming with any details she learns."

Clarissa had lost the green tinge to her skin, without gaining any pink. But her eyes had calmed. "You think me mad."

"I find that term imprecise and insulting. If you mean that I think you are mentally unsound in some way—no, I do not." Diana hesitated, uncertain how honest to be. When the head-mistress continued simply to look at her, she threw caution to the wind and said exactly what she was thinking. "I think you have a very sound mind, and a very sad past. I think that the imminent end of the war is causing a great many of us to experience . . . to feel things we have tried not to feel for a long time. Obviously you learned once how to cope with great loss. I am certain you will learn how to cope once more."

"You must think me very pitiable. Poor little rich girl, lost her brother ages ago. How many children die in England each year, do you think? In 1915, it was one hundred and fifty thousand children under the age of five. How many of their sisters have the luxury to sit around and mourn endlessly? And you, well you have seen death in numbers so great as to make individual tragedies seem . . . trivial."

"No death is trivial," Diana said, heat burning her throat with the words. "And you really must stop telling me what I think."

When Clarissa laughed, it teetered for a moment on the edge of hysteria but only for a moment. It softened into something softer that, despite its melancholy, eased the grip around

Diana's chest. Whatever had possessed Clarissa Somersby had retreated. For now.

"Did you learn plain speaking as a nurse, or did you take it with you to France?"

Diana let out a huff equal parts relief and amusement. "My mother says my first words were telling her she'd burnt the toast. Sometimes an authoritative voice was all I had to get a terrified or enraged soldier under control."

"You feel that you need to get me under control?"

"I feel that researching annual childhood-mortality rates is not a healthy coping mechanism for loss."

With pursed lips and narrowed eyes, Clarissa appeared to be debating with herself. She stood up suddenly, her own authority back in place, and walked to a side table that held a number of silver-framed photographs. She took one up and lightly passed a finger across it before handing it to Diana.

"That is my brother Thomas. It was taken just eight weeks before he disappeared. It is a story much passed around in the village and, no doubt, the school with all the variations that time and curiosity can create. I wonder . . . I find I am in need of a detached observer. A nurse, if you will. An unflappable, intelligent mind that can see past emotional complications in order to view things in their proper relationships. I would like to tell you about Thomas and my own reasons for remaining at Havencross."

When Diana didn't immediately reply, Clarissa added, "Not now. It's been a rough night and a difficult morning. You must see to Austin Willis, and I must see to my school. Perhaps you would join me for tea tomorrow or the next day?"

Diana looked from the boy, frozen forever just before a smile, to the woman who still grieved enough that she hoped to find ghosts. "Of course I'll join you. I'd be honored."

Maybe by then she could think of something to say that wouldn't be dismissive or dishonest.

After checking in with Beth—Austin had fallen asleep and she was keeping both boys out of class for the day—Diana went to the infirmary and tidied away the linens from Austin's stay. Next she sat down to update her notes. She got no further than the date before exhaustion and melancholy swamped her and she put her head on her crossed arms on the desk.

She slipped somewhere between daylight and dreams, into that nebulous space where everything harsh and sharp recedes and all is muffled in cotton wool. She drifted in that half-pleasant, half-stultifying state until jerked upright by the sound of an enormous crash behind her.

Diana whirled out of her chair and was not surprised to find an empty room.

She *was* surprised to discover one of her file cabinets on its side. Diana touched it with the tip of one shoe; it was solid oak. Even empty she'd only been able to move it by throwing her shoulder against it and shoving it with the whole weight of her body. She doubted there was a boy who could do it. The faculty?

But none of that answered the question of how the person had vanished so suddenly.

Rolling her eyes, Diana grudgingly accepted that, whatever her fears, she would have to explore Joshua's secret passages. Whatever the difficulties, there must have been some added to the medieval sections, now lost from present memory. It was the only explanation that made sense—even if it did leave out the why of the whole thing.

As though he'd read her resolution from afar, a knock on her door was followed by Joshua's entry. He had his mouth open to speak but switched what he'd meant to say when he saw the fallen file drawer.

"More pranks?" he asked.

But even as Diana shook her head, the expression on his face changed and he strode across the room, the hitch of his left leg noticeable in his haste. "What happened?" he asked more urgently.

"It fell—" she began.

But Joshua had taken her chin in one hand and angled her face up and away. "A file drawer didn't do that."

Diana raised a hand to her neck, only now realizing that it stung. She pulled away from Joshua and fetched the hand mirror she kept in a drawer.

Angled from her left ear down her neck, which had been exposed while she dozed at her desk, were four red streaks. Diana had never seen anything quite like them before but she knew instantly what they were: sharp fingernails had raked her skin hard enough to draw beads of blood.

CHAPTER SIXTEEN

ISMAY
DECEMBER 1457

For the first time in nearly a year, the entire York family gathered at Ludlow Castle in the Welsh marches, including Anne (though she came without her husband, who was far too firmly identified with the Lancastrian cause.) While Elizabeth and Margaret fawned over their sister, Ismay kept five-year-old Richard entertained and tried to keep eight-year-old George from slipping away to harass his older brothers for stories.

Edward, give him his due, was an affectionate big brother who happily recounted stories of tournaments and battles to George—until he was distracted by an attractive kitchenmaid or visiting daughter or sister of local gentry. Edmund was less easily sidetracked and spent as much time as possible with his little brothers and Ismay. Which she was even more grateful for when Duchess Cecily's family arrived for the holiday.

Ismay had only seen Johnny Neville a handful of times since the uncomfortable proposal meeting two years earlier. Since then he hadn't done much to press his suit personally beyond remembering her name and asking her about Havencross. Ismay was less afraid of Johnny than of his brother, the Earl of Warwick. Fortunately for her, Warwick was stuck in Calais, so she had to deal with only the second-most-frightening member of the Neville family: Warwick's father, the Earl of Salisbury.

Although they'd met several times, Salisbury always treated Ismay like a new pet his sister Cecily had taken into her family. Ismay thought that was the most humiliating thing he could do to her. Until Christmas day.

After mass and a feast in the great hall, Salisbury summoned Ismay to sit next to him while carolers sang. It was clear that Warwick had learned his techniques from his father, for Salisbury looked her up and down twice before deigning to speak.

"You're growing up nicely," he said, in a tone that left no room for mistaking his intent. "Not many women can bear like my wife or sister, but I think my brother-in-law is right—you're worth the chance."

You mean Havencross is worth the chance, Ismay thought darkly. "And what does Johnny think?" she asked.

"Younger sons and orphaned wards are much the same," Salisbury answered. "They do what they're told."

Before Ismay could decide whether she most wanted to shout or to burst into tears, Edmund intervened with the warmth that was particularly his own. "Uncle, may I steal Lady Ismay from you? I'm afraid Richard refuses to go to bed until she tells him a story."

After a moment in which Ismay mentally crossed her fingers, Salisbury transferred his hard stare from her to his nephew. "Far be it from me to deprive a child of comfort," he said drily. "It speaks well for you, girl, that you have made yourself so essential to this family."

"Lord Salisbury," Ismay said, bobbing a hasty curtsey and forcing herself not to run as she followed Edmund out of the hall into an empty corridor. She immediately collapsed against the wall with only the bare minimum of melodrama.

"Thank you," she said.

"I didn't do anything."

"Considering Richard isn't meant to be in bed for another hour, you did me a great favor."

"In that case, come hide with me for a little. Someplace no one will bother us."

"Where?" She laughed. "The castle is crawling with people."

He extended his hand. "I know a place."

Ismay hesitated. The thought of holding Edmund's hand, however he meant it, felt weighted with meaning. And the longer she waited, the heavier the pause became. The fear of Edmund changing his mind made her brave. She took his hand. "Show me."

He led her outside and across the inner bailey, the muddy yard frozen and slick, to the west tower. The great ovens for the household were located on the ground floor and kept the storage rooms above warmer than might be expected in winter. They advanced up the spiral stairs for two floors and came out into a space that had been divided into storerooms. The largest looked west into Wales and contained only empty barrels and a highbacked oak settle that concealed them both from passing sight once they were seated. Indeed, it was so perfectly arranged to hide two people that Ismay just knew that Edward had shown it to his younger brother. Probably as a favorite place of his own to dally.

The thought of dalliance made her flush, and she realized

they were still holding hands. Edmund looked at her with unusual intensity. "Ismay, can I ask you something?"

"Yes."

"You don't have to answer if you don't like." He swallowed without ever breaking eye contact. "Do you want to marry my cousin Johnny?"

She could have answered in so many ways, but there was only one word that mattered. "No."

"He's of good birth," Edmund pointed out. "It would please both my parents. He's not terribly old. A good soldier. My sisters say he's handsome."

Ismay drew away her hand from his. "Have your parents or uncle sent you to persuade me?" she asked coldly.

Edmund dropped his head into his hands. When he looked back at her, all his assurance had vanished. "Good God, why am I so bad at this? No, I'm not trying to persuade you. Quite the opposite."

With a dawning understanding that made her fingertips spark, Ismay turned the question back on him. "Edmund, do *you* want me to marry Johnny?"

"No, I don't."

This time Ismay was the one brave enough to reach out, laying her hands on top of his. "Why?"

He bit his lip, and in a swift movement captured her hands between his and brought them to his chest. "Because I love you, Ismay. Do you not know that?"

"I . . . I hoped," she whispered.

"Do you . . . is there someone you want instead of Johnny?"

Ismay would never have thought herself so bold, but she seized the moment and tilted her head up. Edmund's kiss was as gentle and kind as Edmund himself, but Ismay could feel the depths of something larger and fiercer stirring within her.

The kiss broke, and she rested her forehead against his. A little shakily, Ismay said, "I love you, Edmund. And I will never marry Johnny Neville."

But even while Edmund held her, delirious in the first flush of being loved, Ismay offered a desperate plea to heaven: *Please God, don't let Warwick ruin things.*

CHAPTER SEVENTEEN

JULIET
2018

Only when the sun had risen in a watery blue sky did Juliet open her bedroom door, an event that required moving a desk, a chair, and the suitcase that she had shoved in front of it.

She didn't know why she thought any of that would stop a ghost.

Maybe he was a polite ghost, though, because the rest of the night had passed without any incident except those imagined in Juliet's head. She'd never been so aware of the sounds an empty house could make. And ten thousand square feet of house only amplified the sounds, and the fear.

She'd very nearly broken down and called Noah Bennett. Which might be considered progress, considering she hadn't thought about calling a man other than Duncan in ten years. But she'd had enough self-preservation not to call a good-looking man in the middle of the night and say, "Sorry to wake you, but I saw a ghost in the corridor. Or possibly I'm hallucinating my own dead son."

When in a state of rattled exhaustion, start with food and coffee. Juliet gratefully toasted some of Rachel's homemade bread. And after three cups of coffee, her head had cleared enough to make a to-do list:

1. *Pull myself together before Noah arrives.*
2. *Ask him about noises in the furnace and water pipes.*
3. *Get him to tell me about the Havencross ghost.*
4. *Find my makeup.*
5. *Destroy this list so as not to humiliate myself.*

Starting from the bottom up, within thirty minutes Juliet had changed into a pair of velvet leggings and an oversized cashmere sweater, had brushed her hair, and had applied concealer, mascara, and lipstick. It was the longest she'd looked at herself in the mirror in months, and she was glad to note that the pregnancy weight, compounded by depression eating, had begun to drop off. Her olive-toned skin no longer looked sallow, and her dark hair had something of the same sheen to it that she'd seen in the photos of a young Clarissa Somersby.

Once ready, she set up in the cavernous Victorian kitchen with the scrapbook of Thomas Somersby's disappearance and her notebook—it was either pretend to do research or sit on the front steps like a teenage girl waiting for her first date.

The thing about being a historian was that even pretending to research could easily turn into the real thing. It only took one tidbit to catch the imagination—usually buried in a mass of details. Gradually Juliet compiled a timeline.

Sir Wilfred Somersby had passed Christmas and New Year's at Havencross with his second wife, Sylvia, their two daughters and baby son (ages four, three, and one), and the children of his first wife, thirteen-year-old Clarissa and nine-year-old

Thomas. Also present for the holidays were two of his sisters with their husbands and children. A grand total of six adults and sixteen children.

It seemed their planned departure had been hastened by an oncoming blizzard and the threat of the bridge being flooded over. Reading between the lines of the local news stories, Juliet got a strong impression of an unruly scene: the North's early sunset mixed with heavy clouds and rapidly increasing snow-fall, almost four dozen people (counting the servants), horses being harnessed to carriages, children being loaded separately from parents, too many people shouting too many orders with too little organization . . .

Only when the last of the carriages arrived at a Newcastle inn was it discovered that Thomas had been left behind. As at least five servants had remained at Havencross, so it was assumed the boy would be petted and spoiled. How he would enjoy being the only child there until the weather cleared.

It was three days before anyone realized that Thomas was not at Havencross. Or at least, not in the house. Searches were set up, and every foot of ground for five miles around was scoured. The only thing they found was a single shoe, on the banks of the high-rushing river.

By keeping a severe focus on her note-taking, Juliet avoided losing herself in the pathos of the lost boy. *This was research*, she reminded herself. And if she intended to write about the influenza epidemic at the boys' school, she'd have to get used to reading about suffering children.

An editorial published three weeks after the search had been suspended offered the intriguing tidbit Juliet had been hoping for.

Odd happenings are not new to Havencross. The estate passed rapidly through various families from the days of the first Elizabeth until the end of the eighteenth century when it lay

*empty for decades. All properties of great age accumulate ghosts—
at Havencross, it is said to be the spirit of a young boy. Supposedly
he haunts both the house and the grounds, though he is reported
to be of a mild nature.*

Juliet was scribbling down notes rapidly, already wondering
how she could weave this into her research, when she heard
footsteps followed immediately by Noah Bennett's voice.

"Are you home?" he asked rhetorically, since he already
stood in the kitchen doorway. "I used the knocker on the front
door but figured you'd never hear it if you weren't nearby. But
then you didn't seem to hear me knocking on the scullery
door either."

She stood up too quickly, nearly knocking over her chair.
"Sorry! I get this way when I'm reading. Or researching. You
could set off fireworks behind me and I'd never notice, so my
husband always said. Ex-husband."

Shit. So much for doing her makeup and impressing Noah—
he'd been here twenty seconds and she'd already babbled about
her failed marriage. She wouldn't be surprised if he walked
straight back out the way he'd come.

But he just said, "Enviable trait. I have to wear noise-
cancelling headphones if I want to concentrate for more than
fifteen minutes at a time. More research about the school?"

"Not directly. I was reading the news clippings about Thomas
Somersby's disappearance in 1907. Most of them refer to the
ghost boy of Havencross, the one your great-aunt says might
date back to the Wars of the Roses, but one of the reporters
also talked about tunnels constructed by the original medieval priory. They were supposedly used as hideouts or escape
routes during the Scottish wars, and I'd like to look into that.
Secret tunnels could easily provide answers to some supposed
hauntings."

"Absolutely. And secret passageways. Havencross supposedly has some of those."

Juliet felt a chill at the base of her neck. She was already living entirely alone in a house with more rooms than she'd bothered to count and at least three staircases—did there really have to be hidden passages for her to worry about?

Not that ghosts need hidden passages, she reminded herself.

Not that ghosts are real, she shot back at herself.

Anxious to change the subject, Juliet asked abruptly, "Did you need to look at the furnace? Water heater? Or whatever it is you're here for. I don't really know what a surveyor does."

A different man—Duncan—would have taken offense. At her words, at her tone, at something only he could discern that was wrong in her.

Noah just laughed. "I wouldn't say heating and plumbing make up the bulk of my work, but having grown up in an old farmhouse I have plenty of experience troubleshooting. I'll be glad to take a look at the furnace."

Although she wanted nothing more than to flee, Juliet tagged along when Noah invited her. Maybe pretending to be fascinated by heating systems would shake her into normal behavior.

In the end she admitted that it was more interesting than she would have guessed. (She would have guessed she'd have less than a zero-percent interest, so it was a pretty low bar to clear.) The heating system hadn't been updated yet, and the Edwardian boiler that squatted in the cellar could have been an alien species from some sci-fi movie. Noah talked her through the basics of how it operated and showed her how to restart it if necessary.

"Of course, the advantage to old houses is that you have an abundance of fireplaces," Noah added. "I'll get Rachel's boys to help me bring a load of firewood to stack in the scullery. Worse comes to worst, do you know how to start a fire?"

"Uhhh . . ."

"I'll teach you."

She eyed him skeptically. "That can't possibly be part of your surveying job."

"No, but if I let you freeze to death, then I can't ever get you to go out with me."

Wait . . . what?

The only reason Juliet didn't instantly combust was that Noah didn't stop to judge the effect of his words. He just kept on with what he was doing. "Let's take a look at the electrical while we're down here. That's something you're very likely to lose in a bad storm."

He flashed a grin at her over his shoulder. "And yes, I am going to make sure you have plenty of torches and batteries and candles at hand. It's simply logical to make all the preparations you can."

Logic. Duncan hadn't been much for logic. He'd had the ability to completely contradict himself within two minutes without the slightest acknowledgment that he'd done so. And when Juliet pointed out such a lapse in his logic—usually having to do with her behavior—he'd either fly into a fury and accuse her of undermining him, or look at her blankly and flat-out deny one or the other of his statements. There'd been times Juliet had wanted to record him for later proof, but she figured even that wouldn't help. It would just hand Duncan one more weapon to use against her.

And the sad part was, Juliet had begun to doubt her own instincts.

Also unlike Duncan, Noah didn't seem anxious to press her for a response. Not that he'd actually asked her anything. Yet. What would she say if and when he did? By the time Noah had showed her how to reset the electricity (much simpler, since even she could recognize a fuse box) her nerves had settled and Noah had her talking about her career.

As they climbed up from the cellar, she even felt comfortable enough to say, "An adjunct professor isn't much of a career. You're the lowest of the low in academic departments, although no university could teach its students without adjuncts."

"I get that—but don't tell me it's adjunct teaching or academic infighting that you care about. You didn't come to the farm and charm Aunt Winnie and drag boxes from our attic just because it will make you look better in a job interview. I saw your face. Whatever it is about Havencross that's caught your attention, it shines out of your eyes. That's what I want to hear about."

When was the last time anyone had asked her what she loved? Almost shyly, Juliet said, "It's people that I like, knowing about people in the past. How they lived, what they talked about, the things that frightened them and made them happy. History is just people. We've organized it into dates and politics and wars and governments, but in the end it's all just people making choices, making mistakes, hating and loving just like we do." She caught herself and cleared her throat. "Anyway, Havencross is a beautiful building, but I want to know about the people who lived in it. Especially the boys and staff who were here in 1918. The war is dragging to an end, life is supposed to be getting back to normal, and bam! Out of nowhere a virus explodes and rocks their whole world. That's the story I thought I'd write. Except . . ."

She hesitated. Tell him about the ghostly links or not?

"Except what?" Noah prodded.

"Except, just like all history, the 1918 flu isn't a discrete event. It had influences from the past woven in. One of them seems to be the disappearance of Thomas Somersby in 1907. And the stories of his disappearance talk a lot about the ghost boy of Havencross."

He shot her a sharp and knowing look. "You've been listening to Aunt Winnie. What did she tell you about me and the ghost boy?"

"Just that I should ask you about him. Sometime."

With a wry smile—how many different smiles did he have?—Noah said, "No time like the present, I suppose." He cast a look around the cellar and blew out his breath in a way that made Juliet's throat catch. "If I'm going to tell you a ghost story, this isn't the place for it. Can we go to the medieval part of the house?"

Where her bedroom was. Where she'd seen . . . whatever it was she'd seen last night. "Sure."

Something about traipsing through the vast ground floor and up the dramatic Gothic staircase made Juliet very aware of the house's size and emptiness. She'd managed thus far to keep her attention focused only on her immediate surroundings in Havencross, and wondered if she'd be able to sleep at night if this new awareness stayed with her. All of that space—with only her own breath and heartbeat for company.

When they crossed into the thicker-walled corridor of the medieval core, Noah saw the open door that led to her bedroom. "You chose to sleep up here?"

She thought she understood his subtext. "You're wondering why?"

"I am, rather."

"Because this is where you saw him." Juliet realized this answer could be misconstrued. "I mean, I didn't choose it *because* this is where you saw a ghost. But you're wondering . . ."

Would he say it, or would she have to? Duncan would never have been able to follow her thought process.

Noah said it. "I'm wondering if *you* have seen something."

The thrill of being understood pulsed through her. "I think I'd like to hear about your experience before I share mine."

"Fair enough. You know Havencross has been empty since Clarissa Somersby's death in 1992. All that time my family's acted as caretakers, making sure it didn't burn down or flood, putting plywood up over broken windows, keeping down the rodent population, things like that. Both Rachel and I would tag along at times. I was ten years old the winter of '99. Came with my dad to check things over after a snowstorm."

He motioned to the door at the end of the corridor. "We were up on the attic level, the medieval solarium, where one of the window frames was leaking. Have you been up there? I mean, you must have; it's part of your job."

"I go up once a week," she said.

"Right, so you know how empty it is up there. Boring for a child. I left my dad working and came down the spiral stairs to amuse myself in wider spaces. It was here that I saw him." He indicated with his hand the corridor in which they stood—the corridor that had lightened so inexplicably last night.

Juliet bit her lip. "What did you see?"

"At first, just an impression of light. I couldn't figure out where it was coming from. But then the light settled and coalesced into the form of a young boy, about my age, with fair hair and wide-set eyes." Another of his too-sharp glances. "Does that sound familiar?"

She nodded, not afraid, exactly. More awed.

Noah nodded back. "And then I heard him, without him ever opening his mouth. He extended his hand and he said—"

"Come hide with me," Juliet said, word for word exactly with Noah.

With a wondering, admiring expression, Noah said, "You *have* seen him."

"Last night. Scared the hell out of me," she admitted. "I spent the rest of the night with everything moveable shoved in front of my bedroom door."

He laughed. "I shouted so loud my dad came tearing down

the stairs thinking I'd broken my leg. He told me I was just imagining things. Aunt Winnie believed me though. And I never cared to come back to this part of the house again. And yet . . ."

It was his turn to hesitate. But Juliet felt she knew him well enough to finish his sentence: "And yet, the boy does not seem threatening. Just lonely."

"Right again." Without the least self-consciousness, Noah extended his hand, and she took it. "Does that mean you're going to keep sleeping up here?"

"I think so. For whatever reason, I like this part of the house. It feels the most . . . loved. Maybe I just like that it's small and easier to see into every part. Sleeping in that grand front bedroom would feel like being on display in a deserted museum. And despite my initial shock, I'm not afraid of a lost little boy."

When he looked at her with a question in his hazel eyes, Juliet almost told him why—about her own lost little boy and the grief that had driven her to Havencross. But talking about Liam was one step too far for today.

Noah's expression lightened. "I don't suppose your contract requires to you spend every waking minute inside the house. I mean, you came to the farm. Would you like to go dinner some night next week? You could come to Newcastle, or I could meet you in Hexham."

So he hadn't just been teasing.

"I'd love to see Newcastle."

CHAPTER EIGHTEEN

JULIET
2018

After that rather extraordinary afternoon with Noah, Juliet spent the next few days in flat-out physical labor, exhausting herself so thoroughly that she had no trouble falling—and staying—asleep.

She kept remembering what he'd said when she'd asked him why the ghost boy couldn't be Thomas Somersby: "Whoever the boy was in life, he wasn't Thomas." She didn't know why she should find that so reassuring—wouldn't a ghost who'd been stuck on Earth for even longer than a hundred years be that much more demanding? However, Noah's strongly voiced certainty had rung through her with rightness, suggesting she'd found the path to follow.

A path that seemed to be mixed up with Clarissa Somersby's interest in the Wars of the Roses. *Maybe.*

All right, Juliet conceded.

Her own memory of the ghost boy and Noah's description—"Tall but slight. Fair hair. Carrying a candle and dressed in a white shirt with embroidered cuffs and a cloak."—were by no means definitive of an age. Noah had even sketched the boy for her, though he admitted cheerfully to being much more use as a surveyor working with lines and shading than with portraits. And indeed, the face was indistinct and the clothing, as Juliet pointed out, had commonalities with almost every period of the last six or seven hundred years. It didn't prove anything.

"It tells us he's not a monk from the old priory," he'd said. "Yes, I know. Thomas Somersby might have worn something similar enough. And of course, that's what I thought at first. It's not like I talked to him, but I was wondering, you know? In my head. And when I thought 'Thomas Somersby,' the boy looked disappointed."

So Noah Bennett was either extraordinarily sensitive to the supernatural, or he had a boundless imagination. Or Juliet's taste in men had moved on from controlling and scary to, at best, creative storytelling and, at worst, out of touch with reality.

Of course, Juliet herself might be out of touch with reality. Anyone from the outside would certainly say so. Thirty-year-old female, newly single, history of depression, recent stillbirth, living in seclusion, blah, blah, blah. Already prone to dreams that bled into waking hours, why wouldn't she hallucinate in a well-known haunted house?

Against all that, Juliet had only one defense. (Two, if you counted Noah Bennett's obviously well-grounded sanity.) It was that, despite everything she'd gone through, she felt better than she had in years. She had no idea how worn down she'd become during her years with Duncan. They'd been together since her second year of college, and everything she knew about long-term relationships had been filtered through this single experience. With the recovery of her body from months of pregnancy and the hormonal aftermath of a wrenching delivery, she realized that she even moved differently now. Always so cautious around Duncan, always bracing herself for an attack of words and emotions she never—or always—saw coming. Now she ran up and down the palatial staircase at Havencross without thinking twice. The muscles she worked hauling boxes or packing books or dragging furniture she loosened with stretching, and they were restored in a day or two.

Most critically of all, she could think.

How long had it been since she could think rationally about anything to do with herself? She'd always managed to do her work, to prepare lessons, lectures, and critique essays with a measure of confidence in her subject matter. History had already happened. But anything beyond those narrow confines had been shadowed and weighed down by Duncan's opinions. Duncan's criticisms. Duncan's ever-so-offhand commentary had been an anchor she dragged everywhere. He might say, "I thought the dean's wife looked a little flabby today" while meaning, "Work out harder and eat less so no one ever thinks *my* wife looks flabby." Juliet should flatter her department head more, Juliet should never be accused of flirting, Juliet should lengthen her hemlines and raise her necklines and never wear gold and never color her hair pink . . .

God, no wonder she'd been so tired for so long.

And now she wasn't. She was awake, and she was thinking, and there was no Duncan to cast doubt on her grasp of reality.

She had seen things. She had heard things.

Now she wanted to figure out what it all meant.

On Wednesday she left Havencross at 4 p.m. to meet Noah for dinner. Already the sun was so low that crossing the narrow bridge across the river felt perilous; she wondered how she would manage in complete darkness. Maybe she'd just park on the far side of the river and walk across when she returned.

Even with her nerves about driving and navigating in an unfamiliar city, Juliet was early enough to walk along the river and admire the Tyne bridge before arriving at the Quayside pub. She hovered nervously outside, hoping her black jeans and tweed blazer were appropriate, feeling exactly like she had the last time she'd had a first date. She had to keep reminding herself that she wasn't twenty years old anymore and Noah was nothing at all like Duncan.

Noah came striding up just five minutes later, leaving her both relieved and flustered. Did he always look so delighted to meet someone, or was it just her? He immediately complimented her outfit, asked about the drive, and said, "Do you mind if I kiss you on the cheek?"

Sexy, polite, and respectful of boundaries. As he brushed her cheek with his lips, Juliet knew she was in the best kind of trouble.

"This is really your first English pub?" he asked after they'd ordered and had wine in hand.

"I only arrived in England the day before I reached Havencross. I haven't been anywhere except Heathrow and whatever roads I took to drive up here. Everyone told me I should spend a few days in London first, but I didn't really feel like sightseeing on my own."

"London's well enough," Noah said with a distinct lack of enthusiasm. "For a visit. But nothing beats the North."

"Have you always lived in Northumberland? I suppose Newcastle is still in Northumberland?"

He fake-clutched his heart. "Woman, you've wounded me! Forget the flu pandemic, we've got to set you studying the most noble and ancient history of Northumbria. Yes, Newcastle is in Northumberland. Ignore those who will want to tell you about the modern county of Tyne and Wear."

"I promise," she said solemnly.

"Seriously, I was born in Hexham, lived all my life at the farm until I went to the University of Edinburgh."

"Farther north," Juliet pointed out.

"Right. Then I came to work here in Newcastle. I could maybe be persuaded to go as far south as York, but that's where I draw the line. What about you? Had you always lived in the same place until you came over here?"

"No. I grew up in Pennsylvania, went to university in Massachusetts, and worked at various colleges in Maine ever since."

She was afraid he would ask her about her marriage next, but the food arrived and conversation became a little less personal if no less entertaining. At least four times Juliet wondered how it was that Noah didn't already have a partner or girlfriend. Maybe she'd ask Rachel about her brother's romantic history.

Over a shared dessert—Juliet pointed out that American pancakes were usually eaten for breakfast—Noah said, "If you're still interested in trying to place our ghost boy in history, I've got an old roommate from university who works at a museum in Berwick. His specialty is medieval history. I could put you in touch with him if you like."

"That would be great. I'm not giving up on the influenza book. But no historian worth their degree would leave a research path until they've exhausted every possibility."

"I'll let him know you'll be calling and text you his info. If you don't mind giving me your number, that is."

"You've fed me authentic English fish and chips. I think I owe you."

He walked her to where she'd parked, and they lingered by the car.

"You'll be all right getting back in the dark?" he asked.

Juliet was too happy to remember her earlier misgivings. "I'll be fine."

"Would I be overstepping if I asked you to text me once you're safely back?"

"Not at all. It's nice to have someone care."

"Care," he repeated. His voice softened and his eyes swept her face. "If I wanted to kiss you good night . . ."

She caught her lower lip with her teeth, a habit of adolescence. Feeling more bold than she had in years, she said, "It doesn't have to be on the cheek."

"Good."

He kissed her with a thoroughness that left her shaky. Whatever his romantic history, he clearly had one—Noah Bennett knew how to kiss. She imagined he knew how to do a lot of things. She let herself imagine a few of those while she drove back to Havencross, humming as she went.

Even the bridge wasn't as terrifying as she'd feared. It was a clear night, the moon was full, and her headlights provided a steady path across the river. Juliet floated into the house and up the stairs, and listened to herself humming until she reached her bedroom.

Where she heard something else. It was the same sound she'd caught four or five times since she'd arrived, at odd hours of day or night. Something rhythmic, almost like drumming, but less familiar. It came, as always, from the door that led to the medieval solar.

Still buoyed by the pleasure of the evening, Juliet got as far as opening the door to the spiral steps. No way in hell was she going up that tightly enclosed spiral in the dark—she just thought she might hear more clearly with the door open, maybe identify the sound as coming from the boiler pipes. Or something on the roof. It had almost an animal feel, as though raccoons or dogs were running across the highly-peaked roof.

Horses.

Juliet didn't know where that thought came from, but she knew instantly it was right. It was horses she could hear. Obviously not on the roof, but heard through the windows from the solar above her: the drumming of hooves on packed earth, the creak and murmur of leather saddles, the iron jangle of armed riders.

Seized by an impulse to race up the stairs—*How many riders? Whose men?*—Juliet had gotten three steps up when her phone sounded a text alert. Immediately everything else fell silent. Backing down slowly, afraid to start that unsettling experience again, Juliet eased herself into the corridor and shut the door.

"That was terrifying," she said aloud. "Little ghost boy, whoever you are, tonight would not be a good night to show yourself."

At least hearing her own voice yanked her back to reality. *Text alert, right.* It was probably Noah, checking on her. She fumbled the phone out of her bag and looked.

It was not from Noah. It was from Duncan.

Do you remember when we went on the haunted trolley tour in Boston? Five years ago tonight. Do you remember what we did later in the hotel? I miss you, Jules. I've never loved anyone the way I love you. Please tell me you forgive me.

CHAPTER NINETEEN

DIANA
NOVEMBER 1918

"You sure you want to do this?" Joshua asked.

Diana was very much sure that she did *not* want to do this. In fact, she could think of twenty things she'd rather be doing on the first Saturday of the half-term holiday than voluntarily walking into an enclosed space.

But she'd been desperate on Wednesday to distract Joshua from the scratches on her neck, and exploiting his interest in the hidden passages had been the first thing that came to mind. Not that he'd looked particularly deceived, but he'd allowed himself to be redirected. For the moment. She suspected it would come up again. Maybe later today, when they walked to his family's farmhouse to take tea.

So now the two of them stood in a third-floor storeroom holding industrial torches, a mostly empty school beneath them. Fifteen boys remained for the holiday: scholarship students or war orphans with no easy homes to retreat to. The masters had gone too, except for Joshua and Luther Weston. This morning Clarissa herself had joined Weston and Beth Willis in accompanying the left-behind boys on an expedition along Hadrian's Wall, leaving Diana and Joshua to their exploring.

It wasn't fair that Joshua looked even better in flannels and a hand-knit sweater than he did in a suit. Diana kept fingering the scarf tied around her neck and then dropping her hand hastily before Joshua could be reminded of the scratches. At least they were healing nicely.

She must have done it herself. It was what she'd said to Joshua and what she kept repeating to herself over and over.

Maybe soon she'd believe it.

"Well," Joshua said, "let's see how good my memory is. If I'm right, this is where Clarissa and I emerged all those years ago when she showed me the secret passage."

He and Diana had to move boxes of old agendas and pieces of worn-out desks and chairs to get to the passage's opening. No one had bothered to conceal it beyond the piles of junk—it was simply a low rectangle cut into the wall that levered open to reveal, not the matching servant's room next door, but a narrow corridor between the two rooms. It couldn't be much wider than Joshua's shoulders, and she saw him raise his eyebrows at the sight.

"The space was certainly much bigger when I was young," he noted, but his grin belied any hint of apprehension he might feel. "Good thing I've got you. If I get stuck, you'll have to find an ax or something."

You're putting a lot of faith in a woman whose last experience in an enclosed space left her paralyzed and choking. She would never tell Joshua that. She would never tell anyone that.

With considerable sarcasm, she retorted, "Yes, I can see myself explaining to Miss Somersby now: 'No worries, just one of your masters is stuck inside the walls of your house, and I'm going to ax him free. You don't mind if I bring down a ceiling or two in the process, do you?'"

Joshua laughed and touched her hand with his. "I'll go first."

Although his hand had only rested on hers for a moment, it felt cold when he withdrew. She watched his strong, straight back moving carefully down the hidden passage and, with a quiet sigh, followed.

It wasn't so bad. Although narrow, the passageway was the same height as the rooms it was carved out of and was constructed of the same wood and plaster. Their torches shone brightly, and for some time Diana saw little but dust.

"I knew it." Joshua's satisfied voice floated back to her, and she moved up to where he'd stopped.

He leaned his back against the wall, allowing Diana to see past him to where a second passage angled off from the straight path they were on.

"That direction"—Joshua gestured with his torch to the straight path—"leads to the stairs that go down to the second-floor linen closet in today's staff corridor. That's the direction Clarissa brought me years ago. She didn't tell me where this other passage leads."

"Maybe she didn't know," Diana offered.

"Let's find out, shall we?"

In spite of how tight her entire body was held, Diana felt the first thrill of curiosity and wondered how much of that she was picking up from her companion. Either way, she said, "Let's."

Unlike the path they'd been on, the offshoot passage rambled in twists and turns until Diana had no idea where they were in the house. Still on the attic level, at least—until they reached a stone staircase so tightly wound she couldn't see more than two steps at a time.

Joshua continued to lead the way going down, but now Diana kept close enough that she kept bumping him with her torch. She was not about to let him out of her sight in this confined space. Already her blood pulsed so loudly that she was sure he could hear it. She thought maybe he had when he began to narrate what he could see. Since there was nothing to see but stone, it was less informative and more just comforting hearing his voice.

"It's odd, don't you think," Joshua said, "that the spiral stairs were constructed of stone when the passageways are more like regular corridors. Only smaller and hidden. Maybe Gideon Somersby had a thing for the medieval and wanted to put touches of the old house into the new one."

"Where no one could see it but him?"

"Exactly. Possessive. A very Victorian male thing to do."

The staircase ended in a vestibule-type space that was just big enough for Joshua and Diana to stand together. She took his torch and directed both lights onto the wall where he pressed and prodded until finding the right catch. Cautiously, he pushed the door open just enough to peer through.

They were definitely in the family section of the house—unless Clarissa outfitted her schoolmasters' bedrooms in rich velvet drapes and thick carpeting. Diana turned off the torches as Joshua eased the door wide enough for them to slip through.

It was not only empty, but had the impersonal air of a room long unused. Although everything was clean and dusted—Diana ran a finger along a carved end table—the single-size bed was unmade, the mattress shrouded in heavy linen. The heaviness of the décor had a masculine feel to it and, on a hunch, Diana crossed the room and opened the door on the opposite wall.

It gave onto a room nearly three times as large, with an enormous mahogany four-poster bed and a matching wardrobe. The bedding was fresh, and the array of things—books, slippers, bedrobe, brushes—were a dead giveaway: Clarissa Somersby's room. And before it had belonged to her—

"Gideon Somersby, the original owner." Joshua had followed the same train of thought. "A very Victorian male in every way, including the dressing room off the marital bedroom that he could sleep in when his wife didn't want him."

"Allowing him to use his own private staircase to access the servants' quarters," Diana finished. "What do you want to bet only the prettiest maids were assigned to that attic bedroom?"

"I'm feeling pretty glad that my female ancestors who worked here lived at the farm," Joshua answered, a little absently. He had taken a step into Clarissa's room but no farther.

Diana felt the same hesitation, but her curiosity had sparked with the realization that Clarissa Somersby had a direct—and private—route to the school side. Even if the other end of that passage didn't go to the medieval core, coming out in the attics would allow her to get to the infirmary and Diana's bedroom without passing through any inhabited or heavily traveled corridors.

But why? Diana fluttered her fingertips at the silk around her throat as she tried to imagine the elegant, reserved headmistress creeping through that claustrophobic passage in order to slam things, knock on doors, and move objects.

And slip so silently across the floor that she could rake her fingernails down Diana's neck without her knowing?

No, the headmistress would not do such things.

But the grieving sister? The woman obsessed with rumors of a ghost boy? The daughter whose father was threatening to take her away from Havencross?

Diana stepped lightly through Clarissa's bedroom, not touching anything, just scanning it all to turn over later in her mind. She didn't see anything obviously suspicious or out of place. Volumes of classical literature, academic studies on private schools, bound school records by year, novels in French and German. Diana felt stupider by the minute.

There were two photographs framed in old silver on the bedside table, where they would be the first things Clarissa would see in the morning and the last things at night. One was an old-fashioned family portrait: Diana recognized a much-younger Sir Wilfred Somersby, with his wife surrounded by two little girls and a fat baby on her lap, and two older children standing on his other side—Clarissa looked twelve or thirteen, the boy next to her around the same age as the first-year students.

The same boy was the sole figure in the second photo. He had dark hair and the round face of the young, and despite the stiff clothing and pose, he looked ready to burst into laughter.

The lost Thomas. He reminded Diana of her own little brother. Unlike Clarissa, she might know where to physically find Harry today, but he'd lost the irrepressible joy of youth somewhere in France.

Joshua came up beside her. "You ready to go back?"

The thought of returning to that enclosed space was too much. "There's no point. We've mapped out the possibilities of that passage. Servants' quarters, staff linen closet, and head-mistress's bedroom. The linen closet is boarded shut, and I highly doubt boys are sneaking in and out through here under Clarissa's nose."

"Are you all right, Diana?"

He was way too perceptive. As unhurriedly as she could, Diana moved across Clarissa's bedroom to the outer door. "I think we should leave the private wing before anyone finds us. If you want to go back through the passage, I'll meet you in the attic and we can put everything back the way it was."

"Diana—"

"Then we can cross off that passage and move on. Do you think Clarissa has the original house plans? Maybe she'll let us look at them."

Joshua stopped her by simply stepping in front of the door. "If you don't want to talk about it, Diana, that's all right. God knows there are stories I don't tell. But I don't want to keep throwing you into spaces that you don't . . . that aren't . . ."

His obvious care in trying to select the right words, and the two little creases between his eyebrows as he thought, forced a tiny crack in Diana's well-guarded defenses. "You're right, I don't love tunnels and darkness. Maybe someday I'll tell you all about it. And in the future I'll confine my exploring to maps— you can do all the legwork." Diana tried to match one of his grins, probably looking more demented than sexy. "Seeing as how we worked so hard to save that leg in the first place."

Where did he learn to look at a woman like that? Never mind, she thought hastily. *I don't really want to know.*

For a dizzying moment, she thought he'd kiss her. His eyelashes lowered as though he were looking at her mouth, and they both moved ever so slightly inward. But then his mouth quirked into one of his myriad smiles.

"Clarissa likes us both," he said, "but I don't think that will help if we're caught here."

Right. Clarissa. School. Tunnel. Ghost.

Diana shook away all the disparate thoughts in her head and followed Joshua out the door. He definitely had a better grasp of the house's physical layout because he led her out of the private wing and back into the school spaces without a single wrong turn.

And none too soon, because the boys were trooping through the great hall as the two of them came down the main staircase.

Behind the mass of boys came Beth Willis, walking with her young Austin, and Clarissa Somersby bringing up the rear at her most imperial. She wore a divided skirt of dark plum tweed, the matching jacket impeccably tailored to her frame. Next to her, the perfect country gentleman in gray flannel with cap in hand: Luther Weston looked as though he'd been speaking to her for some time.

Why did Diana feel that Clarissa—as her eyes caught her nurse and assistant headmaster standing on the stairs—could review everything she'd been doing? It was probably a trick she'd learned in one of those school leadership books in her bedroom.

But it was Luther Weston's stare that truly unnerved her. Besides his evident dislike of Joshua, he seemed to have developed an irrational animosity toward Diana as well. She wouldn't put it past Weston to play tricks on her in the night. Or at least to use those tricks against her. Already he'd said Diana was too "imaginative"—not a quality one wanted in a school nurse. She would just have to keep any future ruses between herself and Joshua for now. As much as she wanted to believe that she'd scratched her own neck in her sleep, Diana would rather die than allow Weston to imply the same thing in public.

CHAPTER TWENTY

DIANA
NOVEMBER 1918

Joshua tried to convince Diana that she could just go to tea in her trousers and a sweater.

She laughed. "I have manners."

"We'll be walking across fields to get to the farmhouse," he reminded her.

"I can walk in a skirt."

She proved it with a wide-gored skirt in a heathered green tweed and her long-line wool coat in navy blue over a lace-trimmed blouse. One of the older boys playing cricket on the grounds whistled and Joshua shouted, "Decorum, please. We do not treat women like dogs."

"So you don't think I look nice?" she teased.

Joshua offered her his hand and, after a moment's debate, Diana took it. When was the last time she'd held hands with a man? Long enough that it hadn't been a man, that's for sure, but a boy. She felt some of that girlish thrill now, deepened by her awareness of Joshua's very masculine presence.

"I think," he said deliberately, "that I cannot properly express my appreciation for how you look. It would set a very bad example in front of these schoolboys, because I don't feel at all like being decorous."

Could he feel the flutterings of her pulse through her hand? Thankfully, Joshua knew how to compliment a woman without expecting anything in return. But she didn't let go of his hand until White Rose Farm was in sight.

"Welcome to my home," Joshua said. "Its roots don't go as far back as Havencross, only to 1699. However, it has been in the same family for all of its two hundred and nineteen years, so that's something."

It wasn't as imposing as Havencross either, which filled Diana with relief. White Rose Farm was low-roofed, with two stories in the center and one-story wings balancing it on either side. The dark slate roof paired well with the pale stucco of the outer walls. The front door was painted yellow and vines framed the door and its flanking windows.

"Climbing roses," Diana identified. "White, I presume."

"But of course."

"This farmhouse didn't exist until more than two hundred years after Richard the Third's death. So how did a family with a Scottish surname come late to the Yorkist cause?"

"There were Yorkists in Scotland," Joshua pointed out. "Before he became king, Richard was warden of the North and a particularly respected one at that. By both sides. My granddad always claimed the Murrays bought this land because of an old connection to the Yorkist cause."

"Is there any part of the North that doesn't have connections and causes and claims to the past? My mother would say it's because none of you know how to live in the modern world."

She expected Joshua to laugh. When he didn't, it sharpened her attention.

"London has just as much history weighing on it as the North," he retorted. "Londoners simply build on top of it and pretend it isn't there."

Diana didn't have to think up a reply, because the cheery front door had opened to disclose, in rapid succession, a dog, three cats, a pleasant-looking woman of middle age, who must be Joshua's mother, an adolescent girl, who would be his fifteen-year-old sister, Alice, and a small hurricane who threw himself headlong against Joshua's weak leg so that he had to firmly brace himself on the good one.

"Be careful, Tom!" Alice scolded. "You'll knock Uncle Joshua to the ground."

Tom turned out to be the four-year-old son of Joshua's older sister. She had been widowed by the Somme and now worked in a factory in York while her son stayed at the farm. Looking at the little boy's grin was to get a glimpse of Joshua as a child.

A glimpse of what Joshua's own child might be . . .

Definitely not following that train of thought, Diana told herself firmly.

The Murray family was as welcoming as Joshua, though in slightly different ways. Alice seemed very grown-up for fifteen—at least compared to Diana, who thought guiltily of things like stealing her brother's motorcycle and sneaking cigarettes at Alice's age—but she brought the same attentive questions as her brother and seemed genuinely curious about Diana's life during the war. Edith Murray was the same age as Diana's mother, and her quietness was in no way shyness. Having seen too many of the fussy, neurotic mothers who fluttered around their wounded sons as though they were broken birds, Diana approved of Edith's steadiness and ability to allow her children to live their lives.

Joshua's grandfather was a hearty, energetic northern farmer of seventy-two. Moving with an ease his grandson no longer possessed, he probably looked the same since he was forty. And though Joshua's father could only greet her from the low daybed in the parlor, he had the same open, welcoming face. He was still recovering from a stroke, but to Diana's professional eye he looked to be healing well.

It had been a long time since Diana had shared a family meal that didn't include arguments, debates, and criticism. Her mother would have thought the Murrays hopelessly uncultured (although she would never have been so rude as to say so directly). The food was also amazing—the benefit of being on a farm, she supposed. When Diana expressed appreciation for the bread, Alice—who had made it—blushed with pleasure and immediately offered to teach her how to bake.

Caught by surprise, Diana said, "I don't know that I'd be any good at baking. What if I forget the salt or burned something?"

"You literally saved my life," Joshua said, "and you're afraid of burning bread?"

"Don't be so dramatic," she shot back. "I spent thirty minutes getting you prepped for surgery, that's all. It's the surgeons and the rehabilitative staff that got you back on your feet."

He looked at her intently, as though they were completely alone—like he had on the moor, and in Clarissa's bedroom this morning. "There's more than one way to save a life. Your work's not done yet, Nurse Neville."

With the exquisite judgment of a mother who knows how to defuse potential emotional explosions, Edith Murray said, "Joshua tells us you are interested in the history of Havencross, Miss Neville. Whatever questions you have, I know my father-in-law will be delighted to answer."

"Please call me Diana," she reminded. "And I don't want to be pushy. But Northumberland and Havencross are so different from anything I've known. I'm dreadfully curious."

"Hear that?" Joshua's grandfather asked the table at large. "Finally, an intelligent woman for me to talk to. Don't worry about being pushy, Diana. You're more likely to beg me to stop talking long after I've exhausted your curiosity."

She wasn't pushy, and he could talk a lot. But luckily for her he was a born storyteller and luckily for him Diana was delighted to have found an absorbing interest far removed from the battlefields of France.

Not that the stories didn't have plenty of violence. "It's the borders," Mr. Murray said easily. "There's always someone to fight. Even as far back as the thirteenth century there were lots of raids. Christian or not, priories were wealthy places and fair game for soldiers and reivers alike. The monks quickly learned to protect their wealth and their people. In Ireland they built round towers as far back as the Viking age to which they could retreat. Havencross did the opposite—they tunneled."

Of course they did, Diana thought. "Escape tunnels?"

"They were more places of retreat than of escape," he conceded. "Whatever outlets they might have had are lost to time. At least so far as archaeologists have learned. Which isn't much since the Somersby family put up that house. They prefer to keep their land private. But I've got drawings from the survey done before building that identify a number of foundations from the original priory. Including the chapel. And there was a dig conducted fifty years ago a few miles from here that seems to have been an exit point to an old tunnel. The police went looking for it when young Thomas went missing."

"They thought he'd gone into a tunnel?"

He shrugged, the wearied sadness on his face a reminder of

his age and the death he'd seen on both large and small scales. "He went somewhere. Just nowhere any of us could follow."

It was a curious word, that—*follow*. Diana would have expected a more prosaic finish, like "nowhere any of us could find." *Follow* implied Thomas Somersby had stepped through some sort of unnatural or otherworldly veil, crossing a threshold that mere mortals could not.

Passing straight from boy to ghost with no steps in-between.

Diana shivered as she thought of Austin Willis and his brother and the dozens of other boys now at Havencross. Whatever was at work there was disturbing them, and she wouldn't let it go further.

The return walk to Havencross was quiet for the most part, Diana thinking about tunnels and choking and Joshua lost in his own world. When they parted on the upper landing, with the house settled into the end-of-weekend hush around them, he held her hand as he thanked her for coming with him.

He kept holding it when he'd finished speaking, long enough for the same alive awareness that had descended in Clarissa's bedroom to return.

In another moment, Diana thought, *I will kiss him.*

He kissed her first. A gentle, almost-brotherly kiss on the cheek. But there was nothing sisterly in her reaction to the bristly roughness of his jaw or her sudden wish to lead him to her secluded corridor and bedroom.

They parted without speaking again, and Diana fell asleep with a hand to the cheek he'd kissed.

She woke, as she'd too often done these last weeks, to a burst of freezing air as her covers were yanked off the bed. Diana almost made a grab for the quilt but a realization that it would not be wise to engage in a tug-of-war with something she couldn't see stopped her.

When she tried to turn on the bedside lamp it too was yanked from her grasp. *I must have knocked it over*, Diana thought as it crashed to the floor. But she knew better. She knew. There was someone in her room. Someone who wanted her gone. Someone who hated her. Someone who had dragged their fingernails across her neck, drawing blood.

Someone who could not be seen.

Not that Diana could see much of anything. But even the shadowy outlines of her room began to fade, as though a vortex were coming from the outside in, sucking away all light and heat. And she knew what came next, the terrible choking on dust and darkness to the point where she couldn't breathe and she would never be able to breathe again or see or move—

Someone pounded on her door with an urgency that spoke of danger. "Diana!"

In an instant, it vanished. The terror, the cold, the dark.

Diana realized she was sitting bolt upright on her bed, hands at her throat as though clawing for air, but whatever presence had been with her was gone. Her covers were still on the floor along with the broken lamp, but Joshua's voice had banished the rest.

She slid carefully to her feet, avoiding the shards of glass, and threw open the door. Joshua stood there in flannel trousers and a partly buttoned shirt. He looked as though he too had been dragged out of bed.

"What's wrong?" she demanded, pushing past him for the infirmary and her bag, with all her years of practice at switching instantly from sleep to work.

"Jasper Willis has disappeared."

CHAPTER TWENTY-ONE

ISMAY
MAY 1458

Afterward this year was held a counsel at Westminster, to the which came the young lords whose fathers were slain at St. Albans by the Duke of York, and they were lodged without the walls of London. The city would not receive them because they came against the peace. The Duke of York and the Earl of Salisbury came but only with their household men in peaceable manner and thinking no harm. Then the other lords and bishops of the land treated between the parties for peace.

"How do I look?" Elizabeth demanded.

Ismay took her time observing her friend, knowing that Elizabeth's nerves needed a thoughtful and truthful reply. It was no accident that Ismay chose the compliment that would most give Elizabeth confidence: "You will do your mother very proud."

"And my husband?"

Right. It was easy to forget that Elizabeth had been a wife for almost four months. Her marriage had been part of the whole tense affair of the late winter. King Henry had recovered his health and determined to reconcile all England's enemies. It was the only time Ismay had ever heard Duchess Cecily sound anything less than composed. When the summons came for the Duke of York and the Neville family to attend the king in London and account for the Battle of St. Albans, the duchess had said bitterly, "My father, my brothers, my husband, my sons. Will that woman leave me with no one?"

That woman being Margaret of Anjou, Queen of England. If the king, in his mildness, was prepared to both forgive and forget, his queen would do neither. And with a five-year-old son to fight for, she had become only more implacable as time passed.

Which made the fact that they were all presently staying at Queen Margaret's castle of Greenwich extremely awkward.

But Elizabeth was fourteen and newly wed and more concerned with the fit of her golden gown and the straight line of her blackwork-embroidered kirtle that showed beneath the deep V-cut of her bodice. Ismay straightened the edge of one attached sleeve that did not need it and adjusted the short sheer veil that fell from Elizabeth's covered hair. It was odd to have her own hair loosely dressed and showing its rich brunette while her younger friend must now, as a wife, cover her hair.

"Your husband," said Ismay firmly, "could never be anything but proud of you."

He'd better be. John de la Pole may not have married Elizabeth for love, but if he ever wanted his father's estates returned to him, he would shower attention and respect on the Duke of York's daughter.

Ismay grabbed Elizabeth's hand and asked on impulse, "Are you happy?"

Astonishment was all the answer she needed. It conveyed both the "Of course I am" uttered by Elizabeth and the unspoken *What has happiness to do with any of this?*

Swallowing a sigh, Ismay followed Elizabeth out of the small bedchamber that she shared now with only ten-year-old Margaret, and into the social battlefield that was the English court.

Within ten minutes of entering the crowded hall, noisy with talk and music, Ismay saw two people that put a huge smile on her face and reminded her that not everything was terrible this spring. John Neville, twenty-six and eternally restless, stood attentively next to his brand-new bride, Isabella Ingaldsthorpe. The elegant and self-possessed seventeen-year-old was a stranger to Ismay but currently her favorite person in England. Queen Margaret's ward had a larger inheritance than Ismay, and her marriage into the Neville family was another intended way to bind the warring camps together.

Better her than me, Ismay thought.

And immediately regretted it when Edward appeared at her side. "So what do you think of Father's newest proposal?"

The honest answer was *I'm trying to forget it*. But she wasn't prepared to be quite that honest with Edward, and he had the unnerving ability to see right through lies and equivocations. So she turned it back on him. "You must be pleased it's not you threatened with an eleven-year-old bride."

"I didn't mean Edmund's proposed marriage to Margaret Percy—awful as that is, poor boy, he'll have to wait years to get her in bed."

It was no use being offended by Edward's frank talk. Ismay simply pushed the image away, as she had grown adept at pushing away many images she didn't like.

Edward's blue eyes searched the crowd as he continued. "No, I meant the proposal that you marry Lord Egremont."

"It has not gone as far as a proposal," Ismay retorted.

"Hasn't it? Are you sure? Because I don't think my father considers your assent a necessary part of the whole thing. The king wants peace. Father wants to keep the lieutenancy of Ireland and his place in the succession. He's already wed Elizabeth to a Lancastrian. What better way to prove his commitment to peace than marrying both his son and his ward into the devilish hands of the Percys?"

He put a hand on her shoulder and pointed. "And there he is. Thomas Percy, Lord Egremont. I suppose he's not so bad. Could be older. Could definitely be uglier. How will you like being the wife of a man twenty years your senior?"

Ismay couldn't help but look. She'd seen Egremont before but steadfastly avoided coming to his personal notice. Of course she didn't want to marry him. He was thirty-six, a Percy, and had dark, unfriendly eyes and a face that looked as though he'd never once smiled. Throw in his undying hatred for the Yorks and Ismay couldn't think of anything she'd rather do less than marry Egremont.

"Don't worry," Edward said, with that unnerving air of having read her mind. "You could always ruin your reputation and then no one would have you. Of course you'd end up in a convent, but getting there might be fun. You have only to ask and I'll help you along the path of ruin."

His wicked grin snapped Ismay out of her silence. "If I didn't know you were teasing, I'd slap your face for that. Actually, I'd do it anyway if I didn't want to cause a scene. Go bother some girl who doesn't know you half as well as I do."

The problem with Edward was that you could never stay angry with him. He kissed her cheek, like he did his own sisters, and went whistling across the room in the direction of a lovely young wife standing alone.

Ismay shook her head, as much to dislodge unpleasant thoughts as to express disapproval. There was no point in disapproving of anything Edward did. Where everyone else in the York household—and most people in England—lived in fear of the Duke of York's ire, Edward would simply listen to whatever reprimands his father gave him then merrily go on to do exactly as he pleased.

Probably that was why Edmund was his father's favorite.

As though summoned by her thoughts in the same way as his older brother, Edmund appeared at her side and everything within Ismay tightened and relaxed. She knew that wasn't actually possible, but it was how Edmund made her feel.

With the softest whisper of a touch along her hand, he said, "Come hide with me. The herb garden is particularly aromatic this afternoon."

The herb garden *was* aromatic beneath the fitful spring sun: sweet basil and lemon balm, and white chamomile flowers swaying in the same breeze that tugged at Ismay's hair. Edmund touched the end of one loose plait; it was enough for her to swing around. And then she was in his arms.

"I missed you." His words seemed to be delivered straight into her heart.

"You saw me yesterday."

"At Mass. Sitting with my mother. Not the ideal circumstances."

Ismay rested her head on his shoulder, the summer-weight wool of his doublet warm beneath her cheek. She wondered how much Edward knew. He and Edmund were very close. And though Edmund insisted he hadn't breathed a word, one could never discount Edward's ability to sniff out secrets. Especially where romance was concerned.

"Has your father spoken to you yet?" Ismay asked.

Edmund didn't need to ask about what. There was only one

topic that obsessed everyone these days: how many marriage alliances needed to be made to create peace.

"Not formally. No one's talking formally right now. We're all just nibbling at the edges, trying to figure out how much we have to give to get what we want, and where we cannot afford to give any longer."

If Edward was a natural soldier and leader and, in his instinctive way, a politician, it was Edmund who had the real gift for politics—the ability to hold the big picture in his head at all times and see how each individual act fitted into the puzzle that was currently English government.

But Ismay had the directness of a girl who knew what she wanted and wasn't afraid to ask for it. "And will your proposed marriage to Margaret Percy soon be moved from the edges of discussion to the center? Or is that something your father is not prepared to give?"

What she meant was, *Is it something you're prepared to give? Are you ready to sacrifice what you might want today for the needs of your family?*

Maybe it was because she was an orphan and an only child, but Ismay couldn't see how one family member's wishes could command everyone else. Even if that family member was hovering closer to England's throne than was comfortable.

Then again, she had already watched Elizabeth—one year younger than herself—marry with no qualms except the quality of her gowns and the public esteem in which her bridegroom was held.

"Ismay." Edmund shifted so that her head came away from his shoulder, and he dipped his own head to meet her eyes. "I'm not worried about my father's position on the matter of my marriage. Not yet. Why worry about what he thinks when I don't know . . . when I'm unsure . . ."

Sometimes she marveled that two brothers so wildly different could be the best of friends. Had Edward of York ever once considered that a girl—any girl, any woman—might not be head-over-heels in love with him?

"Edmund, do you think I'm in the habit of casually kissing any man of my acquaintance?" Ismay asked, a little asperity in her voice.

He, so much fairer of skin and hair than she was, blushed. "No, of course not. But we are apart so often. Indeed, we have spent many more days separate than together. I would never hold you to a kindness that might change over time."

"My love is not a kindness. And I suppose," she said, with growing confidence, "I shall simply have to keep reminding you of that every chance I get."

With that, she went on tiptoe—Edmund was nowhere near as tall as Edward but still a good five inches taller than Ismay—and kissed him. Softly, at first, but not at all timidly. She would never be afraid of Edmund, or afraid of herself with him.

Ever the gentleman, Edmund responded gently at first. But they were both fifteen, old enough that a rush of desire could spark a raging response. His hands went from her shoulders to her waist, and he pulled her against him. The sensible (Scottish) part of her warned that they were in a public garden—all too easily stumbled upon—and that this was hardly the way to introduce the subject to the Duke of York. But that sensible voice sounded as distant as though it were coming from Scotland. In the end it was Edmund whose common sense prevailed, and the kissing stopped. But they clung together for a few moments, breathless and trembling, and Ismay wondered if one could die from sheer delight.

"Well, well, well."

The shock of another voice spiked through Ismay like

lightning, and she jolted away from Edmund. But even in that movement, she'd recognized the voice and knew they'd been discovered by perhaps the only person in the world who wouldn't immediately ruin things.

She squared her shoulders and turned fiercely to Edward. "You of all people should know better than to sneak up on a clearly private moment."

"Not that private," he said, and in his amusement ran a thread of warning. "I may have the gift of defying father, but how would he like it if he knew his favorite son and his wealthy ward were embracing in the very heart of Greenwich Palace, where any Lancastrian could see and take advantage of such knowledge?"

"There is no advantage to be taken," Ismay shot back, "because there is nothing to know. Everyone knows how close I am to your family."

"And yet I've never been the recipient of such kisses. More's the pity."

Edmund might have been quieter and calmer by nature than either Ismay or his brother, but he could not be bullied. "You know I would never compromise Ismay's honor or that of our family," he said steadily. "Our feelings are private, but my intentions are not. I intend to marry her, if she'll have me."

"Really?" Edward asked extravagantly. "Will you have him, little Ismay?"

"I'm not going to propose to her in front of you," Edmund said, as rudely as he ever got. "And do you really want to play the game of who knows the most devastating secrets about the other? I can't even count the number of women I've found you kissing. And a great deal more."

Edward laughed, all warning gone in apparent delight at his brother's show of spirit. "You think any of that would be a surprise to Father?"

"Mother wouldn't like it."

Ah, thought Ismay as Edward's eyes briefly darkened. *A hit. Because if Edmund was the Duke of York's favorite, Edward was patently his mother's.*

"Really, Edmund, you don't know me at all if you think me likely to carry tales to anyone. The only secrets the York family cares about are political ones. And unless Ismay has the means to undo the current government, she's harmless. Love where you will, little brother. But take the advice of your elder—kissing in gardens is one thing; if you intend to take it further, find someplace more comfortable."

He strolled away whistling, leaving Edmund flushed and Ismay wondering if there was anything that could truly touch Edward of York's heart.

CHAPTER TWENTY-TWO

DIANA
NOVEMBER 1918

If the gravity of the situation had not sufficiently impressed itself upon the adults at Havencross, then the headmistress set them straight without a word. Clarissa Somersby, cheeks stained with color and eyes glittering almost feverishly, had set up command in the great hall in preparation for a search. And if you weren't looking at her, you might think she was simply an incredibly prepared headmistress, right down to the appropriate martialing of search parties.

And she was prepared—with maps of each section of the house as well as the grounds ready to hand and with notations about places easily overlooked. Diana would have been impressed if she didn't have such a vivid mental image of Clarissa spending years creating and poring over these maps and every hiding place they represented. Years in which she had never stopped looking for her little brother.

That was what you saw when you looked at her—the bereaved sister thrust back into her greatest nightmare.

Except Thomas had been gone eleven years. Tonight it was Jasper Willis they were looking for. And the advantage of that was Jasper had nowhere near the familiarity with Havencross as young Thomas once had.

Clarissa designated Joshua to stay with her and help conduct interviews with Jasper's classmates, including the three boys who shared his room. Diana managed to pull Joshua aside long enough to say, "Do what you can to direct the questioning yourself. I'm afraid she'll frighten the boys."

He'd nodded once, agreement in his expression, and told her to be careful. She wasn't thrilled to be paired with Luther Weston, but he kept his mouth shut as they took heavy torches and threaded their way back to the medieval section of the house. From what was now a kitchen storeroom, they let themselves down the ladderlike stairs into the cellar.

The dampness hit her first, wrapping around her like the chains of an anchor. There was no other smell like that of damp, heavy soil.

Diana didn't know she'd stopped until Weston bumped into her from behind.

"Sorry," they both said automatically, and Diana shook her head hard to force back the choking fear trying to worm its way in through her skin and nose.

"Don't like cellars?" Weston commented.

"Not ones that began life five hundred years ago. At least it's empty."

She swung her light, seeing only the rock walls and packed earth where casks of wine and barrels of produce had been stored at one time. It had long since been cleaned out—no forgotten bottles, not even a forlorn potato or apple. Nothing—and nowhere—to hide.

She was pretty sure Weston eyed her thoughtfully when they

emerged from the cellar, and she took in three deep breaths in quick succession. "Split up?" she suggested. "I'll do the back rooms, you cover the front. Meet at the foot of the stairs?"

He agreed, and Diana explored the succession of low-ceilinged, dark-paneled rooms that had once been home to medieval servants wearing their lord's badge, armed men standing guard against the Scots and troublesome neighbors, clerks, cooks, and chaplains. Even the lady of the house had probably been back in these storerooms or antechambers, for this had not been a castle. Just a family home, a family with wealth enough for comfort but not so much as to vault them into prominence through war or judicious marriages.

As Diana was checking inside the last of the store cupboards—no sign of the missing boy—the door to the room slammed shut.

"Weston!" She hoped she sounded furious.

But she knew, even as she strode across the room with more haste than dignity, that he was unlikely to pull a prank in such a tense situation. She grabbed the handle, but the door refused to open. She tugged hard and shone her light to look for any locks or catches. But this was a medieval door, and the handle—smack in the middle—couldn't lock. The only way to secure it was with the bar, and that was clearly undone.

One last pull and the door flew open hard enough that she stumbled back.

She wasn't surprised that no one was there. Or that she heard the tapping of dainty heels echoing away from her down the corridor.

She was, however, beginning to be furious. That energy trickled through her veins like an infusion of drugs, and she let it fuel her as she marched to the staircase. Weston had not found anything in the rooms he'd searched, and they continued to come up empty as they scoured the next two floors. He respected the infirmary and her bedroom to the point of not touching anything, but he kept a close eye on her while she rummaged through everything, even the most absurd of hiding places—really, why would Jasper Willis have closed himself inside her empty luggage case? Did Weston think her likely to be complicit in hiding a child and turning out the school in the middle of the night to look for him? Ridiculous.

Like the cellar, Diana had not been up in the attic space of the medieval section before. Unlike Victorian houses, the uppermost floor had almost certainly not been set aside for servants but used as comfortable accommodations for the family. Not quite a castle keep but adhering to the general rule that the lower floors were for household work and business, and the upper ones for guests, diplomacy, and privacy.

Also for retreat during an attack.

If Jasper had chosen to retreat here, he hadn't stayed long. The space was intimidatingly bare. Diana could see every foot of it from the top of the enclosed spiral staircase.

And yet . . . even as she told herself *It's empty*, vague outlines began to form. All suggestion and shadow, but Diana swore she could see furniture forming before her eyes. Very specific types of furniture: enormous coffers with carved sides, high-backed settles flanking the fireplace, a trestle table against one wall, and a smaller table that looked like a desk. And dotted throughout the room and in corners stood tall candlestands of iron.

Diana took a step forward and heard a rustling at her feet. She jumped back, but when she looked down she saw only bare wood under her feet.

Impatient, Weston took advantage of her hesitation to push past her. Diana tentatively placed one foot in front of her and this time not only heard but felt the rustle of straw. The floor was covered in rushes. Invisible rushes. Because whatever imagination in her had conjured up indistinct outlines of medieval furniture didn't stretch so far as seeing straw on the floor—just hearing it and feeling it.

As Diana took another careful step, her frightened fascination with the rustling at her feet was swallowed up in a multitude of other sounds: the drumming of hooves on packed earth, the creak and murmur of leather saddles, and the iron jangle of armed riders.

Seized by a terror outside herself, Diana flew across the room and threw open a window. If the inside was a shifting jumble of impressions, both here and not here, outside was decidedly in the "what the hell is going on" camp. A fact that Diana noted only very vaguely in the part of her mind that remained under her control.

Most of her was in whatever moment of terror she'd been possessed by. Frantically, she counted the horsemen and searched for the identifying banner . . .

She'd known what it would be, and yet she'd hoped. For George, maybe, for as detestable as his actions were, he surely held her in fondness and he was by all reports as changeable a man as he'd been as a boy. She'd known him since he was tiny and she could use that, could twist all his mixed-up loyalties against him.

But it was not the royal banner with its three silver bars marking George's distance from his brother's throne.

It was the white bear and ragged staff on a field of red—the banner of the Kingmaker himself, the Earl of Warwick.

She knew, in that moment, there would be no clemency. Warwick dealt only in death.

"Diana? Diana?"

Diana came back to herself with a shock, like plunging into ice water.

Weston had his hand on her shoulder, shaking her. "What's wrong?" he demanded.

She blinked three times, although that did nothing to erase the clarity of what she'd just experienced. But the blinking also cleared away the remnants of her vision—or was it a dream?—and what she saw overrode anything else.

Pointing out the window, Diana said, "That's Joshua Murray's grandfather walking up from the river. And he's carrying a boy in his arms."

Weston spotted them, watching like she did until they were both certain the boy was moving—alive. "You'll be wanted," he said abruptly. "Well done, Miss Neville."

She followed him to the low opening of the stairs, already making a triage list in her head. As she stepped down onto the first tread, something shoved her hard in the back and she fell heavily against Weston. If it had been Joshua in front of her, his repaired leg might have given way, but Weston was solid and only grunted when she hit him.

"Sorry," she said. "I slipped."

Except I didn't, she thought, gripping the rope handrail tightly as she crept the rest of the way down the stairs.

She'd been pushed. Because whatever—whoever—remained in the fabric of this part of the house didn't like her.

No, not a strong enough word.

They *hated* her.

CHAPTER TWENTY-THREE

DIANA
NOVEMBER 1918

Jasper Willis had a broken leg. Though Diana knew she was perfectly competent to set it, she had Clarissa ring the local surgeon just to cover all the bases and provide comfort to Beth Willis.

Dr. Bennett, a man in his midsixties, was Northumberland born and bred with a keen eye and an unusual tolerance for progress if his manner to Diana was any indication. She didn't take his bluntness personally; anyone who'd worked with army officers was accustomed to abruptness. He told Beth Willis that Jasper's leg had been adequately set, which the mother greatly appreciated.

Clarissa had been present from the moment Mr. Murray brought Jasper in. Her hectic appearance had gone, and the competent headmistress had returned. Still, there was something in her eyes Diana did not like, and she determined not to leave her alone with Jasper.

She'd expected the doctor would want to speak to Clarissa about the circumstances of the boy's injury, but it was Diana he closeted himself with after everything had been done.

"What's going on at this school, Nurse?" he asked.

That was more abrupt then she'd expected. "What do you mean?"

"Schoolboys can find trouble locked in the bottom of a barrel, but at the better-run schools you don't generally misplace eleven-year-olds in the middle of the night. Especially not outdoors. If the weather had been any colder, or if it had been raining, you'd have more than just a broken leg on your hands."

"I know."

"Also, I've known Clarissa Somersby since she was born. She's one of the most intelligent people I know, but she's also high strung and prone to obsession."

"If you know the family, then you know about her brother."

"Yes, I helped search. As did Michael Murray, who found your boy today. But back then we got the worst result of all: nothing."

"That's worse than death?"

"Oh yes. And don't tell me you don't agree. It's not those families you wrote to from France telling them about their son's or father's last hours that suffer the most—it's the ones who will never know for sure where those they love lie. I suppose Clarissa believes these ghost stories coming from the boys?"

"I think so. I think . . . she seems to hope that it's Thomas."

"A ghostly boy who wants other boys to follow him—she probably hopes one of them will lead her to Thomas's body. Maybe this house isn't as locked up at night as you think."

She didn't like the implications of that at all. Would Clarissa deliberately leave doors unlocked in order to allow schoolboys to wander at night?

"You should speak to her," Diana told the doctor.

"She won't listen to me. She never has. If she did, she'd have left Havencross long ago and got on with her own life. Keep an eye on her for me, will you?"

After promising to return in two days to check on Jasper, Dr. Bennett departed, and Joshua almost immediately took his place in her office.

"Clarissa has asked to speak with you," he reported. "Are you all right? You've looked rather shaken since the search. Did Weston say anything to upset you?"

"What? No." It was hardly the time to get into the unsettling whatever-it-was that had accosted her in the attic. "We're all shaken and sleep-deprived and hungry and worried. How did Clarissa seem to you during the interviews with Jasper's friends?"

"Definitely more traumatized sister than capable headmistress," he said.

A succinct assessment, and worrying. Diana sighed and Joshua touched her cheek with the back of his hand. "You can't fix everything," he told her. "Surely you learned that lesson in France."

"The very first day," she said wryly. "But I never learned to stop trying."

"And I, for one, am grateful. Be careful with Clarissa Somersby. That kind of distilled grief can pull you down with it."

An apt metaphor—for entering Clarissa's office was a little like stepping to the edge of a whirlpool. Diana could feel the pull of the woman's emotions even before she saw them swirling across her face. She had never seen Clarissa look so alive, or so on edge. She didn't even try to sit down after urging Diana to do so but paced in large circles around the Persian rug.

At least Clarissa asked her the appropriate question first: "Are you and Dr. Bennett both convinced Jasper Willis will recover completely?"

"Yes. It was a simple, clean break. As long as he stays still and exercises it appropriately when the time comes, there should be no problems."

"Has Jasper said anything more about . . . his experience?"

"No. And before you ask, I don't want him questioned any more today."

Clarissa shot her a look keen with intelligence. Whatever her current emotional state, there was nothing wrong with her brain. "You mean you don't want *me* questioning him."

In for a penny, in for a pound. "No, I don't. Certainly not in your current state."

"You think I would frighten a child for my own ends?"

"Not deliberately. But I think you would do almost anything to get the answers you want."

Astonishingly, Clarissa laughed. Far from being offended, Diana's blunt words seemed to have calmed the outward signs of her agitation. She perched on a leather footstool and wrapped her hands around her knees in a surprisingly young gesture. "The answers I want," she repeated. "Nicely phrased. Meaning you think I'm more interested in confirming my own suspicions than in actually knowing what happened to my brother."

"Meaning that I'm worried about you. Of course you can't be completely objective when a boy goes missing for any period of time—no one expects you to be."

Clarissa ignored that opening and stared intently at Diana. "I am more interested in questioning you."

"About what? You don't think I had anything—"

"No, no. I wanted to know if you had any . . . unexpected experiences while searching the medieval part of the house."

"Why would I? I've been sleeping and working there for weeks now."

"You hadn't been up to the solar before now."

Diana narrowed her eyes, meeting Clarissa's gaze head-on. "I take it you have."

"Yes."

"Why don't you tell me about *your* experiences?"

"Ahhhh." Clarissa straightened up, satisfaction in her smile. "So you've felt it."

"I . . . I don't know what I felt. Searching in the dark, worried about a missing boy—"

"That's *why* you felt it! That's when it happens, when she comes, when you're as sick with worry as she was once, terrified for the safety of a child—"

"She who?"

"That I don't know, at least not her name or dates or anything else you would like to know to confirm the reality of what you experienced. Property records get murky past the late eighteenth century. It doesn't matter. Just tell me that you didn't feel the same things."

"The mind is a flexible instrument—" Diana began, and was immediately cut off.

"So you think I'm crazy, just like everyone else does. 'Poor Clarissa. Locked herself away all these years, she's grown mad tormenting herself with guilt, creating ghosts to ease her loneliness.' I know that's what people think. No one except my father has ever dared say it to my face, although Dr. Bennett hints from time to time. Did he tell you to disregard anything I might say about ghostly sounds and elusive images?"

"He told me that you are one of the most intelligent people he's ever known, not that I needed telling. You are obviously sane, Clarissa, if understandably sensitive about ghost stories and missing boys."

"So, passably sane with a very vivid imagination?"

Diana bit her lip, thinking hard about which would do more

harm—continuing to evade Clarissa's original question about the solar, or answering it. "It seems unlikely that I would conjure up precisely the same scene as you did, no matter how vivid my own imagination. I saw . . . shadows. Outlines of furniture. I heard horses and men, and saw a banner. And I felt—" Diana stopped, searching for just the right word.

She said it at the same moment Clarissa did: "Terror."

Clarissa's smile could have powered half of London. It made Diana want to smile back, in spite of the day's seriousness.

"That doesn't mean I believe in ghosts," said Diana. "And I definitely do not believe that the ghost of Thomas is trying to contact you by haunting schoolboys."

If she'd expected to shock Clarissa by using her brother's name, she was disappointed. Clarissa simply looked at her with absolute confidence and said, "Nor do I. Of course not. Why would you think that of me?"

Diana floundered for words. "Because . . . but you've been so interested in the sightings, so curious about how I was being haunted . . . if you don't think this ghost is Thomas, why do you care?"

"Because Thomas saw him too in the last days before he disappeared. I am certain that my brother was following the ghost boy when he vanished."

CHAPTER TWENTY-FOUR

JULIET
2018

On what was Thanksgiving Day back home, Juliet joined the Bennetts for dinner. Rachel had gone all out researching traditional meals and proudly served mashed potatoes, homemade stuffing, and a perfectly roasted turkey.

Rachel made only one apology: "I could not bring myself to make pumpkin pie. Why would anyone want a dessert made out of a squash? You'll have to make do with sticky toffee pudding."

Juliet assured her that was no hardship and spent the next two hours playing board games with Antonia, the three little boys, and Noah. He didn't go so far as to kiss her in front of everyone, but there was enough hand-holding and shared glances going on to make the children giggle and Juliet blush.

Noah had driven her to the farm and gladly accepted her invitation to come in when he returned her to Havencross after dark. There followed an exceptionally pleasant half hour on a squashy sofa in the sitting room across from Juliet's bedroom—one of the few rooms that held any furniture at all. They only stopped when Juliet's phone rang.

"It's my mother," she said, stretching across him to look at her screen. "And it's Thanksgiving. I should probably talk to them all."

He kissed her once more, untangled himself, and stood up. "I'll see you day after tomorrow. If we're still on for sightseeing in York?"

She promised, and sighed with a mix of desire and frustration before calling home.

Though she had no siblings, Juliet had a number of aunts, uncles, and cousins on her father's side of the family who all gathered together on holidays. The phone was passed around from person to person, with Juliet repeating the same few sentences: "Yes, England is lovely." "Yes, I'm enjoying the house and the work." "Yes, I plan to return to teaching next year."

At least everyone in her family was wise enough not to talk about the divorce or Liam. Except, naturally, her mother, who said abruptly, "I saw the photograph online."

At least Juliet could be assured that this wasn't a prelude to her being told to "Quit taking half-naked selfies" or questions like "How drunk were you exactly?" But it was even less welcome.

"Duncan," she said flatly.

"And his student's new baby. I assume this was the same one he was with when you were in the hospital? Or are there more women to come forward?"

"Mom, did you ever pause to consider that I might not have seen that photo? That you might be telling me something I had no idea about?"

"Oh please, Juliet. I know you much too well. Of course you keep tabs on him online. I'm just glad that you managed to finalize the divorce without changing your mind."

"Thanks, Mom. Very encouraging, 'I'm glad my daughter's only a partly hopeless loser.'"

"Juliet, that man had you pinned like a butterfly to a board for ten years. We didn't see you most of those years unless he was perched right next to you, watching every move you made and listening to every word you said. I thought I had lost my daughter for good. I will grieve forever the loss that brought you to your senses. But I will also never stop being grateful that you had enough spirit left in you to walk away."

Her mother didn't use Liam's name. Juliet had screamed at her the one time she had, in the hospital just hours after they'd taken him away.

It was an unusual flood of sentiment from her severely practical mother and, in her newly healing state, Juliet felt a pang of remorse.

"I know, Mom. I'm sorry, you're right. Yes, I saw the photo. And I didn't get drunk or crawl into bed for three days or stop showering. So you can relax. I'm doing well." She knew better than to tell her mom that Duncan had been texting her four or five times a week since the night of that photo. That his texts had thus far remained pleasant enough, dwelling on his own faults and asking for her forgiveness.

Juliet simply deleted them and hoped he would get the message sooner or later.

She thought of what else she could tell her mom as a distraction. "I even have a date on Saturday. He's a surveyor in Newcastle, and his sister helps keep up the house. His name is Noah."

"That sounds very promising. He's not a stalker, is he?"

Juliet rolled her eyes. "I've got to go, Mom. Love you."

November turned to December under steel-gray skies and unrelenting rain that only occasionally crossed into snowflakes.

At least she could still work out—the best thing about a ridiculously enormous house was the ability to jog indoors. The daily workouts had become the first part of Juliet's newly perfected routine. The rest included waking to an alarm, eating salads for lunch, and spending a minimum of four hours a day researching either the Wars of the Roses or the 1918 pandemic.

Her hard work was rewarded the second week of December when Nell Somersby-Sims made a brief visit to Havencross. Juliet expected it to be a little more than a tour of what she'd accomplished so far and, no doubt, judgment about how far she had left to go. Would Nell notice that she hadn't washed down all the baseboards in the old dormitory wing?

Juliet braced herself for the solicitor's London-tailored perfection by wearing a jersey dress she didn't remember packing—maybe her mother had thrown it in—red tights, and low-heeled ankle boots. She straightened her hair, applied makeup (including concealer), and only stopped herself when she considered whether she remembered how to apply eyeliner.

It doesn't matter what some distant cousin thinks of me. Just as long as I don't get fired.

Nell, when she appeared, wore country-casual clothes (black skinny jeans, velvet-trimmed long-sleeved T-shirt, Burberry raincoat, forest-green Hunter boots) and a perfect ponytail. But just when Juliet's confidence began to sink, Nell popped the trunk of her car and grabbed the first of several boxes.

"Family history," she announced. "You did say you were interested in the Somersby past?"

Juliet snapped her mouth shut and swallowed. "Yes, thank you. Let me help."

They placed the boxes on the long table in the Victorian kitchen alongside Juliet's notebooks and the boxes from the Bennett farmhouse.

"This is really very—where did you get all this?" Juliet opened one and saw a number of neatly-labeled folders: *Surveyors' Maps, Renovation Work After 1940, Property Tax Receipts.*

"Someone in the family had to pull everything together in order for the sale to go through. Clarissa Somersby did a lot of the work; I just cleaned it up a bit. It's interesting." Nell was defensive in a way Juliet recognized—it was a tone she'd often heard coming out of her own mouth. Every time Duncan had squinted and cocked his head about one of her interests, for example. She'd never known anyone more able to convey disdain with just the blink of an eye or the scrunch of his nose than her ex-husband.

The memory broke through Juliet's own preemptive defensiveness. "Thank you for bringing all this—I'd have come down to London and spared you the trip if I'd known."

"I'm supposed to check in before winter hits anyway, to make sure you're set up in case there's any trouble."

"I think so. Noah Bennett from the surveyor's office came round, made sure I have firewood and plenty of food stored."

"Noah Bennett? Very nice."

Did Nell sound amused? It had been so long since Juliet had had a friend who teased that she wasn't sure. She cleared her throat. "Anyway, do you want to take a look at the things I've set aside for possible resale or for the family to choose from?"

"You've been very thorough in your lists and photos. I trust you. And I'm heading up to Edinburgh for a conference."

"I'll enjoy going through all this." Juliet waved at the boxes. "Plus, I have an appointment at the Berwick Museum this afternoon. But don't worry, clearing out Havencross is my first priority."

Nell snorted—more elegantly than Juliet would have done, but a snort nonetheless. "You've already done more than expected. Honestly, your presence here is mostly to ensure the place stays standing through the winter. As long as you keep your eyes open to fire or flooding, you can entertain yourself however you like." She arched her eyebrows and added, "And Noah Bennett is well worth entertaining yourself with."

There was really nothing she could say to that, though her reddened cheeks made Nell laugh. For the first time in years, Juliet didn't automatically assume that the laugh came at her expense. Although she did wonder, not as fleetingly as she'd have liked, if Nell knew that from firsthand experience.

Juliet had debated the merits of taking the train versus driving to Berwick and, as traditionally English as a train felt, decided that the convenience of having her car outweighed the experience. She could go Christmas shopping after her appointment.

The Berwick Museum and Art Gallery was located in the redbrick military barracks that formed part of the Berwick Castle grounds. Juliet had to admit the ruins made a fitting backdrop for her queries today—the castle had been here long before even Havencross Priory was built. She went to the information desk and waited for Noah's friend to be summoned.

"Dr. Stratford! Delighted to meet you. Noah's told me all about you." Daniel Gitonga was a solid, broad-shouldered Kenyan with a smile almost as charming as their mutual friend's.

"Noah only met me six weeks ago. And please, it's Juliet. The only person who ever calls me doctor is my dad. Plus, I haven't even finished my dissertation."

"Don't get me started on the pride of parents. Although I'm pretty sure my mother doesn't correct those people who assume I'm a medical doctor."

Juliet asked the question dear to every historian: "What brought you to history?"

"The purity of my heart that despises all things material—like rent money and vacations."

With laughter and mutual understanding, they talked about their respective study and career paths as he led her through a maze of back corridors and staircases leading all the way to the top floor.

"I've got us in a conference room to better view the items I pulled for you." He ushered her in, and Juliet felt the historian's buzz at seeing things last used by those long dead. Even for her though, these items were extraordinary—she'd never gone further back than the eighteenth century.

She and Daniel donned thin cotton gloves, and he gave her an overview from left to right. "These are the items found on the Havencross grounds in 1918: a carved wooden top, eight coins, and a textile livery badge."

"I'd read about the coins and badge, but not this." Juliet touched the spinning top, no longer than her ring finger, and had a sudden, vivid image of a boy spinning it and watching it intently—a tall, fair-haired boy with wide eyes.

She shook her head clear. "Tell me about the coins."

"Five silver groats, two silver patards from Burgundy, and a gold crown ryal."

With a laugh, she said, "Okay, now tell me what that all means. Is it a lot of money?"

"The silver was very common—common enough that you can still buy medieval groats today for a hundred pounds online. One of the groats was minted in 1455 under Henry the Sixth." He pointed at the outline of a crowned man. "The other four were struck between 1463 and 1469, under Edward the Fourth."

He pointed at a crowned figure that she supposed looked marginally different to the first one. "What about the coins from Burgundy? Is that unusual?"

"Not for this time period. They were both struck in 1469—the year before that, Edward the Fourth's sister Margaret had married the Duke of Burgundy. There was plenty of commerce passing back and forth between England and the Low Countries. Silver is silver, no matter the name or face stamped on the coin."

Juliet touched the edge of the gold one. "This is less common?"

"Less common, and obviously worth a good deal more than the silver. It argues that whoever lost or buried these coins was someone of a certain wealth. At the least, a prosperous merchant."

"Or a manor-owning family?"

"Or a manor-owning family," he agreed.

"May I?"

When Daniel nodded, Juliet picked up the gold coin and studied it front and back. Unlike all the others, this had no royal portrait on it. "That's the English royal coat of arms, correct?" She pointed at the shield.

"Correct. Lions and lilies."

"And what's this on the reverse?"

He grinned. It seemed Noah's friends were as good-humored as he was. "Think about it."

"Are those petals?" she asked. He nodded, and illumination burst upon her. "Ah, it's the white rose of York."

"Yes, it is. This coin is known as a rose ryal."

"How much would it cost me to buy today, if one were for sale?"

"Thousands of pounds. More significantly to your research, this ryal was minted in London in 1470. However all these items came to be together, it's a fair bet it happened during the reign of Edward the Fourth."

Warwick's banner floating in the wind . . . the drumming of hooves on packed earth, the creak and murmur of leather saddles, the iron jangle of armed riders . . .

Where had that image come from? Juliet remembered the moment on the stairs up to the medieval solar, that sense of having been seized by something outside herself, hearing sounds she shouldn't have been able to recognize—

"Juliet?"

Daniel was looking at her expectantly, holding the last item.

"Sorry," she said. "What did you say?"

"I said this adds weight to the Edward the Fourth theory. Do you know what a livery badge is?"

"To identify servants, right?"

"Clerks, messengers, men-at-arms—their lord's livery badge was sewn to their clothing and provided recognition and a certain standing. Anyone who bore a livery badge was under the special care and protection of their lord."

"So you think whoever created this little cache was under the protection of a specific lord?"

"I do."

"Are you going to tell me which one?"

"Let me say this—don't confuse a coat of arms with a badge. Coats of arms were heraldic devices meant to proclaim an often complicated family history. They could be quartered and quartered again until they could hardly be deciphered. And there arises the question of multiple brothers—how do you easily distinguish between the male members of the same family? That is where the personal badge comes in. Most every man of status—and a good many women, like Anne Boleyn—chose their own symbol and motto as a straightforward form of identification. Easily seen on the banners of a battlefield, easily carved into stone, easily turned into textiles."

Juliet, distracted by the mention of the famous queen, said, "I think I remember something about Anne Boleyn. Was hers a falcon?"

"Very good. Ironically, she paired it with the motto The Most Happy."

"All right, so I'm looking at a personal badge." Juliet took it from Daniel and narrowed her eyes. The colors had dulled over the centuries it had been buried, but she could still separate white from gold. "The white rose of York." She didn't touch it but circled it with one finger hovering. "What's the gold surrounding it?"

"That is the Sun in Splendor. Before the Battle of Mortimer's Cross, three suns appeared in the sky. To calm his anxious men, Edward of York assured them it was a sign of heaven's favor toward their cause. When his armies were victorious and he became king, he chose to set his York rose in the midst of the sun—in remembrance of Mortimer's Cross."

Juliet pondered that. "So someone at Havencross had the personal badge of the King of England?"

"They did. It begs all sorts of questions—not the least of which is, how did it come to be lost in the earth with a handful of coins and a child's toy?"

CHAPTER TWENTY-FIVE

ISMAY
OCTOBER 1459

In every society this quarrel made an entrance; so that brother could hardly admit brother into his confidence, or friend a friend, nor could anyone reveal the secrets of his conscience. The combatants on both sides attacked each other whenever they happened to meet, and—now the one and now the other—for the moment gained the victory, while fortune was continually shifting her position.

In her six years with the York family, Ismay had grown accustomed to the high tension and major drama of politics. She accepted the heavily armed retinues among which she—with the duchess or her daughters—traveled, and the intensive arms training always taking place at Ludlow when they were in residence. She no longer looked twice at royal messengers or worried about the attentions of court officials, because she knew herself to be only on the edges of the devouring interest. It was York himself, and his wife's Neville brother and nephew, Salisbury and Warwick, who consumed all the crown's attention.

And with Queen Margaret in the ascendant, all the crown's enmity.

Ismay had never felt the air so tense and taut as had filled Ludlow for the last two months. Sometimes she imagined it cutting against her skin as she moved through her days, but all the fears and damage remained mostly invisible. It showed mainly in sharpened tongues and fragile tempers.

The saving grace of all these long, uncertain weeks was that the family was together. Ismay had never spent so much time with Edmund. Even with all the tension, there were plenty of stolen moments together, making everything bearable.

Everything except goodbye.

The royal army had been sent against them. The Earl of Salisbury and his men had been ambushed at Blore Heath but managed to fight their way free to Ludlow. Salisbury, his son Warwick, and the Duke of York had been named traitors. And tomorrow, outside the walls of the town, it would all be decided by men wielding swords.

Men including Edmund and Edward.

The afternoon was passing quickly. Ismay's hands trembled as she searched the castle forecourt crowded with men and horses. Servants preparing to join the Yorkist army dug in against the town walls. How many of these men would be alive this time tomorrow?

Keep him safe, keep him safe, keep him safe.

She spotted Edward, always the easiest to see as, even at seventeen, he towered over every man Ismay had ever known. He was in a corner between the stable and the outer wall, talking to a pretty girl. Edward would be talking to a pretty girl on his death bed. But he saw Ismay and tipped his head in the direction of the chapel.

The shadows inside the round chapel dedicated to St. Mary Magdalene made it hard to distinguish anything except the fair head where Edmund knelt before the altar. She drew closer, moving softly so as not to disturb his prayers.

"I'm not praying," Edmund said without turning his head. "Or at least, not in the way the priests would have me pray."

"What are you doing?" Ismay knelt beside him.

He angled his head sideways and gave her a look so filled with longing it warmed the very air between them. "I cannot offer petitions tonight. I can only make demands. That we win. That we lose none we cannot bear to. That the town is safe. That the castle is not breached."

Ismay nodded.

Edmund drew in a long breath and let it out shakily. "May I give you something, Ismay?"

"A question?" she teased. "I thought you could only make demands tonight."

"Of God. I would never make demands of you."

"Of course you can give me something."

He pulled an object from his pocket, small enough to enclose in his fist. He took her right hand, palm up, and released it.

A ring. Of dark, heavy gold with a square gem set in it. There was not enough light to make out anything more.

"A garnet," Edmund said. "And it's inscribed."

"What does it say?"

"*My loyalty is fixed*. Which it is, forever." He bit his lip, a gesture that always made her want to kiss him. "Will you marry me, Ismay?"

"Edmund," she said, her throat too tight for her to speak.

"I'd do it tonight if we could. I'm not afraid to die, Ismay. I am afraid of not having loved you long enough. Of never getting to . . ." He sat back on his heels and ran his hands through his hair. She'd never seen him look so frustrated.

He dropped his hands. "Sometimes I think Edward's right. I think too much and let it get in the way of what I want. Not that I would ever take advantage of you—oh God, I don't know what I'm saying. Except this: I will come back to you. It's just a battle, Ismay. My father, Salisbury, and Warwick are the best soldiers in England. We'll come through it, I promise. And when we do, I'll tell father everything and we'll get married. He can't object on account of our age—mother was only fourteen when they were married. That is, of course, if you want to marry me?"

She took his face in her hands. "Yes," she said, and kissed him, forgetting that they were in a chapel, forgetting everything except her fear and love, and her desire to violate every rule of decency and modesty. She wanted to have this memory to keep with her always.

Ironically, the only person at Ludlow who would have cheered them on was the one to stop it.

"Sorry," Edward said, silhouetted in the chapel doorway, "but Mama is looking for Ismay, and Father is ready to join the men in camp."

Ismay took care to conceal the ring in the pocket tied beneath her skirts before joining the family in the forecourt. The family leave-taking was brisk and professional—no doubt anyone with more personal things to say had found a private place to say them. Like her and Edmund. She fingered his ring while she watched them ride out of the large castle gate and down the hill to where their army was encamped by the River Teme.

She spent the next several hours helping with George and Richard (which mostly meant keeping them from escaping their bedroom in order to spy out what was happening), and only when the younger boys had fallen deep asleep was Ismay released to her little room nearby in Pendower Tower. With all of the Duke's daughters elsewhere she had it to herself, and Ismay spent a long time crouched over a candle flame trying to stamp the poesy ring on her memory. She could not wear it, not yet, so she threaded it through the rosary chain she wore around her neck and tucked it beneath her shift.

She did not expect to sleep, but she must have because she woke later to the sound of many raised voices. She listened for a minute, wondering if this was a natural occurrence the night before a battle. But she could feel the wrongness in the air. Something had happened.

Ismay threw on her simplest gown over her shift, lacing it quickly, and lit her candle. The middle of the night was no time to wander Ludlow Castle in the dark; there were too many additions, wings, and traps for the unwary. As it was, she tripped twice before reaching the great hall.

She had seen the hall filled with people on many occasions, but never like this. No tables or benches were arranged, only the rush-covered stone floor and dozens upon dozens of anxious men. Ismay blew out her candle and set it down against a wall then went on tiptoe looking for Edward.

It was the Duke of York she found first, standing slightly apart from everyone except for the woman in his arms whose hair cascaded around her shoulders. It took longer than it should have for Ismay to identify her as the duchess. She had never seen Cecily Neville so . . . unbound. As Ismay watched, the duchess touched her husband's lips with her fingertips, and into Ismay's head came a phrase she'd heard long ago to describe Cecily as a girl: the Rose of Raby, she'd been called.

Turning away from that most private moment, Ismay hastily shifted her gaze and marked Edward against the far wall. He was in close conference with Salisbury and Warwick, but Ismay didn't falter because Edmund was there too. She didn't care what rumors she sparked tonight. She had to know what was wrong.

She slipped in behind Edmund and touched his arm.

He spun around like a spooked horse. "Ismay! What are you doing up?"

"What has happened?" she asked. When Edmund did not immediately answer, she shifted her gaze to Edward. She had never seen his mobile, affectionate face set so hard.

"We've not got time for women and children," Warwick said dismissively.

Edmund rounded on the older man. "It's the women and children who will have to watch Ludlow fall tomorrow, *cousin*, because of your man." If Edward had never looked harder, Edmund had never sounded harsher.

Taking her hand, Edmund strode away from the group and kept going until they'd left the hall and found a quiet space in the solar. The tapestry of a hunting party that Ismay and the duchess had been halfheartedly working on loomed on its frame against one wall.

"We've been betrayed," Edmund said simply. "One of Warwick's commanders has taken his men over to the Lancastrians. It leaves us hopelessly outnumbered, besides the fact that Trollope knew all our battle plans. Father's given our men leave to slip away how and as they can. No sense in wasting lives."

Ismay thought of the duchess touching her husband in public in a way she never did. "You're running."

"If we don't, then tomorrow my father's head will be piked on Ludlow's wall with Salisbury and Warwick. And probably Edward and I as well."

She forced away the horrific image of Edmund's bloody head and asked, "Then why are you still here?"

"We had to make a few plans. Salisbury and Warwick will go south and take ship back to Calais—Edward will go with them. My father and I will ride west through Wales and make for Ireland, where his rule is solid."

"If you are taken—"

"We won't be. Edward and I spent our childhoods riding through these hills, and the Welsh are loyal to our cause. We'll be all right. And so will you be," he added. "If we had time, we'd try to get you and Mother and the boys to an abbey, but really you need not fear more than rude manners. Neither side makes war on women and children."

It's the women and children who will have to watch Ludlow fall tomorrow . . .

"And the town?"

He hesitated—answer enough for Ismay.

From the hall, someone shouted for Edmund. "I have to go," he said. "Be safe, Ismay."

He kissed her long and desperately, and her cheeks were wet when they reluctantly pulled apart. Would Edmund be safe? Would she ever see him again? She had thought watching him ride into battle would be horrible, but this was excruciating. How long would she have to wait for news? How long until she knew if he was safe?

He kissed her once more, perhaps as afraid as she was, and that delay gave those in search of him time to come upon them together. Sadly it was not Edward but someone much, much worse.

Warwick.

The earl stood just inside the door and looked the two of them over in a leisurely manner that made Ismay wonder how long he'd been standing there. But perhaps his own imminent danger kept him from making malicious comments.

"It's time to go, cousin," Warwick said smoothly.

Ismay stood with the duchess in the inner court and watched the two little bands of horsemen slip out the postern gate. One group for Calais, one for Ireland.

The Duchess of York allowed Ismay to slip her hand into hers. "They will be all right," Ismay said, with more confidence than she felt.

"Yes, of course they will." With a nearly visible effort, the duchess composed herself and said briskly, "You should know, Ismay, before he left, my lord asked me to tell you that, should you think it wise, you are free to accept the king's offer of clemency. Your estate is far from here, you have no husband, and no men committed to our cause. He would understand if your primary concern were to protect yourself."

Ismay knew, from her tone of voice, the duchess would *not* understand if she made that choice. Not that such consideration weighed in the balance. There was no choice in this matter, not for her.

"Yours is the only family I have had since I was ten years old," Ismay said firmly. "I stand with York to the end."

CHAPTER TWENTY-SIX

DIANA
NOVEMBER 1918

After Clarissa's shocking revelation about Thomas and the ghost boy, which left Diana gaping like a landed fish, someone knocked on her door and the telephone rang and the headmistress was swept away into a whirl of business.

Diana grabbed a cup of tea and two slices of toast from the dining room that was filled with unusually subdued boys before returning to her room. She fell into an uneasy sleep, dreaming of vague impressions of galloping horses and bloody banners.

She woke unrefreshed before noon, took a quick bath, and checked in on Jasper, who was sleeping much more peacefully than she had. Laudanum would do that.

Emerging from the infirmary, she found Joshua once more hovering in the corridor. When Diana saw how he was dressed— heavy trousers, chunky knit sweater, waterproof mackintosh and boots—she groaned aloud.

"I'm going to regret having just bathed, aren't I?" she asked. "Where are we exploring now? Hopefully, by your coat, in the wide outdoors."

"I thought we should take a look around the area where Granddad found Jasper. Whether a ghost or something else led the boy there, we should check it out."

Diana couldn't argue with that logic. And the thought of being in the open air beneath Northumberland's skies appealed. Surely that would wipe away any lingering effects from the medieval solar this morning. It might also wipe her away, she realized, after ten minutes walking through a scouring wind that made it hard to breathe.

Joshua eyed her sideways. "Wishing you were back in London?"

"At least I don't have to trip over a hundred people just to get where I'm going. Speaking of which, where exactly are we going?"

Joshua pointed to some feature of the landscape that Diana couldn't distinguish. "Granddad walks the wall every day at sunrise—rain, shine, or blizzard. This morning he decided to check out the old icehouse, probably because he was telling you about it yesterday."

Diana squinted as they got closer to what looked like just another jumble of rocks, trying to trace a design. "Old icehouse?" she asked skeptically.

"Medieval, actually. All of this land belonged to the priory of Havencross. The icehouse was built around 1300, but when it became a private house it was deemed too far away and something nearer was constructed."

Diana studied the area doubtfully. "Jasper came this far? Alone and in the dark?"

"Certainly argues for a very persuasive ghost."

"If your grandfather hadn't come this way, it might have been another hour or so before he found him. With this wind—" Diana shook her head. "We've got to put a stop to this, Joshua. Or someone's going to die."

"I know. That's why we're here."

At Joshua's insistence, when the first pass of roughly twenty-five feet in diameter revealed nothing of note, they examined it again on their hands and knees. Diana wondered if he had a magnifying glass in his pocket, planning to whip it out like Sherlock Holmes if he found a clue.

She wasn't finding clues. She wasn't finding anything except heather, dying thistles, and sharp stones. Diana sat back on her heels and stretched. The ache of exhaustion had settled behind her eyes, and she blinked away the collection of dark spots that danced before her.

Instead of disappearing, the spots coalesced into an opening between two of the stones precariously stacked on the old icehouse foundation. Diana couldn't have said what caught her attention. Perhaps its angle? Gingerly, she worked one hand into the opening and pulled at the top stone.

It came out all of a sudden, knocking her off-balance and alerting Joshua.

"Found something?"

"I don't know. Probably just some animal burrowed into the ground here." But even she, London born and bred, could tell very quickly that this opening hadn't been made by animals.

After half an hour of concentrated work, they had moved enough stones—and used some of the sharper ones to dig into looser soil—to uncover an opening that was at least three feet across with inlaid brickwork around its edge.

"The outlet of a secret tunnel." Diana sighed. "I knew I was coming to the edge of the known world up here, but I didn't expect to be transported to an adventure novel."

"Priories, convents, and monasteries were wealthy places—some of them, anyway," Joshua said, repeating his grandfather's words. "They always had to keep in mind the threat of soldiers and marauders. It might even have served simply to hide portable wealth."

"Whatever its original intent, it's definitely the kind of thing that appeals to boys. Do you think—is there any chance this is what happened to Thomas?"

"Trapped in a tunnel? Not this one, at least. Not from this direction. I doubt anyone's moved those rocks since the archaeologists my granddad referenced from 1870."

"Then why was Jasper Willis out here?"

The eternal, unanswerable question. Except that Jasper had answered it: he said the ghost boy had led him to this spot. Even accepting the unbelievability of that, what would be the purpose?

Joshua was sifting through the loose soil they'd moved around the opening, his face closed off in thought. Diana allowed herself to watch him, appreciating his capable hands, his palms toughened by regular riding, the line of his jaw, and the hollow beneath where his jaw and ear met. She imagined pressing her lips to that spot and felt herself flush when Joshua's hands stilled. Had he realized she was watching him?

But he didn't turn to her, not right away. Instead, he used just his fingertips to brush at something that had caught his eye in the debris.

"Well, well, well," he murmured.

"What is it?"

Joshua plucked the object and held it between his fingers for Diana to see.

"Is that . . ." She narrowed her eyes and leaned closer, staring at the thin disk. "Is that a coin?"

"An old coin," he corrected her. "Possibly Roman. They still turn up from time to time around here." He handed it to her. "For luck."

She stared at the dark circle, grimed with age. It didn't look particularly lucky.

Joshua stood, his left leg catching. He expertly rebalanced and offered Diana a hand. She allowed him to help her up and then kept hold of his hand.

A million things swam through her head: Jasper's broken leg, the possibility of open doors at night, how to stop vulnerable boys from conjuring ghosts when she herself had seen an entire troop of medieval horsemen riding into Havencross this morning. And was the war ever going to end, and would the terrible tension that she felt snap when it did end?

Joshua didn't pry, didn't push, didn't try to pretend. He simply pulled her close and wrapped his arms around her. And for just a few minutes, Diana was at peace.

CHAPTER TWENTY-SEVEN

JULIET
2018

The morning after her Berwick visit, Juliet woke to Rachel's cleaning and gladly accepted a freshly baked scone with her coffee.

"I owe you," Rachel said. "My boys are deliriously happy at seeing Uncle Noah so often, even if it is just hello and goodbye."

"Oh, I'm not trying to—I told him he doesn't need to come over so often. Any questions I have I can ask by phone or email. Really, he's been very helpful."

When Rachel murmured amused agreement, Juliet threw caution to the wind. "Is he . . . does he . . . he must have had girlfriends. Or boyfriends," she added hastily.

"He had a partner, Allie, for three years, but she emigrated to Australia eighteen months ago. Noah doesn't even want to move to London, so that was the end of that. I imagine he's not lived the life of a monk in Newcastle, but he hasn't talked about anyone like he's talked about you all these weeks."

"That's nice," Juliet managed.

Rachel had an eye roll that spoke volumes. "You are lame, the pair of you. Do you know what he's been asking me? 'Do you think I'm moving too fast, Rachel? Do you think Juliet's over her divorce?'" With the stern tone of a mother, she added, "Get on with it and don't make me lock the two of you up in this house together."

Juliet flushed and laughed. Her breath swooped in a way she hadn't felt since her earliest days with Duncan—anticipation and desire and hope mixed into a concoction that could make one feel drunk.

Focus, she told herself. *Work*.

She had just about reached the end of the war in the school nurse's records from 1918 and picked up her reading there. The weekend before November 11th, a third-year student had apparently broken his leg while outside the school during the night. The nurse didn't offer a lot of commentary in her entries, but to this one she'd added: *Must proceed gently with Jasper re. ghost boy. And find a way to barricade the outer doors.*

Barricade the outer doors? Juliet wondered if that was about keeping outsiders from coming in—or keeping the boys from getting out. Considering that this boy Jasper had been outside in the middle of the night, probably the latter. And it seemed to be connected to the Havencross ghost.

She told Noah about that entry when he called that night, then answered his questions about her visit with Daniel. He made all the appropriate noises of satisfaction and interest she could wish for. "What's your next step?" he asked.

"I thought I'd explore the chapel ruins. The solicitor who hired me brought up some boxes of Somersby family history, including the original site plans from when Gideon Somersby had the property surveyed before building the main house. I think there might be tunnels marked on this old survey, so I thought I'd take a look."

"What a pity you don't know a trained surveyor who could read your old map and help you decipher it."

She thought of Rachel's advice and Duncan's years of cutting comments and her own fragile but growing confidence. "Noah, would you like to read my map and come exploring with me?"

"I'd love to," he said. "Tomorrow's a slow day. I'll take it off. I can drive to the farmhouse tonight and come over first thing in the morning. Deal?"

When had she last felt so happy? "Deal."

The night passed with only a handful of minor incidents: the sighing sound before speech, the distant thunder of horses in her dreams, the impression of light coming from the corridor outside her bedroom. It had become so familiar that she wondered if she'd be more disturbed if she didn't experience anything.

She dressed warmly in the morning and had the nineteenth-century plans spread out on a 1950s army desk in the old school dining hall when Noah arrived.

The first thing he said was "Rachel told me to bring you back for tea today, and I'm pretty sure she's going to beg you to spend Christmas with us, so be ready with strong excuses if you don't want to. She's worried about you being all alone without family."

It had been years since Juliet had spent Christmas with anyone but Duncan—and last year he'd left at noon and hadn't returned for hours. Mentally, Juliet started making a gift list for all the Bennetts.

Noah had brought a clean copy of his Havencross surveyor's map and used it to mark symbols from the Victorian map as he explained to Juliet what they meant.

"Property boundary lines, the current house, the river and bridge, road." He pointed out each one as he spoke as Juliet nodded. "Those are all marked with lines. The abbey ruins are the ones indicated by the dashed lines."

She touched the outline of a small circle that lay on the far side of the medieval chapel. "What's that?"

"The original well. It's been covered over for at least a hundred and fifty years. When they ran water lines to the house, they found that the sides of the well had collapsed in and made it unusable."

"I don't suppose there are any topographical symbols for concealed tunnel openings?"

"They wouldn't stay concealed if they were marked on a map," he pointed out reasonably.

"All right, let's get to work. What exactly are we going to do?"

He grinned. "We're going to behave like Rachel's boys—turn over everything of possible interest that catches our eyes. And get good and dirty in the process."

He wasn't joking. By the time they'd covered the tumbled foundation walls for two of the abbey buildings—the cloister and chapter house he called them—Juliet was sweaty and sore.

"Who knew crawling around on your hands and knees, poking into every possible crevice, could be so exhausting?" Juliet leaned back on her heels and used one gloved hand to brush a strand of hair out of her face. "Oh wait—I totally knew that. It's why I'm a historian and not a landscaper or builder."

Noah's laugh reached in and scooped out her breath. It was a laugh she could listen to forever, because there was nothing cynical or ironic or cruel behind it.

"Short of digging up the ground, I'd say we've exhausted the possibilities here. Like you, I think the chapel is our best bet. It's a sacred space that was supposed to give invaders pause. Didn't work that way in practice, but it still seems the easiest place from which to smuggle objects or hide people underground."

"Shall we have lunch first, then tackle the chapel?"

"Perfect—because Rachel sent food."

It was Juliet's turn to laugh. "I love your sister."

It slipped out naturally and before Juliet could feel awkward, Noah said, "I think she feels the same about you. Even though we grew up here and she loves raising the boys on the farm, she gets lonely during the week without Antonia."

"Pity I'm only here for the winter."

Did she imagine that Noah's eyes lingered as he helped her stand? "A great pity."

After a fortifying, warming meal at Clarissa's Formica table in the small kitchen, they tramped out back to the chapel. The roof was long gone, but it retained its walls up to ten or twelve feet in places, and there were flat slate grave slabs along both long sides of the nave.

"So, if you were a secret tunnel entrance where would you be?" Juliet murmured.

They quartered the space systematically, guided by Noah's expertise. He started at the doorway end, and Juliet at the altar end. When she took a break to get a drink from her water bottle, he stretched in an unfairly alluring way and joined her.

"You hum when you work," he noted. "Did you know that?"

Juliet bit her lip for a second. "I know. I forget that I'm doing it. It must be so loud if you could hear me! I know it's annoying."

Noah caught her by the arm. "Who told you that?"

"What?"

"Who told you that your humming was annoying? Because

a) they're wrong, and b) why are you hanging out with anyone who would say such a thing?"

"I'm not . . . I mean, I'm not hanging out with anyone these days. Except ghosts."

"I'm serious, Juliet."

Did she dare? Juliet swallowed, keeping her gaze locked on Noah's kind hazel eyes. "My ex-husband was a fan of silence. Except when he was talking. I used to sing to myself when I was alone, ever since I was little. Most of the time, I honestly don't realize I'm humming. I'm sure it can be irritating."

He dropped his hand but remained standing near enough for Juliet to see the rise and fall of his breath even beneath his coat. His eyes were so unfairly lovely, but it was his expression that stopped her. Had anyone ever looked at her with such a mix of affection and concern? It caught at her throat, and she almost turned away.

"Juliet . . ."

Her phone rang, breaking the moment. Juliet fumbled to get it out of her coat pocket and stared at the unknown caller alert. At least answering would give her something to do. Noah had already turned his attention away to a grave by the north wall, dropping to hands and knees to feel along the base.

Juliet answered. "Hello?"

"Hello. Is this Juliet Whittier?"

"Stratford," she corrected. "Who is this?"

"Right, sorry. This is Kelsey Thorn? Ummm, from the university?"

Duncan's Kelsey, the one with the new baby—no wonder she sounded tentative, as though she expected Juliet to scream and throw things at her even from across the Atlantic.

"What do you want, Kelsey? If it's congratulations on your—" She choked on the word *son*.

"No! No, I'm sorry. I'm really sorry. I know the last thing you must want is to hear from me, but there's something I thought you should know."

"What?"

In a rush of words and breath, Kelsey said, "Duncan's looking for you. He's angry. Really angry. Mostly he's angry at me at the moment—I wasn't thinking when I posted the photos, the university saw them and figured out he'd been . . . that we'd been . . . while I was still his student. Anyway, he thinks it was you who told them. He's been suspended, pending an investigation into our relationship. When he found out, he was gone for two nights. Then he came home furious and drunk, and I threw him out. He was ranting about you, about how this would never have happened if only you'd understood him, you should never have left him—"

"I'm well aware that Duncan blames me for everything." Juliet paused, an unwilling concern prompting her to ask "Are you safe? You and the . . . he hasn't hurt you?"

"Pushed me against the wall. But I'm okay. I've gone home to my parents. He can't get to us here. But I think he's determined to get to you."

"I wish him luck," Juliet said drily, thinking of the ocean between them. "I suppose I should thank you for thinking of me. Finally."

She could hear the flush of shame in the girl's voice. "I really am very sorry. I didn't mean to . . . He can be very persuasive."

Juliet closed her eyes, remembering Duncan's gift of focusing on you so intently that you believed there was no one else in the world he'd ever looked at in the same way. His teasing, caressing hands, his voice smoky with desire . . . She suddenly snapped into anger. "You should keep away from him, Kelsey, for good. I'm not saying that as a jealous ex-wife either. I'm saying it as a woman. Keep clear of Duncan Whittier."

She cut off the call even as the girl fumbled out a thank-you. "Juliet?"

Noah's voice wasn't smoky in the least. It was bright and clear, like sunlight dancing on a stream.

She prepared to make excuses for the interruption, but despite the heated conversation he'd heard half of, Noah wasn't even looking her way. He squatted next to a grave slab, his hands resting on the top edge. No, not resting—lifting. She came closer as he lifted and shoved the slab away from him to reveal a hole. But not a hole filled with a coffin or bones.

"I think we found it."

CHAPTER TWENTY-EIGHT

ISMAY
SEPTEMBER 1460

And this same year came the Duke of York out of Ireland and landed in Lancashire. And there he sent for trumpeters to bring him to London, and there he gave them banners with the royal arms of England. And so he rode forth into London 'til he came to Westminster to King Henry's palace.

And there the Duke of York claimed the crown of England.

Ismay had been arguing with Father Pierce for half an hour now. If she hadn't known and loved the priest since before she could walk, she would have simply issued an order and dared him with a stony stare to defy her. Cecily of York had imparted some very useful lessons over the years.

As a seventeen-year-old girl, her orders did not carry the same weight as those of a duchess in the wider world. But Ismay was not currently in the wider world; she was at Havencross. She was Lady Ismay of Havencross, home for the first time in seven years to oversee her estate in person. And no matter the opposition, she would not back down on this.

Truth to tell, Ismay still felt a bit bewildered by how she'd ended up here. She had dutifully—gladly—kept her word to the duchess and stayed with her and the boys while they were moved to London by the Lancastrians and kept under house arrest. In December, a rushed Parliament declared every York and Neville lord not only traitors to the crown, but outlaws. They and all their heirs were now legally dead, their property forfeited. All of these boys and men—whether Ismay liked or loved or hated them—had long been entwined in her life, and all had become "lords of time past."

Which was when Duchess Cecily took charge. Never had Ismay more admired the woman than in those weeks after the fall of Ludlow and the vindictiveness of Parliament. Another woman might easily have collapsed beneath the weight of such blows, but not Cecily Neville. They could take away her title, but they could not take away her strength or intelligence.

Ismay knew that information managed to flow between London, Calais, and Dublin—plans were being made, money was being raised, pawns were being set in their places for when the Yorkists once again came to the chessboard.

Apparently Ismay was one of those pawns. And, for the first time, her use wasn't solely as a reluctant possible bride. In fact it involved something Ismay wanted so much that she couldn't quite believe it was being offered to her. "We need you at Havencross," the duchess had told her. "For the future."

And just like that Ismay returned to Northumberland for the first time since she was ten. The Lancastrian Earl of Somerset sent two dozen of his men to escort her, and Ismay knew that if she'd been any less female, any less single, any less young, the Lancastrians would never have allowed it. She had no doubt that Somerset was angling now for her guardianship, either to enrich himself or one of his retainers. He saw in her nothing but a vulnerable girl.

His mistake.

Ismay had spent the first three months proving to her steward and her housekeeper that she knew how to run an estate. Who wouldn't, having been tutored personally by the most formidable woman in England? She then spent the next three months raising a company of armed men. The Duke of York had more than once availed himself of the hundred men that owed Havencross fealty, but in his farseeing wisdom had never attempted to completely pull them into his own ranks. That served him well now, for Ismay was the Lady of Havencross and her parents had both been beloved. The men would follow any orders she gave.

And then it was only a matter of waiting. The worst thing about being in Northumberland was how far she was from everything that was happening, and how long it took to get even the briefest of messages through. Edmund had managed it twice from Ireland—his letters for her passing through his mother's hands in London before making its way north and reaching her in May. It was much creased but the wax seal looked more or less intact, and Ismay decided not to worry about anyone else having read it. It's not as though she would deny anything if asked.

In the last week of June, Edward crossed the channel from Calais with his uncle and cousin. Between them, Salisbury, Warwick and the now eighteen-year-old Edward, the Earl of March, entered London without violence and then routed the royal army at Northampton. With the king firmly in their control and Queen Margaret fled to her power base in the midlands, all of England waited for the Duke of York to make his move.

Ismay had one brief note from Edward in London, which she thought kind of him considering how busy he must be running around fighting and, no doubt, whoring. The next message gave her little warning, for it had been sent by courier just twenty-four hours ahead of its sender. It announced that Edmund and the Duke of York had landed near Liverpool on the ninth of September and Edward had ridden to meet them. And now the brothers were coming to Havencross, having convinced their father he needed Ismay's men to join his army.

Edmund's note had been warm but brief, eager to see her but never willing to presume anything. It was Edward who had scrawled at the bottom: *Better find a priest if you want one. We've not got much time.*

Hence today's argument.

The conflict between her and the priest was straightforward: Ismay had asked Father Pierce to perform a marriage ceremony. He had declined.

"You are too young," he said.

"My mother was fifteen when you married her to my father," Ismay countered.

"Three weeks of banns are required beforehand."

"There are allowable exceptions, as you well know."

"You are all alone here," he said, "with only a single maid and no ladies to aid and advise you."

"As far as I am aware, only one woman is required for a marriage."

"You are deliberately and with intent deceiving your guardian."

And there lay the priest's true objection: the Duke of York.

Having spent nearly nine months in Ireland—keeping safely out of reach of the vindictive Margaret of Anjou—the Duke of York was ready at last to make the final gamble for the

English throne. The Yorkists expected their recent victory at Northampton to be the first on their path to ruling.

Northampton, Ludford Bridge, Blore Heath, St. Albans—Ismay sometimes thought she marked the passing of her life more by the record of battles fought than the calendar. Especially since the duke's two oldest sons were now of an age to fight. And not just fight. The victory at Northampton might be credited to the Earl of Warwick, but it was Edward of York, just eighteen, who had crossed from Calais with his cousin and by all accounts fought brilliantly. Not that Ismay planned to tell him so; Edward had a high enough opinion of himself without needing to be flattered by her.

But no matter Edward's skill, it was Richard, the Duke of York, who looked set to once again be the most powerful lord in England. Ismay understood Father Pierce's reluctance to offend him. But she would not be budged. She might not plan to flatter Edward, but knowing that she had him on her side was a comfort.

On *their* side. Edward liked Ismay, but he loved his brother Edmund almost as if they were twins. Though incredibly different in temperament, they were as devoted to one another as any brothers could be. It was a relationship that sometimes made Ismay wistful for what she had missed not having siblings. Elizabeth and Margaret of York were her friends, but it was not the same.

She could guess, because she knew them both so well, how the conversation between the brothers had gone about this plan.

Edmund: *I will have no one but Ismay. No matter what Father says.*

Edward: *So have her.*

Edmund: *In marriage, brother.*

Edward: *Fine. A priest it is. Unless you want to make di praesenti vows? It's quicker. And still ends in bed.*

Edmund: *Ismay's priest at Havencross has served her family since before her birth. We can marry there. But I will need your help to get away from Father for the necessary time.*

Edward: *It would be so much easier if you had just come with me to Calais and enjoyed all the pretty girls there. But if Ismay is the one you want, then I'll do all in my power to help you secure her.*

The Duke of York would be angry. But not, perhaps, as angry as he could be. With all the distractions of royal displeasure and battles, the duke had greater things on his mind than his ward's marriage. And though his three daughters were either married or officially betrothed, his older sons remained available. Ismay may not be his first choice for Edmund, but it could be much worse. Presented with a fait accompli, she thought the duke would accept the marriage. If anyone protested, it would be Duchess Cecily.

But Ismay refused to be afraid. She had wanted Edmund since the moment she'd met him at Ludlow as a miserable orphan. So she simply smiled at Father Pierce and said, "I expect the Earl of March and the Earl of Rutland to arrive tonight. The marriage will take place first thing tomorrow."

In the end, Ismay was fairly certain she prevailed not because of the authority she'd learned from Cecily Neville, but because she'd gleaned when to smile and nod so she could then go ahead and do exactly what she wanted, just like Edward.

Ismay haunted the third-floor solar for hours, afraid to miss even a moment's sight of Edmund arriving. She spotted the brothers just before sunset, riding without banners and with only two men-at-arms accompanying them. She flew down the spiral stairs so quickly that she was outdoors as they were just riding through the open gate. It seemed to take an age for Edmund to dismount, but it was probably only seconds before she was in his arms.

They wed the next morning before the door of the priory's old stone chapel. Father Pierce had made no protests to the brothers, and Ismay knew why—both Edward and Edmund had grown sharper and warier this last year and carried with them an air that she recognized from the Duke of York: *We know who we are, and you cross us at your risk.*

She had returned the ring to Edmund for the ritual of the ceremony, and when they had made their promises to each other and to God, Edmund held the garnet and gold ring and took her left hand in his.

"With this ring I thee wed," Edmund said clearly. "This gold and silver I give thee. And with my body I thee worship, and with all my worldly goods I thee endow."

Edmund touched the ring to her thumb: "In the name of the Father." To her index finger: "And the Son." To her middle finger: "And the Holy Ghost."

He slid the ring onto her fourth finger and squeezed her hand. "Amen."

It was a very moderate celebration afterward, for Ismay had sent most of the servants away. Ismay's steward and his wife and Father Pierce entertained Edward at the table, or the other way around—he had some very inappropriate stories from Calais—while Edmund and Ismay had eyes only for each other.

She didn't even realize the others had left the room until Edward announced, "Off to bed, you two."

"It's hours until nightfall." Ismay thought she should at least pretend to be scandalized.

"It doesn't have to be done in the dark, you know, or in a bed for that matter." Edward would always say the things no one else would. "We leave at first light tomorrow, my sweet sister. If you wait, you're severely limiting your opportunities. Don't worry, I'll keep myself busy."

"Edward, don't you dare go trawling for girls around here," Edmund said sharply.

"Me? I've promised to play chess with the good priest. Go on then, my lord and lady of Rutland, take to bed. And I'll wager five groats that neither of you will want to leave it in the morning."

He would have won that bet. Ismay was shy at first, but Edmund, though not practiced like his brother, was possessed of an innate generosity. Both young and eager, they knew they must make the most of their time together. Also, Edward had probably enjoyed instructing his brother.

As the sky began to lighten to dawn, Ismay, wrapped in a heavy bedrobe with her hair loose around her, watched Edmund dress.

"Where will you go from here?" she asked.

"London. We'll likely send your men on to Sandal for now, until we know where to best position them. But Warwick's in London. And the king."

"What is your father going to do?"

His fingers, doing up the laces of his doublet, hesitated. "I don't know. But this conflict must be stopped."

"With war."

"Yes, probably."

"When will you come back?"

"As soon as I can. The moment wider affairs are settled, I'll confess all to my father and come claim you properly as my bride. The Countess of Rutland." He caressed her cheek with the back of his hand. "You will wear the title well."

"I don't care about the title, or any title. Except that of your wife."

She would not go down to see them off, for she did not want Edward, with his knowing eyes, assessing her this morning.

Instead she climbed back up to the solar and watched the company ride out, Edward at the front, Edmund bringing up the rear.

As he passed out of sight, Ismay swore she saw a small shape form in the spot where he had been. The form of a child.

CHAPTER TWENTY-NINE

DIANA
NOVEMBER 1918

Diana woke Monday morning, grateful that her nightly tormentor had left her alone for once. Either the living person had left the school for the holiday or the nonliving whatever was as aware of the terrible tension as everyone else at Havencross. She really wanted to pull the covers over her head and go back to sleep, not to get up again until, preferably, the world had righted itself. But nurses ran on duty, so she rose out of bed.

Diana had just finished putting the last pin in her coiled hair when she heard a soft knock.

Joshua looked unusually remote, as though he either had no emotions or had buried them exceptionally deep. Diana's greeting died on her lips.

"Miss Somersby wants all the adults in her office in five minutes," he announced.

She started to ask why, but he shook his head. "I don't know."

They walked silently together through the bare, medieval

corridors into the opulent Victorian ones. By the way Joshua kept clenching and unclenching his hands, Diana thought his tension was also at the breaking point.

Please, she prayed silently, *please let this be what I hope it is.*

Clarissa Somersby wore every bit of her headmistress, upper-class armor this morning. The five masters and staff currently in residence—Joshua, Weston, Beth Willis, the cook Mrs. McCann, and Diana herself—stood before her desk like soldiers on review while Clarissa sat, palms down on the desktop before her.

"I have been on the telephone for nearly two hours," she told them, "confirming the news from Newcastle to London. By every reliable report, an armistice will be signed by noon today."

The announcement dropped into perfect silence. Diana almost wondered if she'd imagined the words, dreamed them into an auditory hallucination. Then Joshua gripped her hand, uncaring of any audience, and she felt the same fine tremble in him that was running beneath her skin.

Clarissa cleared her throat to break the oppressive silence. "Our first thought is for the students still here. The vicar announced that there will be a service of thanksgiving this afternoon, and likely a parade and more secular celebrations tomorrow. I propose that the masters escort the students into Hexham for both." She looked down at her hands, her voice flat and tense. "Obviously this is an epochal moment in history, but it is also a personal one. Every one of you in this room has sacrificed a great deal in various ways the last four years—I regret that I have not the gift of acknowledging you as I wish to—but please know that I am aware of how . . . complicated this day is. For all of Britain, it is a day of both joy and grief."

The morning passed in a foggy haze for Diana, punctuated by a few clear moments. She sat with Jasper Willis for a bit. His cheeks had gained color, Diana noted; save for the broken leg, he appeared completely recovered from his ordeal. She showed him the coin she'd found. She had washed it to reveal the silver. It was not Roman—it had the face of a medieval king surrounded by Latin: *EDWARD IV DI GRA DEI REX ANGL.*

She let Jasper explain the abbreviations and translate, even though Joshua had already done so for her. "It says, 'Edward IV de gratiam Dei Rex Angolorum' or 'Edward the Fourth, by the grace of God, King of England.'" He was definitely pleased to be instructing the school nurse in Latin.

"Do you know where I found it?" Diana asked casually.

He shook his head.

"At the spot where Mr. Murray located *you* that morning." She watched him, his eyes downcast so that his long lashes almost swept his cheeks. "Why did you go all the way out there, Jasper? Did you know about the medieval icehouse ruins?"

He shook his head again. "No, miss."

"Then what was it?"

"I don't want to say it," he whispered. "You won't believe me."

"Let me guess. You saw . . . someone. Who said, 'Come hide with me.'" She repeated the phrase Austin Willis had told them all earlier. "You think it was a ghost."

"I know how it sounds. I'm not stupid. I was staying in Austin's room last night, cause of half-term, and I didn't want him to be alone. I stayed awake, in case. And I was right, 'cause the ghost boy came back for him, but Austin stayed asleep and I went with him instead."

"You didn't think to alert an adult?"

"Adults don't see him. Adults don't see anything they don't want to."

Diana acknowledged the cynical accuracy of his statement. "That is too often true."

"I'm not making it up," he said defiantly. "I didn't dream it, or imagine it. I could feel him and the whole strangeness of things." He paused. "I don't know how to explain, miss, but it was like I was part here and part there."

Chills ran in waves down Diana's arms and spine. *Most of her was in whatever moment of terror she'd been possessed by. Frantically, she counted the horsemen and searched for the identifying banner.* She cleared her throat and banished the unsettling memory from the solar. "I don't think you're dreaming or imagining, or lying," she assured Jasper. "But you must promise me that you will keep me in your confidence. No more heroic endeavors without asking for help. Is that clear?"

After Jasper promised, she went into her office and made meticulous notes in her case diary. She read three or four medical journals and a month's worth of British public health updates. She also spent long periods simply staring into space. The clock seemed to stall and then lurch ahead until finally it was time for lunch.

She had just entered the vast dining hall, sounds from a small group of students echoing. Standing at the head table, wearing dark gray and with her hands clasped before her like a Renaissance saint, Clarissa swept the students and adults with her gaze across the room before announcing: "At eleven minutes past eleven o'clock this morning French time, an armistice signed by Germany and the Allied leaders took effect. The war is over."

In endless ways over the last four years Diana had thought about this moment. She'd imagined cheering or crying or both, hugging people and giving thanks to God. Now that it was here—

Diana fled. She couldn't even bring herself to go to her room for a coat—she just grabbed one hanging from a hook in the scullery and headed for the moor. There, she walked and walked and walked, afraid to stop for fear of what might catch up with her if she did.

She couldn't walk forever. When Diana realized she'd reached Hadrian's Wall, she looked for a good open spot from which to survey the expanse of nothing. She found a flat-topped rock halfway up a climbing path and, overheated from exertion, shrugged herself out of the oversized—what was it she had actually grabbed? She studied the caped shoulders and waxed cotton, the flannel lining—

"It's a stalking coat, for hunting."

Of course Joshua had followed her. Diana snapped, "Aren't you supposed to be on your way to the church service with the boys?"

"I told Miss Somersby I would prefer to be excused from that duty. Mrs. McCann agreed to go in my stead."

"Why?"

He just looked at her. "I imagine for the same reason you bolted from the dining hall and didn't stop for three miles."

"I thought . . . I thought all of this would be simpler. I thought, *The war will end and it will all be over at last.* Instead, I just feel . . ."

He dropped next to her, and bent his good leg as a prop for his arms. "Unmoored," Joshua offered. "Rudderless. Cast adrift."

"Exactly. As long as there was war, there were so few decisions to be made." Diana found herself leaning into him, searching his eyes as though they would have the answer. "So what do we do now?"

He blew out a sharp breath and said fiercely, "We say to hell with guilt. We say that we can remember the dead without making ourselves one of them." He put a hand to her cheek, his fingers tangled in her hair. "We live, Diana. We live in every way we can."

They moved together at the same moment and met in a kiss that exploded through her. She had never been so swept away by reckless desire and she didn't care; there was no one to watch them, nothing to stop them.

Except the damp cold and rocky ground of Northumberland. Even with her borrowed coat spread on the ground, it soon became clear that they couldn't move without courting disaster. Not to mention that they were brazenly exposed halfway up the hillside.

Laughing, Joshua finally said, "I think we'd have to be much younger to find this romantic. We're not sixteen years old and hiding from our parents. We both have perfectly good beds available to us."

"In the school," she reminded him.

"Which, at this moment, is empty of everyone except Clarissa and Beth Willis."

"And Jasper, who's lying across the corridor from my bedroom with a broken leg."

"My corridor is empty." He leaned over her and brushed his lips along her throat.

It drew a soft sigh from her, but she was afraid of . . . she didn't know what.

Joshua knew her better than she did. "You needn't worry that the moment will pass before we reach the house, Diana. I didn't kiss you just because we were in the open air and the war is over. I didn't start wanting you today, and I won't stop wanting you in the time it takes us to walk back."

He got himself standing and drew her up after. Then, his mouth against her cheek, he whispered, "I will never stop wanting you."

Wise Joshua, because Diana discovered on the walk back to Havencross that there was something to be said about a purposeful delay to a desired experience. With each mile her anticipation increased until, by the time they entered his bedroom and he pulled her to him, all she wanted was to lose herself in whatever followed.

Apart from a few hurried, desperate encounters in whatever private corner could be snatched at a field hospital in France, Diana's sexual experience was limited. She wouldn't have thought a schoolmaster's austere room with a single bed conducive to a high degree of pleasure. She would have thought wrong.

"You clearly know what you're doing," she laughed breathlessly, as he undid buttons and slid her blouse aside to kiss her bare shoulder.

"Are you flattering me, Nurse Neville?"

"It's only flattery if it isn't true."

His laugh had an edge to it she'd never heard before; it made her breath catch.

With a catch in his own breathing, Joshua said, "You are so beautiful."

"That *is* flattery. I'm not beautiful. Clarissa Somersby is beautiful. I'm simply passable."

Joshua held her face in both hands and forced her to look at him, his hazel eyes dark with passion. "There is nothing the least bit simple about you, Diana Neville. And I have never wanted anything or anyone in my life the way I want you."

After that, neither had breath enough for speaking.

When the world at last righted itself and Joshua lay propped on his side, watching her, he brushed a thumb over her wet cheek. "You're crying."

"Am I? I don't know why."

"You don't have to know."

It was such a relief not to have to explain or defend or even understand her own feelings. With Joshua cradling her close, Diana cried until she fell asleep with his hand resting on the curve of her hip.

They rose, reluctantly, when they heard the sounds of returning boys, voices high and excited.

"You're sure your corridor is empty?" Diana asked, buttoning the high collar of her blouse.

"I'm sure. All the masters who share this wing went home for the holiday."

He opened the door and checked, just to make sure. "Clear."

She stepped into the doorway and kissed him, not wanting to stop. But if she kept clinging to him, they were going to end up right back on the bed and someone was going to miss her before long . . .

"I already miss you," Joshua whispered into her hair.

"How sweet," someone drawled from nearby.

Luther Weston leaned against one wall, arms crossed and with a bitter smile.

Joshua stepped away from her. "What do you want, Weston?"

"I don't really remember now. What a pretty little secret I've stumbled upon."

"This has nothing to do with you."

"Maybe not, but I bet Miss Somersby would be interested. Doesn't set a very good example for impressionable schoolboys, after all."

"Enough," Diana said in the tone that brought threatening soldiers under control. "I will speak to Miss Somersby myself about my own actions. I'm sure you don't want to gain a reputation for carrying tales."

"No, I'd much rather have a reputation for screwing the school nurse."

Weston anticipated Joshua's punch but not the vicious twist of the arm that followed when Weston blocked him. With a shove, Joshua pinned Weston against the wall, arm at his throat. "Apologize, and get the hell out of here before I really lose my temper."

Looking over Joshua's shoulder, Weston said, "I apologize, Miss Neville. I'm sure your reputation is deservedly unstained."

Somehow the three of them managed to separate without further violence or insults. They even managed to appear at dinner, where Diana listened to the boys' happy chatter about Hexham and the mayor in his robe and chains of office, and the bells ringing for the first time that some of them could ever remember.

Though she would have liked nothing more than to attach herself to Joshua after dinner, Diana's exhaustion was real and urgent and she didn't want to give Weston a reason to go to Clarissa before she could talk to the headmistress. She bid Joshua a decorous good night in the dining hall—warmed by the positively wicked grin he gave her in turn—and checked that Beth Willis meant to spend the night in the infirmary with Jasper.

She reached her door ready to sleep for a solid ten hours. She was so tired that, at first, she couldn't properly take in the state of her bedroom. Drawers had been violently ripped open and their contents flung far and wide. Books and loose papers covered the floor and the contents of her wardrobe had been strewn about in trails of wool, cotton, and silk.

Diana thought it could have been done by Luther Weston. For whatever reasons, he detested Joshua and her, and seeing them together might have pushed him over some edge. But she didn't really believe it. Jasper's voice from earlier today came back to her: *I don't want to say it. You won't believe me.*

If she were brave enough to enjoy Joshua's bed, Diana decided she was brave enough to tell herself the truth: that the malice she could see in the attack on her bedroom matched the malice she'd felt on the solar stairs. Whatever invisible force had seized her in a vision and then attempted to push her down the stairs was the same force that had done this damage.

And yet, Diana was not afraid. She remembered the outside terror that had possessed her as she'd watched a band of hostile horsemen descending on Havencross some long ago century, and she felt only compassion. She knew about terror. She knew what someone might do in the grip of it.

With a sigh, Diana put her things back in a semblance of order. To her own surprise, she then spoke out loud: "I'm not your enemy, whoever you are. I don't want to hurt you, and I'd appreciate it if you'd just leave me be."

That speech—heard and understood or not—sufficed to allow her to fall asleep in peace, her body humming with memories of Joshua's touch.

She wasn't even surprised when she woke in darkness to the sound of knocking. When was the last time she'd simply woken up in the morning like a normal person? She checked her watch and saw it was 4 a.m.

She wouldn't say that she expected it to be Joshua, but the unpleasantness of facing Luther Weston served to fully wake her up. "What do you want?" she asked, keeping one hand firmly on her door, ready to slam it in his face.

The curl of his lip showed that he appreciated her suspicions of his intent, but he didn't offer the expected insults. "Believe it or not, your nursing skills are required. Lawrence Dean is unwell and running a noticeable fever."

"Which room is he in?" Diana asked. "I'll meet you there."

He told her how to find Lawrence Dean and left. Diana

dressed quickly and snatched her medical bag from her office. *Just a fever*, she told herself. Boys get fevers all the time, especially after a day of overexcitement.

But keeping pace with her every step was a line from one of the health bulletins she'd read earlier today: *an outbreak of epidemic influenza has been reported at Birmingham.*

CHAPTER THIRTY

DIANA
NOVEMBER 1918

Lawrence Dean, a tall and robust ten-year-old, had a temperature of 103 degrees. In a French field hospital, that number would have set off a panicked attempt to allay a possible infection in an already weakened soldier. But children could spike high fevers with the mildest of illnesses and be fine the next day. If the fever had been the boy's only symptom, Diana would not be greatly worried.

But he also had a headache and a sore throat. His joints hurt so badly he whimpered when she touched him.

Damn it, she thought.

"Influenza?" Weston asked from the doorway.

"Why do you say that?" she asked, stalling.

"I had influenza in the spring. Half my unit was down with it at some point. Nasty, but over quickly."

I hope so, she thought. But she remembered another phrase from the medical bulletin about Birmingham: *there are an unusual number of fatal cases.*

"I suppose you'll want him in the infirmary," Weston said.

"No. Not yet, at least. I don't want to expose Jasper. Will you stay with him while I alert Miss Somersby?"

Although Weston hardly seemed to even tolerate the boys most days, she admitted that he made no protest at being assigned nursing duties.

Diana leaned over Lawrence, careful not to touch him. He smiled gamely at her when she said, "I'll be back soon with some medicine to help your fever and let you sleep."

"Thank you, miss," he whispered.

Clarissa Somersby woke to Diana's knocks with the ease of a woman who has trouble sleeping, and listened to the report without interruption. She looked amazingly composed for a woman in a silk bedrobe.

"I'll phone Dr. Bennett," Clarissa said when Diana had finished. "I assume that you'd like his opinion?"

"Yes, and please ask him if there are other cases in the area. That's the most critical thing to know at the moment."

"I'll also try to reach the boy's aunt in London."

"She shouldn't come running," Diana cautioned. "If it is influenza, even of the common sort, it's best to limit contact. There are other measures we should take, but I need to see to Lawrence's comfort first. I'd suggest a meeting with all the adults in an hour?"

Clarissa agreed, for she had the blessed gift of taking in essential information and acting on it without demanding to be loaded down with extraneous details. And it augured well for the immediate future that she was willing to take orders from Diana.

In her office, Diana collected the items she needed: aspirin for fever, salicin for pain, and masks for herself and whoever was in close contact with Lawrence. Before leaving, she peeked through the half-open door into the infirmary and saw that both Jasper and his mother were still sleeping soundly.

Lawrence's temperature had risen half a degree, but his pulse and breathing were still normal. He'd had a bloody nose while she was gone. She gave him the aspirin, wrote everything down in her case diary, and sat by him while he fell asleep.

Just before 5 a.m. Mrs. McCann arrived to summon her. "They're all in Miss Clarissa's study," the cook said. "I'll stay with the lad."

Despite everything, Diana brightened when she entered the headmistress's study and saw Joshua leaning over a chair, hands braced on the back. His smile was for her alone, and she had the sudden memory of him smiling down at her while one hand traced a line on her bare skin from neck to hip.

Then Weston cleared his throat, and Clarissa said, "Let's not waste time. Miss Neville, the floor is yours."

"Have you spoken to Dr. Bennett?" she asked first.

"I have. He'll come this morning to check on Lawrence and speak to you. And he said that there have been more than three dozen cases of influenza in the district in the last week."

"Is it the same flu that tore through the armies six months ago?" Weston asked.

"We can only hope so," Diana answered. "Because in that case, you and I should be immune. I had influenza in Amiens in May."

"That's good news, right?" Joshua asked. "That flu was vicious but short-lived."

"Mostly. But there have been reports in medical journals since August saying that localized epidemics are resulting in high cases of pneumonia and unusually high death rates."

"But that's in older people," Beth Willis piped up. "I thought influenza was most dangerous for the infants and the elderly."

"Usually," Diana said. "They also say that this particular

strain targets a much younger population." She didn't want to be drawn into any more just now, didn't want to give them information pulled from half-remembered articles without context. Hopefully Dr. Bennett could help clarify the situation.

Still, there were actions that needed to be taken now even if they proved later to be an overreaction.

"To begin with, Miss Somersby, the students presently at home on holiday should be prepared to stay there longer than for just this week."

Clarissa only blinked and asked, "For how long?"

"Until we are certain that the school is free of infection."

"This is a very large house, Miss Neville, and the infirmary is in the most remote part. If we move Lawrence—"

"It won't just be Lawrence," Diana said bluntly. "Influenza is very contagious. I fully expect it to sweep through and hit all the boys, which means I'll need a much bigger space than the infirmary. I suggest we set up beds in the dining hall. Boys should remain confined to their bedrooms at present. At the first symptoms they can be moved to the hall. If any of them remain symptom-free for a period of four days, they can be sent home."

Clarissa tapped her fingers on the desk. "Some family members might want to rush up here."

"We can wait for Dr. Bennett, but I suspect he'll order a complete quarantine. No one except the doctor should enter Havencross."

Joshua straightened up. "You can't possibly hope to care for more than a dozen patients at one time."

"I often cared for a ward of fifty on my own in France. And we're not on the moon. If anyone's symptoms require it, they'll be taken to hospital."

"Very well," Clarissa said with characteristic decisiveness.

"Mr. Murray and Mr. Weston, you will follow Miss Neville's direction in setting up the dining hall as an infirmary. Mrs. Willis and I will begin notifying parents. Anything else at the moment?"

"For now," Diane said, "only those of us who have been with Lawrence should go into his room: Mrs. McCann, Mr. Weston, and me. If—when—I need further help, I will require you all to be diligent handwashers and to wear a mask whenever you're near a patient. I apologize if that's inconvenient."

"I can cook in Mrs. McCann's place," Beth Willis offered.

"Thank you," said Clarissa. "I'm sure we will all rise to the occasion as required, and remember that any concern we feel should not be transmitted to the boys. They must not be made afraid."

As they filed out of the office, Diana thought, *If only Clarissa could order* me *not to be afraid.*

CHAPTER THIRTY-ONE

JULIET
2018

Juliet would never have expected she could be so thrilled about what was, essentially, a hole in the ground. She chalked that up to Noah, who understood and pointed out the details that made this particular hole unique.

"See the remains of the dressed stones?" He shone his high-powered flashlight down, tracing the outline of what looked like a squared-off stone to her. The light moved on. "And the absolute confirmation—steps."

Juliet rolled her eyes. "They look more like a ladder. A crumbly, medieval-ly ladder."

"Trust me—anything that's survived this long is stronger than it looks."

"Go on, then. Show me how strong it is," she dared him.

Noah eyed her mockingly. "Don't tell me you're not the least bit curious about what's down there. You're the one who got me involved, remember? Is it the dark you don't like, or the enclosed space?"

"I'm not especially claustrophobic, no, but that doesn't mean I want to go exploring without proper precautions."

"Which would be?"

Juliet thought of the things Duncan would be saying to her right now—barbed comments about . . . just about anything, really. He'd never been consistent in his criticisms. One day he'd attack her for being overcautious and the next for being too reckless. She had learned to calculate her choices depending on what she thought Duncan would attack her for. Long ago she'd stopped wondering what she herself wanted.

Faced with a man whose expression was pure curiosity, and with the opening of a medieval tunnel at her feet, Juliet found herself saying, "I suppose I am lighter than you. Fine, I'll test these so-called steps. But I'm not going out of sight of this opening."

"Fair."

It *was* more thrilling than she wanted to admit. She went down sideways, keeping one hand on the packed earth wall and the other on the irregularly sized stone steps as she eased her way down. Thanks to Noah's preparation, she wore a headlamp to give her light.

It wasn't as far down as she'd feared, which she supposed made sense. If one had to hack out a tunnel of any sort in the days before power tools, one wouldn't want to go any deeper than they had to. Her feet hit ground after twenty steps. "I'm down," she called.

"What do you see?"

Juliet turned her head carefully, adjusting the light as she went. "It definitely looks like a tunnel," she reported. "Just one." She oriented herself to the layout of the chapel above and added, "It's heading away from the house. North, I think."

"Nice. A crawling tunnel, or a walking one?"

"I don't think *you* could stand upright. I maybe can if it stays the same size. It's awfully narrow though. Might have to turn sideways."

"How far can you see down the tunnel?"

"I'm a historian, not a surveyor. I don't know—ten feet?"

"All right. Come back up now and we can make plans to explore more thoroughly."

She tipped her head back as she began to climb and halfway up turned off the headlamp so as not to blind Noah. In the sudden dimming, her eyes adjusted. Juliet froze four steps from the top, staring not at Noah's square jaw and steady eyes but over his shoulder at the pale, shimmery outline of a woman in long skirts. As Juliet watched, the woman crouched and slid an illusory grave slab over the opening.

Juliet yelped, and Noah's voice cut through the fog. "What's wrong?"

She blinked and all was normal. "Nothing," she said automatically, and finished her climb.

Noah showed her how the grave slab moved so easily. Although it appeared from above to be the same thick granite as the others, that was only on the edges. Much of it had been hollowed out inside, leaving edges that made it possible for someone to push against and move the slab from below.

Inside, they shed their coats and boots and, after checking the time, Juliet offered him a drink. "We're not expected at Rachel's for another hour, right?"

He quickly agreed, and they took a bottle of red wine and glasses into the little medieval sitting room and its far too comfortable sofa. As they talked about secret tunnels and medieval architecture, and made subtle attempts to discover what the other wanted for Christmas, Juliet's phone kept buzzing. She'd checked it when they entered the house and had seen three text messages from her mother. They'd all said basically the same thing: *Call me, please. We're all fine, but I need to talk to you.*

Finally, Noah asked, "Same person as before?"

"No, just my mom. I can call her later."

"Sounds like she's going to keep calling until you do."

Juliet sighed. "Do you mind?"

"Not at all. I even promise to save you some wine."

She pressed the callback button as she walked down the corridor toward the hidden solar staircase. Her mother answered immediately. Because of course this would be the day the cell reception was perfect.

"Juliet, where are you?"

"What do you mean, where am I? I'm in the middle of Northumberland. Where are you?"

True to form, her mother didn't waste time in snark or answering unnecessary questions. "I had to call the police on Duncan last night. He showed up at our door at midnight, drunk and furious, and looking for you. When I reminded him that threatening a federal judge was a felony, he took off in that stupid convertible of his."

Shit. "I'm sorry he bothered you. He's been suspended by the university—"

"I know. We keep tabs on him. It's you we're worried about."

"Mom, he's hardly likely to drive the convertible across the ocean. Even if he did know where I was."

"I've never thought him particularly stable," her mother retorted. "But if he has nothing to lose, I don't like the thought of what he might do. Sociopaths can be both clever and relentless."

Juliet closed her eyes, swearing freely in her head.

"Juliet, I'm not trying to frighten you. I just want you to be careful."

She wasn't frightened—she was furious. How long was Duncan Whittier going to keep contaminating her life? He'd already cost her ten years and the deepest grief she would ever feel. How dare he worm his way into this fragile new life she was beginning to construct?

Somehow Juliet got off the phone and leaned against the door that hid the solar staircase, an incipient headache coming at the base of her skull. Beneath her anger she could feel other emotions beating—loss and fear and hope and an absolute determination to do what she must to protect what she loved. Juliet could almost feel the weight of Liam in her arms, but instead of grief she felt only awe and gratitude. And when she focused her eyes, the infant she held wasn't pale and still but pink-cheeked and fair-haired, his eyes open and fixed on his mother's . . .

Edmund . . . I shouldn't name him for his father, but how can I not . . . already he looks entirely like a York . . . but not for my son the loss of war and the games of power . . . I will protect him, I will save him, I will hide him from danger . . .

"Juliet?"

Her eyes flew open. She'd forgotten about Noah. She'd almost forgotten herself. Juliet straightened up and knew, with irrational certainty, that those images and feelings had seeped into her from whatever lingered in the medieval solar. Edmund . . . could that be their nameless ghost boy? *Oh God*, she thought, *I hope not. Because if he's a child ghost, it means his mother couldn't protect him from everything.*

Her complicated emotions must have been written all over her face, because Noah didn't say another word. He simply drew her against his shoulder. The simple kindness—missing for so long from her life—undid her. For the first time since the hospital, Juliet began to cry.

At some point she slid to the floor, and he continued to cradle her while she wept out more emotions than she had names for. Slowly, her sobs lengthened out and stopped. Even more slowly, she became vividly conscious of every place she and Noah touched, of the rise and fall of his chest, of the fact that she hadn't been with a man for almost a year—ten weeks into her pregnancy when Duncan had laid a hand on her still-flat stomach and said, "You know you don't really need to gain more than fifteen pounds, right?"

That memory might have put her off, but Noah chose that moment to shift one arm—not to withdraw but to bring his hand to the back of her neck, where he rested it while his fingers stroked the bare skin beneath the collar of her sweater.

Suddenly she wanted nothing more in the world than to be kissing him. She tipped her head up and he met her mouth with his, his tongue flicking in and out until she groaned and moved her hands to the first of his shirt buttons.

Noah drew back and instantly Juliet dropped her hands, face flaming with embarrassment and swollen with tears. "I'm sorry, I'm so sorry, I'm such a fool. Your instincts must be screaming at you to run away from the crazy woman."

"Hey." He waited for her to meet his eyes. "If it were up to me and my instincts, we'd have gone to bed the day we met. I'm too often reckless and sometimes selfish, but I'm not in the habit of taking advantage of women. I wouldn't want you to regret anything done when you weren't thinking clearly."

"I am thinking clearly. I'm thinking that you're the kindest man I've met in years. I'm thinking that I don't deserve this chance after how badly I screwed up my marriage. I'm thinking Rachel would forgive us for missing dinner." She darted a quick, butterfly kiss to his chin. "And I'm thinking that my bedroom is right there and what are we waiting for?"

He pulled her up and swung her into his arms. As they passed into the bedroom, Juliet thought she heard a soft sigh, as though the house itself approved of their decision.

CHAPTER THIRTY-TWO

DIANA
NOVEMBER 1918

One advantage of Havencross for dealing with multiple patients was its size. The dining hall routinely seated more than one hundred people, with the boys crammed together on benches at long tables. Those tables were so long and so heavy, that it was impractical for only the handful of available adults to move them out of the room entirely. They lined them up against the walls instead; covered with linen, they could accommodate everything from extra bed linens and medications to basins for vomiting and other needs.

They brought in twenty beds, enough for every student and staff member, and placed them six feet apart, a luxury of personal space that Diana had never had in France. Best to count her blessings wherever she could.

Diana and Clarissa were making up beds with fresh sheets. Thank goodness for a well-run household; washing the linen of all the boys away on holiday had given them an abundance that made Clarissa say, "We could change their beds three times a day for fun, if we wanted."

No point in painting the headmistress a picture she didn't need yet, such as how many ways these sheets could be stained in the coming days. No point in telling her that any linen they used now might have to be burned afterward.

One apocalypse at a time.

Dr. Bennett appeared in the hall just after noon. "Very nice, indeed," he said, nodding. "Nothing like working with the military to inspire order I suppose, Miss Neville."

"Honestly, it was the nursing supervisors who kept everything orderly. The doctors and surgeons had a hard time looking beyond their own immediate patients. No offense, Dr. Bennett."

"None taken. And I would indeed like to see my immediate patient."

Diana escorted him to Lawrence's room and excused Mrs. McCann. She could hear the other boys in their rooms along the corridor, talking to one another through their open doors, while Dr. Bennett spoke to his patient in a comforting but matter-of-fact way. Diana made note of the changes in pulse and temperature (his fever had dropped a tiny bit to just under 103).

Dr. Bennett smiled at Lawrence. "You're going to feel awful for a time, young man, but I know you'll be a good patient and do everything Miss Neville asks. Right?"

"Yes, sir."

They moved into the corridor and stepped away far enough to discuss without being overheard.

"What do you think?" Diana asked.

"Oh, it's influenza. I just don't like some of the oddities. The high level of pain, for one, and the bloody nose for another.

There have been flare-ups around the country since August with these and other complications."

"Do you want to admit him?"

"The local hospital admitted five people last night, all of whom were either at church on Sunday or at the thanksgiving services yesterday. Which tells me there will be many more cases in the next three days. As long as Lawrence remains stable, he'll get better care here. You know what to watch out for?"

"Difficulty breathing, congested lungs, resistant fever—all the signs of pneumonia."

"Pneumonia cases I'll want in hospital, but I'm telling you right now we might be slow at transporting boys from here."

"We have the wagon. The gardener can come and sleep in the stables. He can transport boys if needed."

"My biggest concern is for you, Miss Neville. If you fall ill—"

"I don't think I will. I had influenza in April."

"In France? From the epidemic that swept through the military? Yes, that's a good sign. But don't try to be a hero. We'll do our best to get you what you need. I'll come morning and evening. Ring my office or the hospital in between."

He had just left when Mrs. McCann, who had been checking in up and down the corridor, reported to Diana that three more boys were running fevers. Diana started three new medical reports and then moved the four ill boys to the dining room. When they were settled with aspirin and cool cloths, and drinking the salty chicken broth that Beth Willis had made, Diana set up a desk at the end of one long table and put everything in order: casebook, separate medical folders for each patient, an oil lantern to light her work when the boys slept at night.

Diana stood up, automatically smoothing her skirt as though the ward supervisor would show up at any moment to check her uniform. Then she folded her hands behind her back and surveyed her domain.

With a jolt, she realized that the last time she'd examined a recovery ward, she'd not been a nurse but a patient. A feverish, frightened, traumatized patient.

It wasn't influenza that had put here there. That was simply a side effect of being in hospital in the first place. After Viliers-Bretoneux, after the high whine of the shells and the screaming of trapped soldiers . . .

She was so shaken that she didn't realize Joshua had appeared until he put a hand on the small of her back. "Are you all right? You look rather pale."

"It's not . . . I'm not ill. It's nothing."

Joshua nodded in the direction of Clarissa and Mrs. McCann gathering bowls and talking to the four ill boys. "Everyone here is set for now. Come hide with me for a moment and talk."

It was probably just that she was tired, but Diana was having a harder time than usual shoving Viliers-Bretoneux back into its box. Joshua pulled her into an alcove beneath the grand staircase and sat her down on the curving bench built into the space. He put his palm to her forehead.

"I don't have a fever," she said sharply.

"I know. You're cold and clammy."

"Very sexy."

He tried to squat down in front of her but his left leg was too stiff, so he settled next to her instead. "Diana, I know shock when I see it. And I know its aftermath. You were shaky when we were in the hidden passageway. Claustrophobia is a common—"

"I'm not claustrophobic!" She got herself under control. "Or at least, I never was. Before."

"Before what?"

She had never talked about it. She'd told her doctors in

France that she didn't remember anything, and insisted the same to her mother before fleeing from her family's smothering concern.

She began slowly. "I was working in a field hospital in Viliers-Bretoneux last spring. We had set up in an old manor house. It wasn't near the front; there'd been no action near us for months. Until, all at once, there was.

"It's the refugees you see first," she told him, and saw Joshua nod in remembrance. "Streaming from the east. The decision was made to evacuate the patients five miles back. I was helping clear the postsurgery ward when I heard the incoming shell."

Her body twitched, a physical manifestation of remembered panic.

"It hit just at the right spot on the manor—the roof and all three floors came down in seconds. I don't remember a lot . . . not that I can describe . . . just that feeling. I couldn't move, I couldn't see, I was buried beneath layers of stone and wood, and there was dust in my lungs, and I was afraid they'd go and leave me and no one would find me."

He held her hand firmly, an anchor in this moment, which was not *that* moment. *Never again that moment*, she reminded herself. She was out. She was safe. She could breathe.

After twenty-seven breaths, she could go on. "Thirteen of us were buried when the shell hit. I was the only one they pulled out alive." She laughed shakily; Joshua looked unconvinced by it. "Anyway, that is the story of why I don't like secret passages or tunnels or anything that has the ability to bury me alive at any moment."

With an indistinct murmur of sympathy, Joshua wrapped his arms around her, and she let herself sink into his steadiness and warmth. Here, she thought, was someone she could trust to hold her up no matter what.

Someone cleared their throat, and Diana pulled out of Joshua's embrace.

Mrs. McCann said, "Miss Neville, Lawrence's nose is bleeding again. And there are dark spots on his face."

CHAPTER THIRTY-THREE

DIANA
NOVEMBER 1918

When Dr. Bennett arrived that evening, he agreed with Diana that both Lawrence Dean and an eleven-year-old with a worrying cough should be transported to hospital. Lawrence had dark red spots on his face, and both boys were beginning to struggle with their breathing. They had the gardener hitch up the wagon and lay mattresses and blankets on the benches to cushion the boys. Diana was torn between going with them and staying with the others, but Dr. Bennett promised to drive his motorcar slowly behind the wagon so he could keep an eye on what was happening.

Diana was accustomed to events moving quickly—field hospitals were nothing but chaos punctuated by brief moments of calm—but even so, the speed with which the flu took hold at Havencross shocked her. Within four days, ten of the fifteen boys had been moved to the dining hall infirmary, and so had the gardener. Dr. Bennett phoned Havencross just before noon on Friday, exhausted and harried, and told her he'd try to come by that evening.

"I've been in hospital all night," he reported. "Your boys are stable for now, but I don't like the look of Lawrence Dean. I've got him on oxygen, but he might be progressing to pneumonia."

"You sound tired."

"So do you. At least I'm not the only medical officer in hospital."

"How many patients are you coping with there?"

"Twice as many as we have room for, and they keep coming. The damned Armistice celebrations might almost have been designed to spread infection. I'll do my best to come round tonight. But I'm telling you right now, unless someone is in very bad condition, they'll get better treatment with you than they will in hospital. I'll do what I can to round you up a relief nurse, or at least another pair of hands."

Her heart sank, but she tried to keep it out of her voice. "I understand. Don't worry—I'm used to functioning in chaos."

Which was true enough, but she'd never borne the sole responsibility of care. And if she'd thought the soldiers she'd cared for too young for what they faced, what was she to make of schoolboys? Wearily, Diana replaced her mask and went to the kitchen to speak to Beth Willis.

She was surprised to find Beth in the scullery, standing in the open doorway and speaking to someone in the yard.

"Who's here?" Diana asked sharply, coming up to Beth's shoulder.

"Mrs. Murray," Beth said, at the same moment Diana recognized Joshua's mother.

"You shouldn't be here," Diana said, glad to see that Beth was also wearing her mask. "We must keep quarantine until everyone's well."

"Yes, Joshua telephoned. I understand. I also understand that only two adults can be relied upon to remain healthy, so how exactly do you propose to care for twenty people on your own?"

"Not all the students are sick, and only one of the staff."

"Today. What about tomorrow? I'm not proposing to force my way inside to nurse. But what I can do is relieve you of some responsibilities. Like meals. Alice and I can cook at home and bring it here. We have a fairly reliable motorcar. That will allow Mrs. Willis to help in the sickroom as needed—if she isn't already ill. She looks a bit feverish to me."

Diana took Beth by the arm and even without touching her face knew Mrs. Murray was right—fever burned through Beth's sleeve. "Damn it," she said, then instantly added, "I'm sorry, Beth. How's your throat?"

"Painful," she admitted. "But I can stay on my feet. It's not like I can make any of the boys sicker than they are."

"No, Mrs. Murray is right. You go straight to the infirmary, and I'll be right there to check you over." She waited until the secretary had gone, then turned back to Mrs. Murray. "I suppose I have little choice but to accept your offer. I'll leave this door unlocked. Whatever you bring you can carry into the scullery and leave. Ring the bell to let us know you've come. And you should wear a mask even at that. I can leave you some in the scullery."

She paused, hearing her own rattle of impersonal orders, and added, "I truly appreciate it. How can I thank you?"

"My son survived the war with both legs intact—and some of that is due to you. I trust Joshua is being useful in return?"

Useful, necessary, absolutely essential to my peace of mind and heart. "Very."

"You'll leave me word if he gets ill?"

"I will." Diana wanted to cross her fingers or throw salt over

shoulder to ward away ill fortune at the thought of Joshua strug-
gling to breathe.

She managed to snatch an hour of sleep before helping feed
broth to the boys who could manage it. She had to admit that
Luther Weston continued to be both helpful and remarkably
silent. Any snide comments he might make these days were
made out of her hearing and she figured Joshua could handle
himself.

In the makeshift infirmary Beth Willis lay in the bed nearest
her younger son, Austin. She could stay there for now, but Diana
was prepared to separate them if either took a turn for the worse.
Dr. Bennett didn't make it to Havencross that evening, but she
felt mildly confident that they'd make it through the night.
Besides Weston, she had Mrs. McCann and Clarissa Somersby
helping in shifts. She had detailed Joshua to watch over the five
boys who were still uninfected, including Jasper Willis, who had
been carried to a room closer to his schoolmates.

As the clock passed midnight, Diana walked the center aisle.
There were two boys she was keeping a close eye on whose
breathing concerned her. One of them seemed to have eased
while he slept, but she could hear stridor breathing from a
thirteen-year-old orphan named Percy Nicholson. When Diana
pressed her stethoscope to his chest, his eyes fluttered open.

"How are you, Percy?" she asked softly.

It took a moment for him to focus on her. "I'm . . . tired."

Her heart sank as he had to stop and catch his breath just to
say two words. She rearranged his pillows to prop him higher
until she could get Weston to boil some water and try to ease his
lungs with steam. She'd give it an hour more, but then it might
be time to call the hospital and get him admitted.

She laid her hand on the boy's cheek. "Go back to sleep for now."

She had hardly stood up when she heard a voice coming

from the opposite end of the hall. At first it was incoherent, and she thought one of the boys must be mumbling in his sleep. But as she paced quickly down the aisle, she made out the words. Except it wasn't words, it was a name—spoken in a voice that made Diana's blood run cold.

"Thomas . . . Thomas?"

Clarissa sat up where she had fallen asleep in her clothes on the last bed to the left. As Diana approached her, she swung her legs off the bed. Even in the darkened space her eyes glittered, focusing on something only she could see.

"Clarissa." Diana used her softest voice, as she did with the boys. "Are you all right?"

"Where are you?" Clarissa whispered urgently.

Moving slowly so as not to startle her, Diana touched her hand to Clarissa's hot forehead.

"Clarissa, can you lie back down for me? I need to take your temperature."

She almost jumped when the headmistress clutched her hand, hard enough to hurt. "Did you see him?"

"Clarissa, please lie down." She didn't want to wake the boys by calling out for Weston or Mrs. McCann.

"Did you see him?"

"Did I see who?" Diana continued to gently press on Clarissa's shoulders, guiding her to lie back down.

"I saw him, I did, I saw him!"

Please don't say it, Diana thought. *The last thing I can cope with right now is the hallucination of—*

"Thomas," Clarissa said with hoarse excitement. "I saw Thomas, I'm sure of it. He was watching over me while I slept. Did you see where he went?"

As a rule Diana didn't believe in coddling unreality in patients. But she was a medical professional with more than a dozen influenza patients and a headmistress who had such a high fever that she was hallucinating the ghost of her dead brother.

"I didn't see him, no."

"I have to go after him!"

Diana held her fast and, with enormous relief, heard the familiar tread of Joshua's footsteps coming toward them.

"Can you help me talk her down?" she asked. "She's got a fever, and she thinks she's seeing her brother."

Joshua cleared his throat and moved to Clarissa's other side. "You can't do anything for Thomas if you're sick, Clarissa. Let Diana help you. And get some rest; Thomas needs you to be well."

His gentleness succeeded. Clarissa submitted to Diana's medical attention, and within half an hour she'd fallen asleep in a clean nightdress, aspirin working to lower her fever.

Diana had barely straightened up from her newest patient's bed when someone called loudly "Nurse!"

Halfway down the dining hall, Luther Weston sat on Percy Nicholson's bed, supporting him by the shoulders and trying to staunch the blood pouring from the boy's nose. In the time it took Diana to get to Percy, he coughed up sputum tinged with more blood.

"Call the hospital and get an ambulance out here now," she commanded Joshua. "Mrs. McCann, help me screen the bed."

The makeshift screens had been lurking along the walls, rolling classroom blackboards draped with sheets. Maneuvered into place around Percy's bed, they would block sight but not sound. She could only hope the others were sleeping soundly enough not to be disturbed.

With oil lamps lighting the bed, Diana dismissed thoughts of any patient except Percy and set about doing everything she could for him. It was precious little. She had no supplemental oxygen available, though she suspected it wouldn't matter. She had seen soldiers deteriorate like this in hospital—falling in just minutes from a tolerable level to the threshold of death.

She directed Weston to sit behind Percy and brace him upright. Joshua returned and she asked, "Is the ambulance on the way?"

"None are available. I rang the farm—Granddad is bringing our automobile."

Diana's heart sank; she knew it probably wouldn't matter. After her first hundred deaths in France, she'd developed an instinct. She'd also developed the ability to work automatically, her body knowing what to do and her mind shutting out everything but the immediate moment.

Fresh linen quickly covered in blood and discarded on the floor . . . Mrs. McCann keeping up a low and comforting murmur in Percy's ear . . . Joshua at Diana's side, handing her linens or basins or a wet cloth to smooth across Percy's face . . . the terrible, distinctive moaning gasp of agonal breathing . . .

Have mercy, Diana thought to anyone or anything that might be present in the cold universe. And mercy was given, for Percy suffered through only three twitching agonal breaths before everything in him relaxed and released. His head canted back against Weston's shoulder and Diana saw the softness of expression that sometimes blessed the dead. Joshua rested his hand on her shoulder, and she forced her hands to open and flex, as though letting go of any hold she had on her patient.

"What else?" Weston demanded.

Diana shook her head. "There is nothing else. He's gone." She checked the watch pinned to her blouse. "Time of death: one thirty-seven a.m., fifteenth November."

"You're quitting?"

"He's dead. How many more ways do you want me to say it?" she hissed through her teeth. "And keep your voice down, unless you want to wake up and frighten every other boy in here."

She needed Weston to stop talking. She needed to keep calm. She needed to move Percy's body before panic could spread.

Joshua read her mind. "If we wrap him carefully, I can carry him to the nearest bedroom." His voice was thin and unsteady, and Diana felt a moment's passionate wish that she could throw herself into his arms and they could weep together.

Diana and Mrs. McCann wrapped Percy in three layers of clean linen, gently drawing it over his face. Joshua carried him to an empty dormitory room. To her dull surprise, Diana saw Weston cross himself. She lingered in the doorway while Joshua laid him carefully on an unmade bed, wanting one moment alone with the boy. To apologize, and say goodbye.

Joshua straightened up and turned to her, his face shadowed. He took a step forward and Diana went to meet him. But she only got close enough to catch at his arm as he crashed to the floor.

When she knelt beside him, he was burning with fever.

CHAPTER THIRTY-FOUR

ISMAY
APRIL 1461

Those that were adversaries and enemies to the Duke of York, on the thirtieth day of December the Year of Our Lord 1460 they fell upon the duke and killed him outside Wakefield, and his son Edmund the Earl of Rutland. When the death of these lords was known, great sorrow was made for them. May God have mercy on their souls.

On the twenty-ninth day of March the Year of Our Lord 1461, on that most holy Palm Sunday, our lord and great king Edward, son of the slain Duke of York, did defeat the enemies of the people in battle at Towton in Yorkshire. Margaret of Anjou and the aforesaid King Henry, being ill-loved by those they claimed to rule, fled to Scotland. The Sun in Splendor now shines over all.

Ismay was not surprised when one of her men told her Edward was coming to Havencross. He'd been in the North for more than a month now, mopping up the last pockets of Lancastrian resistance after Towton. Not that she'd been expecting him to come see her. She didn't expect anything anymore.

Except one thing . . .

At fully seven months gone, there was little chance of hiding her condition. Ismay stood in the forecourt, hand resting on the swell of her pregnancy, and watched England's king arrive at her home.

It was so hard to credit—careless, reckless, impudent, charming Edward as king. His father, yes. Richard of York had been a natural to politics and governing and the kind of worrying that leaders did. Edmund had had some of those gifts, but Edward? She supposed they would all just have to wait and see.

He hadn't taken on royal airs, at least not yet. He swung down from his horse and patted the shoulder of the boy who took his reins. Then he came straight to Ismay and took her hands in his, quick eyes and quicker mind understanding all.

"I am glad," he said, "that there will be something of Edmund still in the world. I am so sorry, my dear sister, that I could not bring him home to you."

Ismay would never have guessed that Edward's kindness would be the thing that broke her. She had not cried when the first rumors reached her of the Battle of Wakefield, had not cried when those few of her men who survived the battle returned to Havencross, had not cried when those men told her of Edmund's brutal death, her seventeen-year-old husband murdered by the Duke of Somerset while attempting to reach sanctuary.

Now she wept. So deeply and for so long that she was hardly aware when Edward easily swept her up and carried her inside.

When at last the flood receded, she and Edward were alone in the small space that had long ago been her father's study.

He handed her a cup of spiced wine and, by the time she'd drained it, Ismay felt scoured clean—and empty. The emptiness where Edmund was not, and would never again be, short of heaven.

"Do you have any questions for me?" Edward asked.

She shook her head. "I know all I ever want to know about what happened at Wakefield."

"So do I," he said grimly.

For the first time, Ismay considered someone else's grief. Edward bowed his head over his clasped hands, and she studied what she could see of his face. His jawline was sharper and his left cheek showed the ravages and scars of recent battles.

"Edward." She leaned forward and placed one hand atop his clenched ones. "I am also sorry. For you, your mother, your siblings . . . oh God, Richard and George are so young still! Your father—"

Edward pulled away. "My father should have stayed put inside Sandal Castle and waited for me to arrive."

She wanted to say something more, to acknowledge the loss of the brother he'd been so close to, something as graceful as he had managed for her. But before her eyes she saw Edward put on the mask of leadership.

Of kingship.

"I can't stay," Edward said abruptly. "I'm expected at Middleham to make decisions about the prisoners."

"I appreciate you coming to see me." Ismay hesitated before adding, "Your Majesty."

He looked almost angry for a moment, but Edward of York, Edward the Earl of March and, it seemed, even Edward IV of England retained his innate sense of humor. His lips twitched into a reluctant smile and he leaned back in his seat, long legs stretched before him.

"I didn't come for you to fawn over me," he said. "We have business, you and I. With my father gone, I'm the head of the family."

For a brief moment, Ismay wondered what Cecily Neville would say to that.

Edward plowed on. "You, Ismay, are a member of my family, and so will Edmund's child be. It goes without saying that, even without those ties, I would consider it a matter of honor to ensure a girl raised in my father's household never lacked for anything. But you are tied to us, legally."

"Do you expect me to announce the marriage now?" she asked. "To trade on the most precious, private hours of my life in order to curry favor at your court?"

"No."

"Then why did you come, Edward?"

"Because I thought it possible that you were pregnant. As you are. Which means you and I need to have a conversation before I return to London for my coronation."

"Why?" she asked again. Edmund, she thought briefly, would have already known. His mind, turned to governing and politics, would have looked ahead, would have known what was coming.

"I am only king today because my father died at Wakefield," Edward explained. "I have no children of my own—not legitimate, anyway. Until I'm married and have sons, my brothers are my successors. If Edmund had lived, he would be my immediate heir."

Ismay refused to understand. "But Edmund didn't live."

"You and Edmund were married. Your child will be legitimate. If that child is a boy—"

"Absolutely not. Never."

"—your son takes precedence. Ismay, you want to think about it carefully. Once decisions are made and written into statute—"

"This child is all I have left. The only thing that this war for England's throne has left me. I am finished with battles and courts and eternal fighting over who should rule. I appreciate what you're offering, Edward, I do. But please, keep me out of this. You haven't told anyone about the marriage, have you?"

"No. Edmund was waiting until . . . until the fighting was over."

"Then don't tell anyone. There's no point to it now."

"You're about to give birth, Ismay. People will think—"

"I don't care what people think. Let them whisper. Let them scorn my child for a bastard. It doesn't matter. The only thing that matters is that I be allowed to raise my child here, far away from other people's fights. Promise me, Edward."

She knew she'd won when he said, with a glint in his eyes, "You might change your mind when people assume the child is mine."

She laughed, something she hadn't thought would happen again. "Just one more on a long list, then."

"Are you certain, Ismay? When I return to London, Warwick will draw up legal papers naming George as my heir until such time as I have sons. You won't regret it?"

Ismay gave a shiver for the ten-year-old George about to be thrown to the wolves. The reminder of Warwick only strengthened her resolve. If there was one person on earth that she never wanted to know the truth about her marriage and child, it was the Earl of Warwick. "I will regret nothing."

"All the same, I'll leave these with you." From the pouch he'd tossed on the table, Edward pulled out two items. The first was a livery badge, to be worn by servants and couriers and those going into battle—such badges were separate from coats of arms. Edward's coat of arms now was the royal one, with its lions and lilies. But his badge, the one he handed her, was different.

The five-petaled white rose of York, so familiar to Ismay, had been placed atop the golden rays of the sun. Even in her isolation and grief, Ismay had heard the stories about the Battle of Mortimer's Cross, how three suns had been seen in the sky before battle, how Edward had given a rousing speech claiming it a sign of God's favor on him.

"The Sun in Splendor," she whispered. And for just a moment, she allowed herself to imagine what a brilliant, charming, cultivated court Edward would create and imagined herself there . . .

But she couldn't imagine herself there without Edmund.

Edward slid a heavy ring onto the middle finger of her right hand. It had a similar design to the badge etched deeply into the surface.

"Your seal?" Ismay asked, shocked.

"A variation of it, for my family and nearest advisors. This way, if you need something to be seen only by me, you can seal it with this and it will remain private."

An optimistic if naïve hope—Ismay wagered that Warwick knew multiple ways to read sealed letters—but the meaning of it touched her. Especially when Edward put his hands on her cheeks and kissed her on the forehead.

"Anything you need, Ismay, for the rest of your life. You have but to ask and England will answer."

It was only as he rode off that Ismay realized Edward had indeed made the jump to king—by equating himself with England.

CHAPTER THIRTY-FIVE

JULIET
2018

Juliet spent the second week of December in a haze of happiness untainted by any of her usual anxieties. Even as a child she'd been careful about showing what she felt, an instinct honed to razor sharpness from the years with Duncan. But Noah Bennett was the most open, unguarded person she'd ever met, and she found enormous relief in letting go and not worrying about herself or him or what was happening or what was going to happen.

They spent the whole of one Saturday entertaining Rachel's three boys. Noah set up a game that had them racing to carry trash from the third-floor rooms to the dumpster, mopping floors, and dusting windowsills. Though Juliet felt a few moments of piercing loss for what Liam would never get to do, mostly she enjoyed this world of uncomplicated affection and belonging.

Noah had to return to Newcastle to work, but they spoke every night and counted down to his ten-day Christmas break.

"Your family doesn't mind you staying with me during the holiday?" she asked him one evening.

"Rachel just grins in a maddeningly know-it-all way, and Aunt Winnie said of course you need company seeing as how you can't leave Havencross at night. Though I'd wager they all know that company isn't the only thing I'm offering."

In between sorting, cleaning, and Noah, Juliet explored the boxes Nell had brought. The solicitor's files were as meticulous as her appearance, which definitely made life easier for a historian.

One collection consisted of newspaper reports and copied field notes from the excavation carried out on Havencross property the summer of 1919—the one from which the coins and livery badge Juliet had seen in Berwick had come. The notes confirmed the likelihood of the ruined icehouse being the terminus of a tunnel, but there had been no recorded efforts to find the opening at that time. Juliet set all this aside for Noah's professional eye and moved on.

She followed the legal property ownership backward, starting with the tangled family trust that had ended with the hotel financiers buying them all out. Nell Somersby-Sims and Juliet's mother were two of five surviving descendants of Sir Wilfred Somersby and his second wife, Sylvia; those descendants had inherited their shares in Havencross after Clarissa Somersby's death in 1992. It was Wilfred's father, Gideon, who had built the flamboyant structure around the medieval core, after clearing out the remains of the Elizabethan and Georgian additions. Although the officials' handwriting grew harder to read the further back the photocopied documents went, the property of Havencross could be traced through previous Somersby owners all the way to Queen Mary Tudor. In 1554, she had assigned "the property and estate known as Havencross, presently held by the crown, in the county of Northumberland, to Henry Somersby, knight, in recognition of his devoted service to the queen in maintaining her right to the throne."

There were a handful of other papers in the same file—two covered with notes and questions Nell Somersby-Sims had made, plus photocopies of two documents written in Latin. With an exaggerated sigh of difficulty—she was really very curious—Juliet opened a Latin-to-English translation app on her phone to double-check Nell's handwritten translation on the back of the page.

The first was brief and direct: on 29 June 1461, Edward IV confirmed "*the absolute rights and honors of the property of Havencross in the county of Northumberland to the Lady Ismay Deacon and her heirs in perpetuity.*"

The second was slightly more complicated.

"*On this first day of November the Year of Our Lord 1471, the property and estate known as Havencross in the county of Northumberland reverts to the crown. Said property to be held by the crown without prejudice or favor in the interests of a proven heir to the previous owner, Lady Ismay Deacon. Said property not to be assigned to anyone but said heir for a minimum of seventy years. By order of His Gracious Majesty, King of England, Ireland, and France, Edward R., signed by his own hand this day at Westminster.*"

Curiouser and curiouser. Juliet talked it over with Noah by phone later as she did her nightly sweep of windows and doors, making sure everything was locked and closed and not leaking as Northumberland sullenly made its way toward Christmas with freezing rain.

"It sounds to me," she said, "like something more happened here than just a simple death. If Ismay Deacon and her family had died out, then why would the king have put in that clause about not giving away the property for seventy years? It's like he expected—or hoped—that someone would show up with a rightful claim to Havencross."

"And," Noah pointed out, "why would the king himself care? That bit about signing it in his own hand—I'm sure he had whole organizations to do that kind of business. You should take photos of all this and send it to Daniel in Berwick. It's his period; maybe he'll have ideas about where to look for explanations."

"Perfect. I know it's silly, and totally not what I came here to do, but every time I get into the research for the flu epidemic at the school, I find myself directed further back. And obviously Clarissa Somersby had some interest in all this, considering the books and things she left behind."

"You don't have to justify yourself to me. I rather think, in my very limited experience, that the best historians are those who can follow their instincts. If you only tread the same paths others have, you'll only ever reach the same conclusions."

"Very poetic," she teased, but it did her good to be confirmed. She had always longed for approval—as much as she disliked that in herself, and as much as she was learning to recognize and follow her own choices, it was still nice to be met with wholehearted support and not critical, cutting questions.

After a few, rather more personal, exchanges, Juliet hung up and finished walking the ground floor. Every door and window down here was securely locked. "Not that it keeps you out," she found herself saying aloud. "Whoever you are."

But whoever you are, I'm not afraid of you. At least, no more afraid than any sudden exposure to the unexpected might make one. She didn't especially want to round a corner and come face to face with the little ghost boy—or the shadowy female that flickered on the edge of her awareness—but she didn't think Havencross or any of its old inhabitants were a threat to her.

She went up the grand front staircase and made her sweep of the second floor, then passed into the medieval section. For the first time since the night of her surprising impression of a woman and newborn baby, she felt something calling to her. It was the sense of something lying in wait, something she half-remembered or dreamed.

Juliet grabbed her bedside flashlight and opened the door leading up to the solar. She commented aloud on her own actions as she climbed, a trick she'd had as a child to keep anxiety under control. "Yes, it's always a good idea to explore a haunted house at night. By yourself. Every movie I've ever seen tells me that this is a perfectly wonderful idea. Maybe there's a surprise party waiting for me up there."

Of course there wasn't a surprise party—there wasn't anything. She'd been up here once a week since her arrival and it was just the same: the light of a single bare bulb and her own flashlight illuminating the bare corners of the space. Empty and echoing and innocent.

She had begun to descend when she heard half-remembered sounds coming loudly and clearly from the windows behind her: the drumming of hooves on packed earth, the creak and murmur of leather saddles, the iron jangle of armed riders.

Men on horseback. The awareness shot through her with the suddenness of a lightning strike, and she dropped the flashlight. It went out when it hit the floor, and she shot back up into the solar. Though she'd already turned off the overhead bulb, it wasn't dark. Light came through the windows as though it were afternoon, not six hours after sunset. It touched and traced and bounced off the outlines of furniture—enormous chests, solid tables—and tapestries along the walls.

Juliet was not possessed. She knew exactly who she was and that something extraordinarily odd was happening, but she was herself as she moved to the windows.

And then, between one step and the next, she was someone else entirely, frantically counting horsemen and searching for the identifying banner—

She'd known what it would be, and yet she'd hoped. For George, maybe, for as detestable as his actions were, he surely held her in fondness, and he was by all reports as changeable a man as he'd been a boy. She'd known him since he was tiny and she could use that, could twist all his mixed-up loyalties against him . . .

But it was not the royal banner with its three silver bars marking George's distance from his brother's throne.

It was the white bear and ragged staff on a field of red—the banner of the Kingmaker himself, the Earl of Warwick.

She knew, in that moment, there would be no clemency. Warwick dealt only in death.

By the time the terror receded enough for Juliet to remember who and where and when she was, she was back in her bedroom with no memory of having reached there. And although she was afraid, it was not for herself. It was for whatever had happened here that was so terrible it still had the power to frighten after centuries. She lay awake for a long time before her heartbeat returned to normal.

She was woken up before dawn, not by anything supernatural but the simple ding of an incoming text. Followed rapidly by several more.

Duncan. Juliet's stomach dropped as she saw that he had abandoned his attempts to be persuasive and reasonable. Her silence had finally provoked him to rage, and venom dripped through every hateful accusation and furious charge he flung at her now. *Never loved me . . . social climber . . . frigid bitch . . . whore . . .*

Dimly, Juliet wondered how Duncan rationalized those opposite adjectives, but his last text pushed all other thoughts from her mind. It was a photograph, taken through an airport terminal window, of a plane pulled up to a jetway.

A British Airways plane.

CHAPTER THIRTY-SIX

DIANA
NOVEMBER 1918

CASE NOTEBOOK

15 Nov., 1:37 a.m.: Percy Nicholson died. Wrapped and placed the body in an empty dormitory bedroom to await transport to the morgue. Joshua Murray ill: temperature 104, pulse 65. No lung rales.

15 Nov., 5:00 a.m.: Ambulance arrived. Sent George Humphrey and Max Lovell to hospital. Undertaker sent for. Clarissa Somersby continues a high temperature of 104.2.

15 Nov., 3:00 p.m.: Percy Nicholson's body removed to local morgue. Mrs. McCann fainted. Temperature 102.6. Nearly had to tie her down to keep her in bed.

16 Nov., 7:00 a.m.: Spoke by phone with Dr. Bennett. Lawrence Dean died two hours ago. Hospital overloaded, will try to send a relief nurse to me.

What is this flu that kills the young and healthy so suddenly?

* * *

There had been no shortage of long hours in France—nurses routinely worked forty-eight hours at a time with only snatches of coffee or twenty-minute naps. But Diana had never felt so close to drowning as she did on that fifth day of quarantine. Only she, Luther Weston, and Jasper Willis remained influenza-free. Leaving the boy and his broken leg in a private quarantine meant two adults to care for thirteen patients.

Dr. Bennett had promised to find a relief nurse for her by the end of the day; there were hours that Diana didn't think she'd make it. As soon as she finished rounds on the ward—taking everyone's temperature and pulse, checking their breathing and pain levels, treating any bleeding, and administering aspirin and salicin—it was almost time to start over again. Plus ensuring the patients were drinking and taking broth, if able, and changing linens . . . Diana hadn't cried on a ward since 1915. She almost broke that streak a dozen times that Saturday.

In France, she'd never known her patients before they needed care. And although she grew attached to a few of them, mostly they moved in and through so quickly that it was all she could do to keep up with the necessities of care for young men that, whatever their age, were officially old enough to go to war. Caring for vulnerable schoolboys, away from their families and trying so hard to be brave, was something else entirely.

Not to mention Joshua. From the moment he'd collapsed at her feet, Diana was forced into the difficulty of professional nursing in the face of personal feelings. She could not allow her feelings for him to dictate differences in how she worked—but God, it was hard! When all she wanted to do was sit by his bedside and will him to get better.

At 5 p.m. the promised relief nurse finally arrived. Miss Bartholomew was an upright, steel-haired retired nurse from Newcastle who appeared almost old enough to have served with Florence Nightingale in the Crimea. But she was sharp and capable of taking temperatures and administering aspirin and fluids. Immediately upon her arrival Diana sent Luther Weston off to sleep for several hours and got Miss Bartholomew adequately informed and up to speed.

When Weston returned to the dining hall at 8:30 p.m. looking remarkably refreshed, Diana didn't have to be told twice to go to bed. For the first time since Tuesday, she made her way to her own bedroom. She stripped off her stained, limp blouse and skirt and tried to decide whether to bathe first or simply fall onto the bed.

At that moment, her wardrobe doors began to shake and bang together.

The sound of footsteps, many heavy-booted feet tramping in the corridor, men's voices, the pounding of steel dagger hilts on closed doors and caskets, reverberating through her head and bones and—

"Stop it!" Diana balled up her skirt and threw it at her wardrobe. It hardly satisfied, so she snatched up her bedside clock and threw that as well. "Stop doing this to me! Why me? What do you want?"

She stopped screaming and listened, chest heaving with half-swallowed sobs. She could still hear the ring of steel and boots, but it had faded a little. Diana could almost imagine . . . something? someone? . . . pausing to cock their head. As though she'd at last caught their attention.

"Please," Diana whispered. All at once she didn't have the strength to stand any longer and she sank to the floor, leaning against the bed behind her. "Please let me be. I'm tired. I'm scared. I just want to save all these boys."

She knew in the tiny rational part that remained of her mind that she sounded ridiculous. But what did she have to lose?

"Can you help me? I don't know, talk to God maybe?"

Although wasn't the point of ghosts that they hadn't moved on to the afterworld? "Or at least give me a break. Just until this is over. Once I've saved everyone, haunt me until the day I die if you like. Just let me rest for now."

The noises stopped. In the end, Diana fell asleep on the floor and, when she woke, had to retrieve her clock from where she'd thrown it. Thank goodness it hadn't broken. She'd been asleep for two hours. She felt stiff and sore but clear-headed. And filthy.

She took a quick bath and was half dressed when someone knocked.

"Miss Neville?" Weston called.

"Come in."

He stopped when he saw she was just starting to button up her blouse.

"For God's sake," she said impatiently, "grow up and tell me what's going on."

She expected a simple recital of current conditions—surely if any patient had dramatically worsened they would have summoned her earlier.

"Miss Bartholomew was fetching fresh water from the kitchen while everyone was sleeping more or less peacefully. I had stepped out briefly to check on Jasper Willis."

It wasn't like Weston to draw things out. "And?" she prompted.

"Jasper's fine. But when I returned to the dining hall Austin Willis was not in his bed. Or in the washroom."

"Shit."

"And," he continued, sounding unnaturally subdued, "Clarissa Somersby is also gone."

"Are you kidding me?" Diana scrubbed at her face with her hand. Beyond caring what anyone thought of her language at this point, she swore like the soldiers she'd nursed. "What the fuck does Clarissa think she's doing?"

"I imagine it's exactly what you expect. She's gone in search of Thomas. And I'm afraid she's taken Austin with her."

"Shit, shit, shit." Diana considered the matter, the hour, the weather, then began to unbutton her skirt. "If you're offended by my female body, you might want to turn around. I'm not trawling the countryside in the middle of the night in a skirt."

She pulled on her motorcycling trousers and threw on her warmest sweater before grabbing a coat and knit hat. "I've got to check in with Miss Bartholomew," she said. "If everything's calm, then I need you to help me search. They couldn't have gone far."

Turned out, a seriously ill woman and a nine-year-old boy could get a lot farther than one would think, even in the rain and wind and dark. Sweeping beams of light around them with their torches, they quickly cleared the courtyard, the old stables, and the gardening shed.

Diana considered the matter quickly, knowing every minute was crucial. She had nothing concrete to go on, only suppositions and rumors, but wasn't that the plane on which Clarissa was operating? Her search for Thomas was powered by imagination, not logic.

Come hide with me in the icehouse.

The words resonated inside like the aftershocks of the explosion that had vibrated through her body in Viliers-Bretoneux. Why did she envision them being spoken in her ear by a young woman with long skirts?

They had to start somewhere. "Mr. Murray found Jasper Willis almost a mile from here at the remains of a medieval icehouse," Diana said. "Clarissa believed Jasper was following the same ghost her brother followed—she'd likely head that way. Taking Austin as a guide, maybe, hoping Thomas will appear to him. What do you think?"

"I've no better ideas. Can we get there in the dark?"

Since they had to do exactly that, Diana didn't bother to answer. The best thing that could be said for the weather was that it wasn't actively raining. The trek through the dark, damp, freezing landscape—with only their two darting torches providing light—was both miserable and too slow. Diana ached to run but knew that would only result in her or Weston stumbling or falling, and she could not afford to injure herself or the last healthy adult at the school.

They found Clarissa well short of the ruined icehouse walls, the white hem of her nightgown nearly glowing beneath a borrowed man's coat. She'd at least had the sense to pull on rubber boots, but the moment Diana saw her face she knew that common sense wasn't currently playing a big role in her decision-making.

"Diana! I'm so glad you've come!" Clarissa gripped her shoulder. She had no gloves, no torch. How the hell had they made it this far without any light?

"You've got to come back with me," Diana said as soothingly as she could manage through her fear and anger. "We'll get you safely back in bed, and warm. Clarissa, where is Austin?"

"He ran ahead. He could see him, the ghost boy, he followed him. I told him to leave me, not to lose sight of the boy."

At that, Diana's temper at last erupted. "Austin *is* the boy! He is the only boy that matters right now. Good God, Clarissa, how could you drag a nine-year-old out here in the middle of the night?!"

"He sees the same child Thomas used to."

"The same *dead* child. That's what a ghost is, Clarissa. And you seem determined to just keep adding to the account of dead boys at Havencross. If Austin is hurt or ill or, God forbid, dies because of what you've done tonight, I will never forgive you."

Clarissa looked like a little girl beginning to realize she'd done something wrong. Her eyes filled with tears. "I just wanted Thomas."

"Thomas is dead, Clarissa. And if you can't put the needs of living children before your dead brother, than you have no business running a school. Weston!"

He looked nearly as bemused as Clarissa by Diana's outburst and eyed her warily. "Yes?"

"Take her back to the house. I'm going after Austin."

"I can do that."

But Diana's expert eye had assessed the woman's physical state. "Clarissa's not going to stay on her feet all the way back," she said. "And I can't carry her. Besides, I'm the one who knows where to find Austin. Just hurry back."

If the small opening she and Joshua had made at the icehouse hadn't been widened, Diana might have missed it in the dark night. But Austin had clearly moved enough stones to get himself inside.

Diana lay with her stomach down on the ground and called into the opening: "Austin? Austin, are you there?"

For a long, terrifying moment there was silence. Then a rush of relief as she heard the boy call back faintly. "I'm here. Miss Somersby?"

"No, it's Miss Neville. Austin, I need you to come out now. I've got to get you back to bed before your mother gets angry with me."

"Ummm . . . I think I'm stuck. The tunnel kind of got thin and uneven, like maybe part of it fell in sometime?"

She batted a burst of panic away. "Stuck like there's no room for you to turn around? Can you just back your way out? I know it's uncomfortable."

"I tried. But I think something's snagged my shirt and I can't quite reach it, whatever it is. Can you help, Miss Neville?"

Diana drew in a deep breath and blew out. And then another. When she was sure she could speak without her voice shaking, she said, "Of course I can help. Just be still and I'll come to you."

Don't think of France, she commanded herself. *This is nothing like Viliers-Bretoneux. This time I'm deliberately entering a tunnel that narrows so much a nine-year-old boy can't free himself. It will be fine.*

Crawling through damp, cold earth with a torch in one hand was excruciating for both her body and mind. Panic lurked at the edges of her awareness, and she kept it back by keeping up a steady stream of words for Austin.

"It really doesn't seem fair of a ghost to want you to come in here," she said. "I don't suppose a spirit has so much trouble getting through narrow spaces. When we're out of here, Austin, we're going to have a serious conversation about logic and responsibility."

Finally her light glanced off the soles of his slippers. Unlike Clarissa, he hadn't managed to put on boots. "All right, Austin, I see you. I'm setting down the light, and I'll come up as carefully as I can and stretch my arm along your side. Which side are you caught on?"

"The right, miss."

Diana wedged the torch against the wall. Although she couldn't so much as crouch in the space, it wasn't as closed-in as she'd feared. It was a mess, though—as Austin had said, it looked as though there'd been some kind of collapse in earlier years. It was that mess of fallen-in debris that had snagged the hem of his shirt—the fabric had caught firmly around a rock and Austin's efforts to free himself had only tangled it tighter.

Diana teased the fabric free. "Okay, Austin, you can back up now. I'm going to crawl back a short way and then you should be able to get past me."

"I can just follow you out."

"Absolutely not. Look what happened when we took our eyes off you for five minutes. You're going out ahead of me so I can be sure you don't take any sudden detours."

"Yes, miss."

She heard the relief in his voice, ample payment for her efforts at speaking calmly. As promised, after they'd both backed up for maybe fifty feet, the tunnel widened enough for Austin to wiggle past her and turn around. Very carefully, Diana managed to get herself turned the right direction as well.

"All right, lead the way," she told him, and set herself to follow his slippers. At least they weren't belly-crawling any longer; they both had enough room to be on their hands and knees.

Diana bumped the torch against the tunnel wall, and in the wavering light, she thought she saw the outline of a boy—one most definitely not Austin. For one thing, he was standing up, with his lower legs sunk into the earth as though rising from a grave.

For another thing, he was transparent.

She yelped and Austin cried, "What's wrong, miss?'

Opening her mouth to ask him to move faster, Diana hadn't made a sound when she felt the vibration and heard the rumble that her body recognized before her brain.

"Watch out!" she called, crouching and throwing her arms up to cover her head. And then there was nothing but the roar of violent collapse and the taste of violent earth in her mouth.

CHAPTER THIRTY-SEVEN

DIANA
NOVEMBER 1918

Oh God, oh God, oh God, oh God . . . Diana was sure she was screaming, but her ears caught only a whimper. Her ears and mouth were full of dirt, and everything was dark and damp, and she couldn't see, and she couldn't move—

That was not her whimper. Awareness kicked her brain into gear. She spit out loose dirt and croaked, "Austin? Are you all right?"

"Miss—Miss Neville? I lost my torch."

"So did I." To her shock, Diana could hear that her voice was steady. *Nothing like a child depending on you to keep you calm.* "Not to worry, the tunnel only goes one place. We can't get lost."

Which was true enough—except Diana rapidly realized that the main fall had come down between her and Austin. No wonder his voice was so muffled and far away sounding.

She took a couple minutes, chatting inconsequentially as she moved, to try and work out how much debris lay between her and the boy. Too much to move quickly on her own, she decided.

"Austin, I need your help." Best to give people a mission, she'd found. Being responsible for someone else could, as she well knew, allay the worst of fear. "I'm going to need help to dig my way out of here. You need to get out of the tunnel the way you got in and get back to the school. You'll probably meet Mr. Weston on your way. Tell him what happened, and that he'll need some kind of tools to dig through to me."

"It's so dark."

"I know. I'm sorry. But I really need the help."

Though she knew she couldn't distinguish such small sounds through the muffling dirt, Diana imagined the gulping swallow that preceded Austin's slightly firmer, "Yes. I'll go. Miss Neville?" He sounded suddenly and sweetly concerned. "Are you all right in the dark?"

"Oh yes. The dark doesn't frighten me."

True. It wasn't the dark that disturbed her as she heard the faint sounds of Austin's movements fade away completely. It was the pressing, squeezing, all-encompassing sense of being trapped, of the earth moving all around her, wrapping around her subtly, sneakily, just waiting to draw her deeper into itself until she was trapped forever, gasping for air and light and life . . . Her head spun, cold sweat broke out along her hairline, and if it hadn't already been completely dark, her eyesight would have dimmed.

"Deep breaths," the doctor had advised. Diana counted and breathed, and counted and breathed, and slowly, slowly she forced herself to take stock of her condition and surroundings. She was sore and her left shoulder and arm had twisted painfully, but she didn't think she was bleeding anywhere or that she'd hit her head. All she had to do was wait.

She'd had to wait before, in much less comfortable circumstances. At least a three-story chateau hadn't fallen on top of her now, and she wasn't trapped with wounded men she couldn't get to, and there weren't enemy soldiers on their way who might get to her before her own people. She just had to . . . wait.

She will come.

The thought was not hers. Diana could swear she felt the breath of the phrase like cobwebs against her skin. And not just once; the words continued to murmur like a hope, a promise, a prayer: *She will come, she will come, she will, she will, she will . . .*

Much sooner than she expected, Diana heard the sound of someone moving through the tunnel on the other side of the fall. "Weston?" she called.

"It's Michael Murray, Miss Neville. Joshua rang the farm and told us what was happening. I saw the young lad squeezing his way out of the tunnel and ran him back to the school in the automobile. Don't you worry, lass, we'll get you out of there right quick."

She could already hear the movement of earth on the other side. She imagined Joshua's grandfather shoveling away, the solid farmer passing out buckets of dirt along the tunnel to Weston, and yet he still managed to keep up a flow of words directed at her. She wondered if Joshua had told him that she was claustrophobic.

Diana wasn't passive—she used her hands to dig what she could from her side. The moment of breakthrough came with a shaft of light from a torch and the nearly imperceptible feel of moving air. She closed her eyes and offered up a wordless thanks. Then she reached up toward the opening and began to dig away from it.

She knew the familiar shape and weight of the coins the moment she touched them. *More medieval coins?* Since she wasn't going to die today, Diana went ahead and pocketed the ones she found among the debris. Then her fingertips touched something unusual. Not stone or metal but a stiff oval about the size of her palm. As the opening widened enough for Mr. Murray's face to come into view, there was just enough light for Diana to realize she had no idea what she was holding. She managed to fit it into her empty trouser pocket and focused on squeezing through the hole before her.

Never had she been happier to step into the open air—not even in Viliers-Bretoneux when, after fourteen hours of being buried, she'd been so traumatized, exhausted, and hungry she hadn't felt more than a dull relief. She stepped away, to allow Mr. Murray to follow her out, and prepared to thank Luther Weston. Standing next to Weston was the face Diana most wanted to see—but not when he was feverish and ill.

"Joshua Murray." She summoned her best nursing voice. "What do you think you're doing out of bed in the middle of November—in the middle of the *night*—when you have influenza?"

He was pale and shivering but steady on his feet. "Do you really think I'd stay in bed knowing you were caught underground? Use your common sense, woman."

His teasing tone was no more serious than her scolding one, and Diana assumed Weston was rolling his eyes as Joshua wrapped his arms around her. Beneath the heat of his fever she felt a trembling that matched her own. Despite knowing what awaited her back at the school, despite her ever-present fear for all the sick boys and adults under her care, Diana felt the same thing she had on her first day at the moors: the assurance that she had come home.

CHAPTER THIRTY-EIGHT

JULIET
2018

Juliet spent the night tossed between dreams of threatening medieval horsemen and threatening ex-husband. At some point, the two bled together. First she dreamt that armed men had invaded the university campus where she'd once worked, and next she saw Duncan looming at her from a corner raising a two-handed sword.

She dragged herself out of bed at eight, wondering why the light from the windows looked so odd. She looked out, and caught her breath at the fairyland spread below: it had snowed in the night. Juliet, who'd lived so long in Maine, judged at least ten inches covered the ground and the priory ruins she could see from her bedroom window.

Throwing on the first sweatshirt she could find, she dashed to the elaborate Victorian bedroom at the front of the house and actually smiled at how beautiful it was outside. The snow smoothed out the rough turf and overgrown hedges, and the stone bridge looked like something out of a misty-hued calendar photograph.

Flakes still drifted lazily down from the leaden skies, and Juliet immediately conjured up a day spent wrapped in blankets and reading to her heart's content until Noah arrived—

Noah. That narrow bridge. And a river that, despite the cold, was still flowing, and whose level had risen dangerously overnight. Juliet ran back to her bedroom, finally noticing that her bare feet were freezing, and rang Noah while pulling on wool socks.

"I hear it snowed up there" were the first words out of Noah's mouth.

"It didn't snow in Newcastle?" she asked.

"Not much to speak of. Six inches or so. You're not worried about me getting there, are you?" he teased.

"A little." Juliet had been checking a weather app while they talked. "It looks like the snow's going to start up again in the afternoon."

"I've lived here all my life, Juliet. I know how to get around Northumberland, even if it's a blizzard. My car has four-wheel drive and it's plenty heavy to navigate safely."

Yes, that heavy, wide car of his. "My worry is the stone bridge," she said. "The water level is awfully close to the track. If it floods over—"

"If it floods over, I can go round to the farmhouse first. We've got a tractor that could get me through Antarctica if necessary. You're not getting rid of me that easily, Juliet."

"That does make me feel better," she admitted.

As they'd talked, she'd kept seeing that image of the British Airways plane Duncan had sent her. It seemed her ex-husband had worked out, at least in a general way, where she was. She told herself it didn't matter. She told herself he liked nothing more than playing games and keeping her off-balance. It was only four days until Christmas. Even Duncan wasn't arrogant enough to think he could just fly to England and find her by instinct. This business about Havencross hadn't come up until after Liam's death, and there was no way her mother would have let slip anything to him. Juliet was perfectly safe. And when Noah arrived tonight, she would be perfectly happy.

"Are you sure you're all right?" Noah asked.

She didn't want to worry him, but she also didn't want to lie. "My ex-husband has been texting me for the last while. He's got problems at the university. Look, if you're really interested, I'll tell you all about our breakup tonight. There's nothing to worry about though. Duncan is an asshole, that's it. I'd much rather think about you."

"If you're sure," he said, a little doubtfully. Noah had an instinct for reading her, even through the phone. It was a warming thought. "Listen," he added, "If the weather does get worse, I'll get out of Newcastle as soon as I can. You remember how to check the boiler and where all the torches and candles are?"

"I remember."

"Even if the power doesn't go out, you might want to light a fire in your little sitting room fireplace. With enough blankets on the floor . . ." He trailed off suggestively.

Juliet laughed and hung up. *Today is a good day*, she told herself firmly. *And tonight will be perfect.*

She dressed warmly, had one of Rachel's homemade scones for breakfast, and began her circuit of the house. It had weathered the night's snowfall without incident, but if the reports were right the next part of the storm would include gale-force winds. For the first time since her arrival, Juliet closed the heavy wooden shutters that framed most of the Victorian windows.

The ensuing darkness was spookier than the nighttime, and Juliet was glad to get back to her section of Havencross, which had been built to withstand both sieges and storms. Nothing would get through the ten-foot-thick walls of the medieval core.

In the little sitting room, she stocked all the necessary supplies for a power outage: firewood, matches, solid pillar candles, two oil lamps, extra batteries for the flashlights, five blankets, crackers and teacakes and protein bars, plus two bottles of wine. She rounded the house twice more, as the shortest day of the year passed quickly toward night, and finished with a visit to the boiler. As far as she could tell it was working fine. By the time she headed back to her room the blizzard had begun in earnest.

Heavy snow was one thing—a blizzard was an entirely different creature. Juliet had experienced three or four blizzards during her years in Maine and knew how quickly a person could get disoriented with snow stinging their face and wind sucking their breath. The vortex of movement could make it seem like the snow wasn't so much falling as attacking from every single direction, including the ground.

Juliet stood at the Victorian front-bedroom window, from where the bridge was no longer visible. She watched the whirling snow until she grew dizzy, then retreated to her cozy little aerie. Setting aside the historian mind-set for now, she lost herself in a classic Daphne du Maurier novel she'd found abandoned in one of the third-floor servants' rooms.

It was 5 p.m. the next time she checked her phone. It also seemed she'd lost cell connection—no bars showing, and no missed calls or texts from Noah. *That's all right. He'll come.* And in case of emergency, she had the landline phone in Clarissa's ground-floor bedroom.

She stretched and considered trekking downstairs to make a sandwich but decided to wait for Noah. At least she could put on something slightly more attractive for later, if only underneath her thermal tee and leggings. Smiling at the thought of Noah discovering her laciest bra, Juliet stepped into the corridor.

The house had been unusually silent today, the hush of falling snow broken now only by the wild winds. But the moment she set foot outside her sitting room, Juliet was enveloped in a swell of noise: *footsteps, many heavy-booted feet tramping in the corridor, men's voices, the pounding of steel dagger hilts on closed doors and caskets, reverberating through her head and bones—*

Juliet yelped and darted across to her bedroom door. Her hand lifted the medieval latch, and through the noise she thought, *I'm sure I left this door open.*

She shoved the door open wider, hoping the corridor noise wouldn't follow, hoping for a space in which to pull herself together and figure out what the hell was going on—

"Hello, Juliet. I've missed you."

Duncan smiled at Juliet from her bed, the predatory smile she'd long had cause to distrust. As she backed away, he slowly stood up, never taking his eyes off her.

"We're going to talk," he said. "And then you're coming home with me."

CHAPTER THIRTY-NINE

ISMAY
MARCH 1471

And then did the Earl of Warwick remove himself from the side of King Edward. First Warwick counseled and enticed George, Duke of Clarence, to wed his eldest daughter without the advice or knowledge of King Edward. Wherefore the king took great displeasure with his brother and Warwick both.

Then did John Neville, brother of the Earl of Warwick, enter into a conspiracy, the object of which was to seize King Edward. As soon as this reached the king's ears by spy, he found himself compelled to consult his own safety and take flight to the port of Bishop's Lynn, in Norfolk. Here, finding some ships, he caused himself and his followers, nearly two thousand in number, to be conveyed across the sea to the Duke of Burgundy. These events took place about the festival of Michaelmas, in the Year of Our Lord 1470, it being the ninth year of the reign of the said king Edward.

In this manner did the Earl of Warwick gloriously triumph over the said king Edward.

* * *

From the moment that rumors of Warwick's doubtful loyalty to King Edward began to filter up to Havencross, Ismay carried a hard stone of dread in her chest. She dealt with her fear in much the same way she'd learned from Duchess Cecily—to prepare as thoroughly as possible for the worst scenario. Long ago Ismay had laid plans for her son's safety, beyond that offered by Edward. Now her wisdom was repaid.

She would never let anyone in England lay hands on her son for political purposes.

Perhaps it had been foolish to name the child after his father, but the moment their son was laid in her arms Ismay had felt Edmund with her. She gave the child her surname, branding him a bastard, but that needn't destroy his future so long as she taught him to keep his expectations in hand.

Which, she admitted, was not much of a problem for a nine-year-old whose greatest excitement was riding his little mare and whose greatest hope was to someday see the great city of York. He had the fair hair and blue eyes of his father and the king, but in features and curiosity he reminded Ismay of the youngest York child, Richard. She liked to think she'd given him his love for Havencross.

When Edward was betrayed by John Neville, forcing the king and eighteen-year-old Richard, his last loyal brother, to flee to Burgundy, Ismay could only give thanks that she hadn't been forced into her first proposed marriage. She wasn't terribly surprised by Johnny's switch in loyalties—and not in the slightest by Warwick's. He had always struck her as too clever, too ambitious, and too proud to stay in a king's shadow forever.

Just so long as the kingmaker kept his ambitions firmly in the south.

It was mid-March when the warning system Ismay had put into place throughout Northumberland and York sounded the first alarms. The warning was simple: the Earl of Warwick was coming to Middleham. Not unexpected—the northern castle had long been his home. But at only seventy miles from Havencross, it was enough to raise her fears.

It was unlikely Warwick would come to Havencross, she told herself. It had been more than eleven years since the earl had laid eyes on Ismay—odds were he had long ago forgotten her. Even if rumors of her bearing a bastard child had filtered through to him, what would he care? Bastards didn't matter.

Still, Ismay followed her plan. The first point of which entailed upsetting Edmund. "No leaving the immediate grounds for now," she instructed her son.

"For how long?" he asked.

"Until I say otherwise."

He thought for minute—like his father, Edmund took time to think before he spoke.

"Do you hear me?" she asked, when he made no reply.

"Yes, Mother."

Unfortunately, Edmund also had his royal uncle's trick of appearing to agree and then doing whatever he wanted.

The second time his tutor had to drag him back from the direction of the old icehouse, Ismay knew she'd have to tell her son something more.

She sat him down in the solar, his mouth and chin stubbornly set and blue eyes refusing to meet hers.

"Edmund, do you remember what I told you about your father's death?"

He couldn't keep from showing interest, for Ismay rarely referred to anything from the past. His gaze shot up to his mother's. "He died in battle."

"Yes."

"There were lots of battles, then," he added. "But not anymore."

"Sadly, Edmund, there have been battles this winter." When he perked up with excitement, she said, "And the only thing you have to remember about battles is to stay far away from them."

He sighed. "Which is why we live here."

"Yes. But sometimes, no matter how hard we try, battles will find us. It is possible, Edmund, that Havencross might be visited by unfriendly men this spring. If that happens, I must be able to find you quickly—and you must be willing to do whatever I ask. You trust me, don't you?"

"Yes, Mother." His eyes were round and wide, his chin stubborn. "But if the men come, I must defend you."

So like his father. "If these men come, Edmund, the only thing that matters is that they not find you. They will not hurt me—armed men don't threaten women." Ismay prayed for forgiveness as she told her son that blatant lie, but she needed him to respond to her every command instantly in case the worst were to happen.

For the next three days, Edmund stayed near her, obedient and subdued, and she prayed that this would be the worst of it. She hated that Warwick had the power after all these years to affect a boy he probably didn't even know existed.

Just in case it wasn't, she sent all the servants away to York with her steward—except for Edmund's tutor, whose help she would need in extremity. When the steward protested, Ismay said, "Have a holiday, buy supplies, go to church and pray. I don't care what you all do. But you are not to return until I summon you. It shouldn't be more than week." After all, how long could Warwick linger at Middleham? He was attempting to take over a country—he would need to be everywhere at the same time.

Two days after the servants left Havencross, the last warning sounded late on a Thursday afternoon as the sun faded rapidly in the west. Ismay found Edmund with his tutor, James Ascham, in the schoolroom across from her bedroom. Keeping her voice light, she said, "Edmund, go and get your warmest cloak and boots, please."

He paled. "They're coming?"

"It will be all right," she told him. "They think to catch us unawares, but they don't know how clever your mother is."

Edmund bit his lip, then tore out of the room to do as he was told.

"Time to go?" Ascham asked.

"You know what to do. Ride west to Carlisle and send a message to Scotland."

"And when I return?"

"Go directly to the old icehouse, where I showed you, and make your way to Edmund in the tunnel. He will be about a quarter-mile along, in a hollowed-out space large enough for him to stand up and move about a little. You know where to take him?"

"Back to Carlisle."

"But only for one day," she reminded him. "If I have not reached you by tomorrow evening, take him across the border. My mother's family will be waiting.

"Lady Ismay, are you sure about all this? It seems unnecessarily complicated to me. We could all ride hard for Scotland."

"There is no such thing as too complicated when it comes to the Earl of Warwick. Don't worry, I doubt it will come down to Scotland. I plan to meet you in Carlisle," she said with forced confidence. "There's no need to frighten Edmund more than necessary. I expect we'll all be safely back at Havencross by nightfall tomorrow."

She could see Ascham's awareness of what she wouldn't say— that with a woman and a small boy in the party, they couldn't outride armed men to the border. Ismay was the delaying tactic, the bait giving her son time to disappear. She could also see that the tutor wanted to argue, to beg her to come with him. She'd known for some time of Ascham's personal interest in her.

"I've made my decisions," she said firmly.

Ascham did as he was told and rode off, and Ismay collected Edmund, who had a small scrip packed with whatever he thought necessary to take on this journey. She slipped Edward's livery badge inside the scrip. She'd given the ring with the king's seal to James Ascham in case he needed it. Even from Burgundy, she trusted that Edward would do what he could for his brother's son.

Then she led Edmund to the old priory chapel, where she'd married his father. "We've done this before," she reminded him. "It's just an adventure. You have plenty of candles and the food we took to the cavern. Remember? Then you wait, for me or James to come and get you. As long as you have food and light, you are not to come out of the tunnel without one of us, is that clear?"

"Yes, Mother." He hugged her and, at the last moment, clung to her hand. "Come hide with me," he whispered, and Ismay's heart broke wide open. *Come hide with me*, Edmund had urged her all those years ago at Ludlow Castle, before he'd kissed her for the first time.

"I can't, Edmund. You have to be brave. And promise me that, no matter what, you won't come out until either James or I come for you. Promise me."

"I promise," he said almost soundlessly.

As his fair head vanished with the lit candle and Ismay dragged the false grave slab over the tunnel's opening, she prayed to the young man she had loved, the sweet boy who had left her with this gift: *Keep your son safe, Edmund. Promise me.*

She had almost taken too long—as Ismay crossed the fore-court, she heard the faint thunder of approaching riders. She left the gate open and fled up the many stairs to her solar, where she had a clear view.

Seized suddenly by the terror she had resolutely kept hidden for so many weeks, Ismay frantically counted the horsemen and, more important, searched for the identifying banner.

She'd known what it would be, and yet she'd hoped. For George, maybe; as detestable as his actions had been, he surely held her in fondness, and he was by all reports as changeable a man as he'd been a boy. She'd known him since he was tiny, and she could use that, could twist all his mixed-up loyalties against him.

But it was not the royal banner with its three silver bars that marked George, Duke of Clarence's distance from his brother's throne. No, the banner floating on the Northumberland wind tonight was the white bear and ragged staff on a field of red: the banner of the kingmaker himself, the Earl of Warwick.

Ismay knew, in that moment, there would be no clemency. Warwick dealt only in death.

CHAPTER FORTY

JULIET
2018

When Juliet tried to retreat into the corridor, Duncan strode across the bedroom and shut the door, keeping his hand braced against the wood. "We're just going to talk," he repeated.

"If all you wanted to do was talk, you wouldn't have broken into my house."

"I wouldn't have had to break in if you'd only been reasonable and answered my texts like you should have."

How the hell had Duncan found me? Juliet let that question settle for later, knowing she needed all her wits about her. He wasn't drunk, but she was pretty sure he'd been drinking. But where? And how did he get himself to Havencross in the middle of a blizzard?

An image fell into her mind, perfectly formed, as though she'd seen it herself: Duncan picking the lock of a side door and hiding himself in the many rooms and passages of Havencross for days. Spying on her, keeping one step ahead of her nightly rounds, waiting for the right moment to confront her.

Tilting her head and aiming for nothing more than a tone of curiosity, Juliet asked, "How long have you been at Havencross?"

"Clever girl," he purred, his gaze stroking down her body in the manner she'd once loved. "Not clever enough to have worked out the tracking app I put on your phone years ago, but still. I've been here two whole days, watching you perform your security checks"—the last two words clearly had invisible air quotes—"listening to you talk to yourself, and on the phone. Who is he?"

He shot the question at her, and Juliet jumped. Realizing she still had her back pressed against the door, she forced herself to step sideways, away from both the door and Duncan, wondering how to spin out the time before Noah got here without further angering her ex-husband. But she was also determined not to play his games. She had tried for years to anticipate Duncan, to placate him, to guess at his intentions and give him what he wanted. All it had gotten her was an empty hospital room and the tiniest of graves.

"Noah's a friend," she said. "His family lives nearby and helps look after the house."

"A friend? I heard the way you talked to him last night. How long have you been sleeping with him?"

"I'm not doing this, Duncan. I don't know what you think you're doing, but we are over. I don't owe you explanations about my life. I don't owe you anything."

He slammed his palm against the closed door. "You. Owe. Me. Everything. Because of you I'm on suspension. Because you drove me out of our bed and out of our house and that bitch Kelsey was just waiting in the wings—"

"Enough! You brought everything on yourself, Duncan. You always have. You're a third-rate professor in a second-rate college, and you think screwing a twenty-one-year-old student makes you hot. But it just makes you sad. You're a sad, bitter man who—"

He slapped her so hard that she stumbled back against her the desk. If he hadn't hit her open-handed, she was pretty sure she'd be unconscious on the floor. Juliet braced herself, one hand at her aching jaw and the other scrabbling behind her on the desktop to find something—anything—useful.

Duncan closed in, his pupils so wide his eyes seemed almost entirely black. Juliet's searching hand closed on the owl paperweight behind her and she tensed, waiting for her moment.

Without a flicker of warning, the lights cut out and her bedroom plunged into darkness. Juliet reacted instantly, swinging the paperweight in Duncan's direction and hitting him somewhere hard enough to shift his position. Knowing her space perfectly well by now, Juliet dashed around him and flung open the door.

The darkness was absolute. The medieval corridor had no windows at all, and if she hesitated she knew she would lose all sense of space and position. Juliet ran to her right, to the door that connected the medieval section with the Victorian. She heard Duncan, swearing freely, begin to follow her.

He would have to be careful. But Juliet could afford to move faster: in her wool socks, any creaks the old floors made were covered by the howling wind outside. She made straight for the main staircase, heading for the Victorian kitchen and Clarissa's old-age suite of rooms beyond. Where the landline telephone waited.

Call the police first, or the Bennetts' farmhouse? The farm was only two miles across the fields; if they had a tractor capable of getting through a blizzard, no doubt they'd be much quicker getting to her than the police would. All she had to do was keep out of reach of Duncan.

Her first check came when she picked up the vintage telephone at Clarissa's bedside and heard nothing—no clicks, no dial tone. *Damn stupid blizzard,* she cursed silently. The second check came hard on the heels of that disappointment: the distinctive, shattering sound of a gunshot.

Where in the hell had Duncan gotten a gun?

"Do you hear that, Juliet? I've got plenty of bullets. Enough to shoot at every shadow and still have one left for you. I know you're in the house. I'll find you. I've been here for two days, prowling around and finding all the places to hide. If only you would have talked to me, it wouldn't have come to this."

He sounded almost sorrowful through the pulse beating in Juliet's ears. She reminded herself sharply that any sorrow he felt was for himself only, and thought frantically about where she could safely hide. She'd never be able to reach the farm in a blizzard, what with all landmarks wiped away. And she didn't relish the thought of creeping through the dark house, trying to keep one step ahead of Duncan.

Outdoors? The old stables were still standing, but she had no coat, no hat, no boots. She'd freeze to death even if she had light enough to make her way carefully from house to stables. Except . . .

Duncan had moved on for now—his voice was getting farther away. Juliet crept through the Victorian kitchen into the scullery, through which she'd first entered Havencross all those weeks ago. Just as she remembered, there was the assortment of heavy outdoor garments hanging on hooks, stiff from age and disuse. There were also two pairs of Wellington boots.

She hesitated, still unsure what was safest. Glancing out the scullery windows told her nothing—it was as dark inside as out. *Help me,* she prayed, perhaps to Liam.

A light began to shine outside, dimly at first but slowly

growing. It was not the light of a farm tractor or car—it was the same shivery, otherworldly light she'd seen in the corridor outside her bedroom once before. Ghost light.

Come hide with me.

Only this time, the light did not outline the shape of a young boy but that of a woman in long skirts, beckoning to Juliet in an undoubted gesture of urgency.

You'll be safe.

Juliet allowed the universe to decide. She shoved her feet into the smaller pair of Wellingtons and shrugged on the heaviest coat, clearly made for a man but waterproof and lined with flannel. There was even a felted wool cap shoved into one pocket that she tucked her hair into. After one deep breath and a final prayer, she opened the scullery door and plunged outside.

The wind stole her breath and the cold battered her. But the light remained, and Juliet set herself grimly to follow it to the stable. She was so focused on the pale female form that she didn't realize they weren't headed for the stables. Only when the form slipped inside the ruined walls, precariously capped with snow, did Juliet understand that she'd been brought to the old chapel.

Her immediate thought was *This is no help at all*, until the light stopped and bent over. It was the same motion Juliet had seen days before over Noah's shoulder—a woman grasping the edges of a false grave slab to move it.

The tunnel, whose opening she and Noah had discovered. The tunnel that she knew she could access safely, and whose opening could be covered and uncovered from the inside. It might not be much warmer down there, but at least it would be dry and protected from the wind. And Duncan would never find her.

Her decision was made by a shout from the house and another

gunshot. "I see your footprints, Juliet. Do you really think you're safer outside? Just come back and talk to me!"

The offer would have been more enticing if Duncan hadn't screamed the last part. Whatever was happening with him, he was clearly on the edge.

Juliet headed into the chapel, trying to make her path look as uncertain as possible. She stamped down, flung snow with her arms every which way, and swept clear as many grave slabs as she could find so that Duncan couldn't be sure where exactly she'd gone. She doubted his first thought would be *secret tunnel*.

She squatted down at the false grave slab and gripped the edges with the sleeves of the coat covering her hands. It moved easily enough to allow her to slip through the space and onto the ladderlike steps. She stopped partway down to slide the slab back into place and paused. Would she have enough air if she shut it completely? Better leave an edge open just in case.

Her biggest worry, though, was unpredictable Duncan and that gun. Like all bullies, he was primarily concerned with his own survival, and she didn't think he'd confront Noah in any kind of fair fight. When a farm tractor blazing light and sound appeared in the fields, Duncan would likely make a run for it. Probably. But he might just be unhinged enough to take shots at someone unaware that he was armed.

After pulling the grave slab as near to closed as she dared, Juliet rested her head on a step and whispered, "Don't let anyone get hurt tonight."

Before she'd even finished, the oppressive darkness lightened. She looked down and saw the same outlined woman making the same beckoning gesture as before.

Juliet remembered the property deeds and royal decrees she'd found in Nell's files: *Said property to be held by the crown without prejudice or favor in the interests of a proven heir to the previous owner, Lady Ismay Deacon.*

"Is that who you are?" Juliet breathed the words into the air between them. "Are you Ismay Deacon?"

If she'd expected an answer, she would have been disappointed. The form—oh hell, thought Juliet, might as well call it what it is—the *ghost* only continued to beckon. There was nothing threatening or frightening about the action, just that sense of urgency. And as Juliet had nothing else to do at the moment but wait for Duncan to grow tired of searching outside or for Noah to arrive, she might as well see what the ghost wanted.

She descended the rest of the steps and faced forward. "Lead on," she said.

It wasn't at all like following someone real—not only was there no noise except Juliet's own movements and breathing, but the ghostly light before her seemed to shrink and grow at will and, sometimes, appeared to be shining from out of the very tunnel walls. Juliet counted steps at first, but got lost around two hundred. Although the space was confining, she hadn't had to do more than stoop thus far. If it came to crawling on her hands and knees, she decided, then she was out. *Imagine being stuck down here, slowly dying and no one ever knowing where you were?*

But when the tunnel changed, it grew larger rather than smaller. And soon Juliet stepped upright into some sort of underground cavern. She thought it might have begun as a natural space, for much of the floor was irregular stone as though water had long ago flowed through here. It had been widened at the sides to create a space where threatened monks could hide with their precious gold and jeweled vessels.

One side had collapsed inward, and that was where the ghost hovered.

Picking her way carefully across the floor, Juliet reached the outer edges of the disturbed earth and saw bricks mixed in with the rest. A structure, then, or—

"The well," she said suddenly. The surveyor's map Noah had showed her was vivid in her mind. The medieval well that had been capped off when Gideon Somersby began building. If Juliet were to draw a line between the tunnel opening in the ruined chapel and the medieval icehouse where it might once have come out, that line would pass very near to the old well.

Juliet thought of how excited Daniel Gitonga would be, and she hoped there would be a proper excavation. And that she could be part of it. She looked up at the ghost, who had stopped both moving and beckoning.

"Is this what you wanted to show me?" Juliet asked, with no expectation of an answer this time.

But the ghost—who seemed to have taken on a more solid outline, whose face was young and whose hair, Juliet could now see, swung free around her shoulders—extended her right hand and pointed.

Juliet followed the pointed finger with her eyes. What was she meant to see? It's not as though the ghost were providing an especially strong light—no theater overheads or spotlights here—but Juliet crouched down and ran her gaze over the rubble of the collapsed well.

Something glinted. Holding her breath, Juliet reached out with a feather-light touch, afraid that it might vanish, but this was no ghostly object. Her hand closed around a ring. The glint came from the gold band, much dulled by time and dirt, but heavy enough that Juliet was sure it was solid gold. There was a dark square stone in the center. Trying to think of the safest place for it, Juliet slipped the ring onto the little finger of her left hand.

When she looked back at her ghost, the pointed finger had not wavered. *So, not the ring. Or not just the ring.* Juliet dropped to her knees for better stability and delicately began brushing at the dirt around where the ring had lain. It took only a minute or two for her fingertips to distinguish a new texture. Not dirt, not stone, not man-made . . .

Holding her breath again, Juliet drew back her hands with care and clasped them beneath her chin. It was an unconscious imitation of prayer, her body's recognition that what she'd uncovered demanded reverence even before her mind caught up.

Bones. The pitted, yellowed, distinctive bones of a human rib cage.

Juliet released her breath in a gasp and looked up at her ghost.

Who chose that very moment to vanish, taking all the light with her.

CHAPTER FORTY-ONE

ISMAY
MARCH 1471

Ismay met Warwick and his men outdoors in the forecourt. She only managed to keep calm because her son's life depended on it, and because she'd spent years watching the Duchess of York in the most stressful moments of her life. She channeled the erect posture, the lifted chin, the neutral expression that Cecily Neville had evinced on the day Ludlow fell to the Lancastrians and she waited for Warwick to come to her.

Though he was more than ten years older than the last time she'd seen him—which had been on that same day of Ludlow's fall—at forty-two, Warwick retained the energy that had always been his most marked characteristic. He dismounted, tossed his reins to one of his men-at-arms, and commanded the dozen others to "secure the gate and the yard. No one leaves until I say so."

"Do you always treat those you visit like you're entering an armed camp?" she asked.

He stood at the base of the steps and studied her with the impersonal manner with which he'd assessed her at age twelve. He didn't smile, but then Warwick rarely did, leaving the charm to his royal nephew.

"My aunt would be proud," he said. "But then, you always had a little spirit to you. You know why I'm here."

"To offer me another Neville marriage?"

"Right now you must be wishing that you'd accepted Johnny."

"John Neville—a man who sold out his king."

"A man who chose his family."

"Edward is your family as well. What does your aunt think of your new allegiances?"

"As one of her sons stands with me, she is . . . pragmatic about the matter."

"Is she pragmatic about your alliance with Margaret of Anjou?" Ismay would never believe that the Duchess of York would accept her nephew's alliance with the hated former queen and the Lancastrian men who'd murdered her husband and second son.

Warwick ignored the thrust. "If you've sent your servants away, as it appears you have, it must be because you don't want me spreading rumors about your son's true parentage."

"It's no secret that he does not carry the name of his father." She couldn't bring herself to openly call her child a bastard.

"Shall we continue this discussion inside, Lady Ismay? Do you really wish to discuss your most personal affairs in the open air?"

"I will not have armed men in my home."

"They will remain here. Would you like me to discard my sword, as well?" he asked with elaborate politeness.

"That won't be necessary." If Warwick wanted to kill her, he'd manage it with or without his sword.

She brought him to the ground-floor study, where she'd met with Edward nine years ago. Warwick chose to lean against the table, arms folded. Ismay remained on her feet.

"I'll admit," Warwick said, "I'd rather lost track of you this last decade. A silly girl who'd failed to seize any advantage from her connections with my family—what did I care what she might be up to? But George, well, George had a very interesting story about the pretty Ismay whom he had been quite attached to as a boy and how she'd shut herself away up north after bearing a bastard child. George seemed to think Edward responsible."

He did smile at her now. "And yet, in ten years I had never heard your name so much as cross Edward's lips. If there's one thing Edward likes to talk about, it's his women and his children. The Woodville witch has shouted about it often enough. And then I remembered the last time I saw you, the night before Ludlow fell. You were clinging to my cousin, all right, all red eyes and trembling lips. But it wasn't Edward you clung to—it was Edmund."

Since he seemed content to hear himself speak, Ismay didn't try to stop him.

"And Edmund was never as cavalier as his brother. He had a romantic streak a mile wide and I considered it highly likely that your bedding came only after marriage."

"Why do you care?" she asked. "Married or not, Edmund has been dead for ten years."

"You were raised among Yorkists; you understand the intricacies of inheritance. Since the moment Edward became king, George has been his heir."

"I understood the queen has at last given birth to a son."

"In sanctuary at Westminster. I'm not worried about an infant. And George is conveniently on my side, being married to my eldest daughter."

"And?"

She would make him say it, a realization he seemed to have reached.

"You want me to spell it out? Royal succession depends both on legitimacy and the order of birth. Edmund was the next eldest brother in his family, George coming third. If Edmund left a legitimate son, that son replaces George."

"None of this matters though, as you've managed to drive Edward out of England and returned Margaret of Anjou's son to England. Conveniently married to your younger daughter."

"I think you know better than that, Ismay. I needed money and men, and she could give me both. Edward turned out to be disappointingly stubborn, in ways George is not."

"The kingmaker wants to rule," Ismay said. "You will use Margaret of Anjou and her son, then rid yourself of them when no longer convenient. And you think George will be more pliable in your hands, especially as your son-in-law."

"Quite. My job is to ensure there are no other Yorkist claimants. At some point Edward will return with young Richard, and they will fall on the field like their father did. Edward's detestable queen cannot stay in sanctuary forever—and infants are notoriously fragile. That leaves only your son, and Edmund's."

"How fortunate for you that my son is dead. He died of a fever this winter."

"I don't believe you."

"Believe what you like. Search where you will. There is no child here."

She had known he would not take her at her word. She had known how hard it would be to lie to Warwick's face, which was why she had sent her servants away. But Ismay realized that she was no longer afraid of Warwick, so long as Edmund was out of his reach.

His men tore the house apart, from cellar to solar, ripping down tapestries and emptying barrels as though she'd hidden a nine-year-old in a cask of flour. Everywhere in her beautiful house was the sound of footsteps, many heavy-booted feet tramping through the corridors, men's voices, the pounding of steel dagger hilts on closed doors and caskets, reverberating through her head and bones until she thought she'd go mad.

It was fully dark by the time they'd cleared the house and the outbuildings. Ismay had been a silent spectator to all of it, kept within arm's reach of Warwick at every turn.

The two were now in the kitchen garden courtyard, the outline of the old chapel against his back. Most of the men she'd ever known gave signs of a slipping temper. Warwick simply struck her with the flat of his hand without warning, hard enough to snap her head to the side.

"Where is he?" he demanded.

"There is no child here." It was the only thing she'd said for hours.

"Do you think I don't know how to make people talk?"

"I think you can make people say what you want to hear, which isn't the same as telling the truth."

"We'll see."

Maybe, she thought, staring at his cold face, *I should still be afraid of him*.

But the man he directed to hold her had barely laid his hands on her when one of the guards he'd left at the gate strode rapidly around the corner with a sweat-soaked, panting courier at his heels.

"What?" Warwick barked.

"News, my lord. Edward of York and his brother Richard, having landed at Ravenspur, have been permitted entry into the city of York."

Ismay couldn't help herself—she started to laugh. She should have guessed that even in his own extremity and without trying, Edward would manage to help her.

Warwick loomed over Ismay, his man still holding her firmly from behind. "I told you that someday you'd regret your lack of enthusiasm for my plans." He gripped her upper arm with his left hand and said to his man, "Take the cover off the well."

Before Ismay felt more than a flash of confusion and fear, Warwick pulled his dagger and reversed it in his hand with a single flip. She realized what he meant to do just before the dagger's hilt struck her in the temple.

CHAPTER FORTY-TWO

JULIET
2018

Juliet woke up in a strange bed and had one moment's disorientation before memory flooded in: *Duncan, blizzard, ghost, tunnel, bones.* Sinking back against the comfortable pillows, she remembered it all.

After her ghostly guide had so inconveniently vanished, Juliet had made her careful way back through the tunnel, keeping both hands on the narrow walls and her head stooped so low that her neck was killing her this morning. The worst part had been navigating her way up the tight, steep steps in the dark and moving aside the hollowed-out grave slab—all the while wondering exactly what awaited her above.

The answer had been the muffled stillness of a landscape covered in two feet of snow. The wind had dropped, and the clouds drifted enough for a shaft of moonlight to reflect off the snow, providing an eerie light. Juliet edged her way along the wall and peered out to scan the back courtyard and the house.

Only then did sound return to the world: the rumble of a tractor engine, Duncan's familiar voice raised in complaint, and another voice that Juliet was not expecting.

"Swear at me one more time, and I'll fire this shotgun over your head. It won't kill you, but the buckshot will sting." Rachel Bennett sounded like an actor in a Western—the righteous sheriff facing down the outlaw.

Duncan never did learn. "Bitch."

Juliet broke into motion and rounded the outside walls of the chapel in time to see the aftermath of Noah's punch. Duncan had fallen to his knees and was spitting blood onto the white snow. It looked as though he'd been tying Duncan's hands with a rope that Juliet could only assume had been in the Bennett tractor.

"Use that word again," Noah said, with no trace of amusement, "and I'll let my sister shoot you. Now for the last time— where is Juliet?"

Things got a little blurry after that. Juliet throwing herself into Noah's arms, Rachel finishing the job of tying up Duncan, the arrival of the police. The officers took statements from both Bennetts and Juliet, and arrested Duncan for breaking and entering and carrying an illegal firearm. Juliet might almost have been sorry for him if he hadn't looked up at her from the back seat of the police car and said, "It's your fault things came to this."

The police officer had obligingly slammed the car door. Then Noah and Rachel bundled Juliet into the cab of the tractor and carried her off to the farm, where she'd been sent to bed.

"Good morning." Noah spoke from the open door. When she looked between him and the empty space next to her in what was properly his bed, he laughed. "You were absolutely exhausted. I bunked in with the boys."

"What am I wearing?" Juliet examined the oversized flannel shirt as she swung her legs out of bed.

"Don't get up," Noah said. "Stay cozy. We'll talk here. The minute you emerge from this room you'll be swarmed by concerned adults and curious children."

He settled on the double bed, leaning against the headboard. Juliet curled up next to him and sighed when his arm came around her shoulders. "They can't be happy about the danger you and Rachel were in."

"Danger? Please," said Noah. "He wasn't going to shoot us. Even if he'd wanted to, he clearly didn't know what he was doing with that gun."

"Speaking of guns, does your sister often drive around the farm with a shotgun in hand?"

"I'll tell you a secret, if you like—it wasn't loaded. Yes, we keep a shotgun in the tractor. Very occasionally there will be animals you need to frighten off. But since the boys came to live at the farm, the shotgun shells are kept locked up in a safe." His arm tightened around her. "I'm not trying to make light of this. I'll admit that finding an American waving a gun around and yelling your name scared the hell out of me. I didn't know if he'd lost you or killed you. What made you think of hiding in the tunnel?"

Juliet closed her eyes and leaned her head on his chest. "You're the only one who will believe me."

She began with the moment the lights went out and she'd made her dash downstairs. She left nothing out—the ghostly woman, the urgent beckoning, the light that allowed her to follow her guide through the tunnel, the pale, pointed finger directing her attention to the collapsed wall and the bones within. The bones were one thing she'd managed to explain last night, though Noah had kept the questions to a minimum.

"I phoned Daniel Gitonga this morning and told him what you'd found," he said. "I imagine he's already at the police station making sure amateurs don't go messing around in a possible archeological site. They'll have to make sure the bones are truly old before releasing them to the historians—"

"They are," Juliet said, remembering the fragile, flaky feel beneath her fingertips. And one thing more . . . She extended her left hand and showed Noah the ring she had pulled from the dirt. She had ever so gently cleaned it before collapsing into bed last night, torn between treating it as a proper historical artifact and the driving need to examine it.

"You found this in the tunnel?" Noah asked.

Juliet removed it from her finger and allowed him to hold it up to the light.

"I think that dark stone might be a garnet," she said. "It's obviously real gold. And there's an inscription."

Noah squinted, turning the ring to try and catch the light at the right angle. "Daniel's going to need a magnifying glass for this."

When Juliet said nothing, he shot her a sharp glance. "Unless . . . do you know what it says?"

She did know. Despite the faintness of the engraving and the unfamiliar spelling, Juliet was certain she knew. Because, as she'd attempted to decipher each individual letter last night, words had floated into her mind and imprinted themselves with surety.

"It reads, *My Loyalty Is Fixed*." Juliet said, pointing to the tiny letters on the inside of the gold band. "And there's a name. A name from more than five hundred years ago."

"Let me guess—Edward the Fourth?"

It was a decent guess, considering everything else they'd learned and especially considering that Edward's royal livery badge had been found deeper in that same tunnel a hundred years ago. But Juliet shook her head. "The letters are a capital *e* and a lowercase *d*, and with another one of those little *d*'s attached. That abbreviation might mean 'Edward,' but it could also mean 'Edmund.' And the next word is not a name, it's a title: Rutland."

When Noah continued to look at her blankly, Juliet said, "I only know this because of the reading I've been doing, following Clarissa Somersby's interest in the Wars of the Roses. See, before Edward the Fourth was king, he was Edward, the Earl of March. And he had a brother—not George, who Shakespeare killed off in the butt of malmsey, and not poor Richard. A brother who was only one year younger than the future king." Juliet touched the ring in Noah's hand and said softly, "Edmund, the Earl of Rutland. He died with his father at the Battle of Wakefield at the age of seventeen, three months before Edward won his crown."

Yes, the ring would have to be dated, and experts would be called in to examine the engraving, and then historians like her would argue for years over its meaning and why it had been found in an obscure Northumberland tunnel . . . but Juliet knew she was right—because her ghostly guide had known.

No, be brave, Juliet thought. *Give the guide her proper name: Ismay.*

It would never be more than conjecture, of course. It was far too long ago, and the written records too few for anything like proof.

Noah returned the ring to her finger for safekeeping. "So what are you going to do now?" he asked casually.

"I still have three months of winter to sit through at Havencross. I'll get started on my dissertation about the flu and probably annoy your friend Daniel with constant questions about what they'll do with the bones from the tunnel. Let the police handle Duncan however they want. I'd be fine just to let him go back to the States. He has enough trouble to face there."

"And when spring arrives and you're no longer needed at Havencross? I suppose you'll go straight back to the States and another university job." He said it without looking at her, as though determined not to influence any possible answer.

"Do you know," she said, snuggling closer to him, "that I never wanted to teach college students in the first place? I always wanted to teach high school kids, or even middle school. But that wasn't prestigious enough for Duncan. I suppose even England might need teachers in . . . what do you call them here? Secondary schools?"

She felt a slight tremor run through his arm. "If you're teasing, tell me now," he warned her.

Juliet turned her face up to his, Noah's lovely hazel eyes wide with appeal. "I'm not teasing," she said, and kissed him.

CHAPTER FORTY-THREE

DIANA
MARCH 1919

Spring came early to Northumberland that year. Although Joshua told her not to trust it—"It's a false spring; there will be snow before Easter"—Diana found the sunshine and temperate breeze a gift after the long winter weeks.

In the end, Havencross School had lost three boys and the gardener to influenza. Watching it sweep across the world, Diana knew it might have been worse. She still woke once or twice a week from nightmares of too many patients and not enough help—but on the other hand, her nightmares about being buried alive had stopped. She knew now how grief would ebb and flow, and ever so slowly the tide would go out as life moved on.

On this Saturday afternoon, Diana sat on the steps with a book in her lap and watched a tumble of boys—some playing cricket, some croquet, and a few of the younger ones engaged in a boisterous game of tag. Austin and Jasper Willis took turns with the camera their mother had given them for Christmas, taking photographs that would be mostly blurry, Diana thought, if their subjects didn't learn how to stand still.

Joshua was at the far end of the lawn, bowling to the cricket players. He'd had the slowest recovery from the flu, but the pallor of illness had at last faded and he was beginning to gain back the weight he'd lost.

Clarissa sat next to her on the steps, arms folded and resting on her knees. She was dressed, like Diana, in a rather informal skirt and blouse. Ever since that night on the moor, Clarissa had softened and warmed. At first Diana had been certain she would be fired for the things she'd said and the way she'd said them, but only once had the matter been referred to. On the day the last patient left the makeshift infirmary and they began restoring the dining hall to its proper use, Clarissa had approached Diana and said abruptly, "I will never forget what you did for me the night I almost killed Austin. Thank you."

Although she had softened, Clarissa had not entirely lost her abrupt manner. Sitting next to Diana now, she said bluntly, "I have news for you."

"Oh, yes?" Diana was only half-listening; most of her attention was on Joshua, whose cricket game had been disrupted by the tag-playing boys. He darted among them with an ease that still surprised her.

"I'm leaving Havencross in June," Clarissa announced.

Diana jerked her head around. "You are?"

"I'm joining my family in London, and taking up a place at Oxford's Somerville College in the autumn."

"I'm . . . Clarissa, I'm so glad for you." And she was, honestly. She was also honestly worried about what that meant for the school and her job.

Clever enough to read Diana's reaction, Clarissa said, "I've no doubt your job is entirely secure, if you want it. I've offered the post of headmaster to Joshua Murray. He's accepted."

Diana swung her attention back to the lawn. As if he could hear them, or guess what they were saying, Joshua paused in his play with the boys and raised a hand in acknowledgment. Diana didn't have to see his eyes to know what she would find in them: desire and amusement and love, wrapped all together in the man she had agreed just yesterday to marry.

"May I ask you a question, Diana?"

"Of course." She braced herself, for talking with Clarissa was a bit like being at sea—one never knew where the next wave was coming from, or how hard it would hit.

"All of those tricks played on you last autumn—the knocking and the breaking things and the scratches on your neck—"

Joshua must have told her about that, for Diana never had.

"—who do you think was responsible?"

"That's very nicely phrased," Diana said. "It could cover almost any answer among the living or the dead."

"I'll admit I cannot reconcile those actions with the stories of the ghost boy who just wanted someone to hide with him."

"No," Diana said. "I don't think it was him. I think . . ." She wondered how best to explain. "You once had the same experience I did, in the medieval solar, right? That feeling of being overtaken by someone else's panic? It was a woman, I'm quite sure, a woman who was afraid for her son. I can't imagine why she should have disliked me so much or considered me a threat, but I'm fairly sure she was the one trying to drive me out of Havencross. I just can't figure out why."

Clarissa looked at her oddly. "If you remember your experience in the solar, then you remember counting the horsemen and looking for a banner to identify them."

"Warwick," Diana said. "Which alone tells you something,

because I wouldn't have had the least idea who Warwick was or what his banner looked like before then."

"The bear and ragged staff," Clarissa said, her expression far away. "The kingmaker, the Earl of Warwick. Quite clearly, from the terror we were both seized by, an enemy to that ghostly lady. And just today I finally realized why her enmity transferred to you."

Diana arched an eyebrow. "You have my attention."

When Clarissa smiled, she looked like the carefree schoolgirl she had never been. "Don't you remember me asking you, the day we met, if you had relations in the North? *Warwick* is a title, not a name."

The answer was just out of Diana's reach, she must know what the kingmaker's name had been . . .

With unaccustomed humor, Clarissa finished. "The Earl of Warwick's name was Richard Neville."

Diana blinked. And blinked again. And slowly said, "Are you telling me I made an enemy of a ghost because my last name is Neville? Because whoever-she-was thought me a threat?" But even as she spoke she remembered the night the tricks had stopped for good. It was the night she'd gone into the tunnel after Austin—but before that, she'd found her bedroom destroyed and had broken down, begging to be left alone until at least she'd saved the boys she could.

Was that what had stopped the ghostly lady? The realization that Diana was not a threat to the boys?

She shook her head. This was much too esoteric for her. She would keep to the world of observable symptoms, diagnosable problems, the lovely man she was going to marry, and the complicated woman next to her who had somehow become her friend.

"Miss Somersby, Miss Neville, look!" Austin Willis pointed the camera at the two of them, and Diana smiled at the future.

CHAPTER FORTY-FOUR

NED MURRAY
MARCH 1490

The horseman reined in on the bank of the river and stared across at the gray stone house. His cousin, Graham, who'd jumped at the chance to escape Carlisle for a day of riding and drinking outdoors, grunted.

"We'll nae be crossing that today," Graham said.

There had been a bridge here, once. No longer. But he didn't need to cross the river to examine the house at closer range. All he had to do was shut his eyes and he could see the house as he remembered it: the grandest, strongest house in the North, the encircling wall tall and thick, the double gate swinging open into a forecourt busy with grooms and maids and men-at-arms, the indoors walled with tapestries and fresh rushes underfoot, the solar on the third floor, from where all the surrounding countryside could be seen. From where, if she were watching, the lady of the house could see him now.

Graham had whistled the dog after him and took his horse to explore farther upstream. Ned remained mounted, remembering.

When he'd realized that he would be in Carlisle twenty years to the day after he'd fled, he knew he had to return. Finally. He'd been back and forth across the border dozens of times in his adulthood without any desire to look upon his home. He knew it was abandoned. He knew it was held by the crown "in the interest of a proven heir to the previous owner, Lady Ismay Deacon." But he had been taught to distrust crowns, especially the English one that changed hands like hot coals.

When he was twelve, four years after the flight across the border, his tutor had given him a ring engraved with England's royal seal and told him his mother had left instructions that it be used in case of dire need. It wasn't until much later that Ned had realized his tutor, Ascham, had been in love with his mother. Had she known and returned the feeling, or had she closed her heart to anyone but his own dead father?

He knew the rumors—widespread among his mother's Murray relatives—that he was a bastard son of the late Edward IV. Ned knew he wasn't. Though his mother had only ever told him two things about his father, it was enough for him to make his own guess as he grew older: that his father had died in battle, and that he himself bore his father's name.

Edmund.

He'd never tried to take advantage of what he knew or guessed. Not when one unknown uncle had followed the other on the English throne. Not now that the English queen was his own first cousin. When he'd realized that Havencross had been invaded by armed men and that, whatever she'd promised, his mother had died because of it—somehow, somewhere—he had thrown off his childhood love of war and glory. He was content in Galloway, farming and trading and making enough money to build his own stone house for his own family.

For one moment, his heart twisted as he gazed upon the

house across the river, and he wanted to say *I wish you could have met Marsali, Mother. She is kind, practical, and beautiful— like you were.*

"Ned!"

Graham came trotting back with the dog running freely across the moorland. "Have you seen all you came for? We'll reach Carlisle in the dark if we don't head back now."

Ned Murray released a deep breath. "I'm finished here."

But as he turned his horse's head, his eyes caught a shimmery, shivery light across the river. It came from the back corner of the house, in the direction of the ruined priory chapel. Ned stilled and watched as the shimmer formed into an outline—a tall, pale boy with fair hair and wide eyes. He didn't have to be closer to hear what the boy said: "Come hide with me."

It was eerie and remarkable, and maybe he should have been frightened, but the Scots had their own appreciation for the uncanny.

As Ned kicked his horse into motion and followed Graham westward, it comforted him to know that some part of Edmund Deacon remained at Havencross, engaged in a long, patient vigil for his mother's soul.

EVENING CHRONICLE
NEWCASTLE-UPON-TYNE

REPORT
17 April 2019
By Tiera Jacobs

BERWICK-UPON-TWEED—Today a forensic scientist and a medievalist from the Berwick Museum and Art Gallery announced the results of tests carried out on two skeletons recovered from the grounds of Havencross Estate. It was at first thought there was only one skeleton, but upon excavation carried out last month, the bones of a second person were found. Both sets were of sufficient age not to be of interest to the police.

The forensic scientist, Dr. Joy Latimer, reported today that the first skeleton was that of "an adult woman, approximately 155 centimeters in height, in probability having borne at least one child, and without obvious signs of disease or injury except for a single blow to the side of the head."

When asked if the woman had been murdered, Dr. Latimer said there was no way to tell at this date if the injury occurred before or after death. "The fact that she was not buried but found in the remains of an old well is perhaps telling," she allowed.

When asked how old the bones were, Latimer would commit only to a period "before 1600."

The second skeleton was much newer—between late 19th century and the 1920s. According to forensics, the bones are those "of a young boy, prepuberty, approximately 120 centimeters in height, without obvious signs of disease or injury." When pressed by a local reporter, Dr. Latimer conceded that the description may well fit that of Thomas Somersby, the child who vanished from Havencross in 1905. She stated that DNA from Somersby descendants has been gathered in an attempt at identification.

Dr. Daniel Gitonga, a medieval specialist at the Berwick Museum, displayed blown-up photographs of several items found with the skeletons. The most intriguing is a ring of the type known as a poesy ring—commonly given by medieval and Renaissance lovers, and with a sentimental motto inscribed within. Dr. Gitonga declined to say if this ring had such an inscription, or what it might say. "We'd much rather be sure of our facts so we can make all our conjectures within the appropriate context."

He is studying the artifacts with the American historian Juliet Stratford, and they intend to jointly publish their findings. It was Dr. Stratford who discovered the skeletons and ring at Havencross in December. She currently lives in Newcastle and teaches history at a local comprehensive school.

ABOUT THE AUTHOR

Laura Andersen is the award-winning author of the Boleyn Trilogy (*The Boleyn King, The Boleyn Deceit, The Boleyn Reckoning*) and the Tudor Legacy novels (*The Virgin's Daughter, The Virgin's Spy, The Virgin's War*). She has a B.A. in English with an emphasis in British history, which she puts to use by reading everything she can lay her hands on. Anderson lives in Boston and is married with four children.